Miss Jenny

Agnes Short's new historical romance is set in the Highlands, in eighteenth-century Edinburgh, and in Flanders during Marlborough's campaigns. Its heroine is Jenny Cameron, whose loyalty to the Old Pretender and whose dashing life story – so startling in the days of submissive young ladies – made her a legend in her own time.

Jenny grows up in lonely Glendessary, running wild with Hugh, son of her father's haunchman. But her father and her uncle Lochiel, head of the clan, have plans for her brilliant marriage, and send her to Edinburgh to be 'finished' by sharp-eyed old Aunt Cameron. Jenny's anguish at the loss of home, glen, and Hugh, and her fury at her imprisonment in Edinburgh's stinking streets and social niceties, are lessened only by Lochiel's momentary vision: that *she will speak a foreign tongue in a foreign land and will one day ride in glory to join Scotland's Stuart king*.

Battles predominate in Jenny's life: stormy battles of will with Aunt Cameron, battles of conscience in a French convent, gun-smoke on the fields of Douai and Bouchain . . . The reports that circulated about Jenny's life were wilder, probably, even than the truth, but they all have some facts in common. On these Agnes Short has built the enchanting story of a loyal and courageous girl whose life-long devotion to the Stuarts, and whose gallant leadership of the Cameron men at the Raising of the Standard, earned her a small place in history.

Also by Agnes Short

The Heritors (1977)
Clatter Vengeance (1979)
The Crescent and the Cross (1980)

under the name of 'Agnes Russell'

A red rose for Annabel (1973)
A flame in the heather (1974)
Hill of the wildcat (1975)
Target Capricorn (1976)
Larksong at dawn (1977)

Miss Jenny

Agnes Short

Constable London

First published in Great Britain 1981
by Constable & Company Ltd
10 Orange Street London WC2H 7EG
Copyright © Agnes Short 1981
ISBN 0 09 464040 8
Set in Pilgrim 10pt
by Elanders Limited, Inverness, Scotland

Printed and Bound in the U.K.
by Mansell (Bookbinders) Ltd., Witham, Essex

to the memory of

JEAN WATERS

Author's Note

In 1746 one Alexander Cameron, a prisoner in Inveraray Castle, wrote a letter to his cousin Colin Campbell in Edinburgh, to which he added a postscript: 'Mrs Jean Cameron's Historie is come to this place written at London. I'll endeavour to send it to you the first ocation ther is but on copie came hear as yett.'

This 'Historie' was *The Remarkable Life and Surprising Adventures of Miss Jenny Cameron, a Lady who by her attachment to the Person and Cause of the young Pretender, has render'd herself famous by her Exploits in his Service: And for whose sake she underwent all the Severities of a Winter's Campaign*, by 'The Rev Archibald Arbuthnot'.

The adventures narrated are certainly 'surprising' – nowadays they would be considered libellous – and it is no wonder that they were thought to be 'evidently in the main fictitious' (R. Chambers, *History of the Rebellion 1745-6*). Other versions followed – all variations on the same theme of intractable childhood, illicit affairs, masquerades in men's clothing, illegitimacies, even incest; in one version, capture by Robert Bruce, King of the Highland Rovers, and a spell as Queen of the same; in others, a nunnery and the Flanders Wars until the Treaty of Utrecht. But all versions agree on two points – Miss Jenny Cameron was daughter of Hugh Cameron of Glendessary where she was brought up freely, until the age of twelve or thereabouts; and she led a band of Cameron men to join Prince Charles at the Raising of the Standard at Glenfinnan. The years between are unknown, as are those which follow. Aeneas Macdonald (*The Lyon in Mourning* Vol.1, ed. Henry Paton) says she witnessed the setting up of the standard at Glenfinnan, a widow nearing fifty with jet-black hair, genteel, well-looking and handsome. She never followed the camp or marched with the army.

However, a list in *The Prisoners of the '45*, 3rd Series Scottish History Society, includes Miss Jean Cameron of Glendessary among the prisoners of note but 'how she and she who witnessed the raising of the standard came to be identified as one I am at a loss to understand' (Chambers). Another source claims the Jenny Cameron in Edinburgh Castle was a 'laundress'. Macdonald quotes a family source (Sir Ewen Cameron of Fassefern) to

7

the effect that 'the lady who made so much noise in 1745-6 as Miss Jenny Cameron. . .sent the Prince a present of cattle at the time of his raising the standard but never saw him herself'. Chambers concludes that if there was a Jenny Cameron in attendance on Charles through his English campaign and subsequently taken at Stirling it was a different lady from Miss Jenny Cameron of Glendessary.

Facts are few and hard to find: those which there are conflict. What is certain is that Miss Jenny Cameron made a great impression on the public mind: a Grub-street novel was composed upon her exploits, she appears in Caulfield's *Portraits: Memoirs and Characters of remarkable Persons*, in an Appendix to the *Life of Dr Archibald Cameron, brother to Donald Cameron of Lochiel*, and in James Ray, *A Compleat History of the Rebellion* from which the quotations in the text are taken, as well as from *The Life of Miss Jenny Cameron, the Reputed Mistress of the Deputy Pretender*, (in *The Life of Arthur Lord Balmerino*, some memoirs etc, London 1746) and *The Memoirs of the Remarkable Life and Surprising Adventures of Miss Jenny Cameron* by 'the Rev. Archibald Arbuthnot'.

The *Scots Magazine* recorded the death of Mrs Jenny Cameron, sister to Captain Allan Cameron of Glendessary, on 27 June 1772, at Mount Cameron in Morven.

Part 1
Scotland

1

Mr Cameron was a Gentleman of very good parts, and bore a good Character in his Neighbourhood; He bestowed a liberal Education on all his Children, but seemed lavish in his Expence upon Miss Jenny, who was his chief Favourite, but out of a mistaken Tenderness for her, was so long before he would put her under the Restraint which her Education required, that some Passions were suffered to take so deep Root in her Mind, that neither Time, Care, nor Expence could afterwards eradicate.

The girl dug bare heels into the horse's flanks and felt skin ripple over bone. It had been a long winter, with fodder sparse. But the garron was used to privation and though the ribs strained like a fast-barred gate against the lungs as the slope steepened, the animal's feet were quick and confident on the precarious path.

The girl rode bareback, like the boy ahead of her, and astride, her drugget petticoats bundled anyhow above her knees, hair flying loose from the riband which had bound it. Ahead of her and above, his outline sharp against the April sky, Hugh Cameron raised a hand in warning and both horses stopped, as motionless as their riders. Hugh turned his head and she saw his lips form the words 'Macdonald country'.

Jenny felt a shiver of excitement. Macdonald had not paid the black-meal. His cattle were fair game and the Camerons accomplished at making a *creach*.

Hugh slipped silently from his horse. She did the same.

With a warning 'Wait!' to the horses, already foraging in the sparse turf, Hugh turned and began to climb the hillside where it rose almost vertical from the path, bare feet nimble as a hare's among the rocks, plaid looped high at the waist to show long, bare thighs firm and strong as a man's. Hugh Cameron, son of Alexander, was fifteen and tall, and though still but half grown, was uncommon strong, with a square golden strength which matched his clear eyes and sunlit hair. Or so thought Jenny, as she lay on the turf beside him below the brow of the hill and felt the chill of frosted rocks creep up through worsted and homespun, and finally linen shift. There were goose-pimples on her arms, her hands and feet were blue, but she would not have changed places with anyone, least of all her sisters sewing dutifully in the upper room at Glendessary in the warmth of a healthy fire, or have been anywhere in the world but in Cameron country, at Hugh's side.

'See,' pointed Hugh now, his voice faltering between manly depth and treble. 'In the far valley . . .'

Jenny followed the line of his weather-tanned hand beyond Garbh Chioch Mhor and Druim Buidhe to the valley of Coire nan Gall with beyond it again the peaks of Sgurr na Ciche and Ben Aden, blinding white in the icy April light. But the valley was in shadow and secret, the dark shapes tiny as fleas on a dog's pelt.

'Cattle,' said Hugh. 'There is a new tacksman in the valley. He brought them with him from Inverness. In the autumn when the beasts are well grown, I will bring you one.'

Jenny's eyes danced with excitement. 'I will come with you, Hugh . . .'

'No.' The boy rolled over on to his back and lay staring up into the sky. 'I shall go alone. I shall capture the best and handsomest of the herd – a young bullock, thick-necked and strong – and drive it home to Glendessary. For you.' He looked sideways to where she lay beside him, on her back now, too, her new-formed breasts round and firm as Monadh Gorm. He felt the quickening of excitement which had disturbed him often lately. He wanted to reach out and touch those breasts . . . Hastily he looked away. 'Then I shall go again, with the others, and bring the whole herd to your father.'

'Macdonald will complain. He sent twice last year to Father with demands for payment for the cattle stolen. *Stolen*, he said, as if it was a sin to take the beasts when Camerons have always done so and no shame to them for that, with their bairns and their womenfolk to feed. But he will not pay the black-meal and he will complain.'

'Then let him,' boasted Hugh. 'And if his men try anything among our grazing, we will send them packing. My father is to give me a Lochaber axe when I take my first beast.'

'And I may not come and see you win your axe?' Jenny's voice was wistful, her eyes soft with pleading.

'No. You will stay at home and watch for me at the window until I come.'

'At *home*?' Jenny stared at him aghast. 'But Hugh, you cannot want me to stay with my sisters, to sit in idleness and ringlets, when I could be in the hills with you? You know I cannot bear to be within walls.' When he did not answer, she added in rising consternation, 'Why?'

But Hugh could not tell her. He could not remember a day

when Jenny had not been there, dark-haired, bright-faced, full of eagerness and courage, and though the other lads had tried at first to shame him out of their friendship, they had long ago accepted Miss Jenny as one of them – strong and wiry as they were and as able to endure. But lately, Jenny's appearance had changed, and, as he averted his eyes from her new roundnesses and curves, so had Hugh's heart towards her. Her absence was a confusing ache, her presence a torment. She was the Laird's daughter, he a mere clansman, but it made no difference. He knew only that her eyes at the window and her gleaming hair were what he wanted to see when he drove his first *creach* home. But in spite of her changing figure, Jenny's heart was as open and innocent as ever. When he did not answer, but blushed and looked away, Jenny tipped back her head and laughed aloud.

'You are afraid that I might make a better *creach* than you! Or that you will miss your beast and I will see your shame. You are like Father's rooster who drives away all rivals lest they show him up. Cock-a-doodle-doo!' and she clapped her elbows tight against her sides and crowed in glee before falling back, laughing, on the turf.

He stared at her with an expression she could not read. When he did not speak she grew instantly sober, scrambled to her feet and stood over him, her head outlined against the sky.

'Swear it,' she said quietly. 'Swear upon your drawn dirk that you will make your first *creach* for me.'

Slowly Hugh rose, his grey eyes steady. From its sheath at his belt he drew a long, straight-bladed knife with curved wooden handle. His eyes still fixed on hers, he raised the blade to his lips and kissed it. 'May I be stabbed with this same weapon,' he said slowly, 'if I break my oath.'

They stood in silence, bound by the solemnity of the moment. Then Jenny tossed the hair from her face, laughed 'Race you to the horses!' and bounded down the hill. In a flash he was after her, sure-footed as she and with twice the stride. He caught her on the slope above the path, where rocks gave way to heathland before falling steeply to the gully and racing stream and they fell together laughing, rolling over and over till they slithered to a halt on the narrow path above the crevasse. They lay a moment close-wrapped and panting for breath, then, before he could stop himself, Hugh kissed her clumsily, full on the mouth. Jenny stared up at him in astonishment, then clasped her arms about his neck and kissed him as clumsily in return. A moment later she had twisted away, scrambled to her feet again and was running to where the garrons stood obediently waiting.

'We'll ride home the long way, Hugh!' She turned her horse

expertly in the narrow space, to ride hard and reckless into the wind while her heart shouted to the hills with happiness. Hugh had kissed her. He was her man now and no one, not even her mother, could part them. When the summer came she would go to the shieling with him, whether he allowed it or not, wrap herself in his plaid and sleep on the hillside with him and the others, under the summer stars.

Her father would not cross her. She had only to tell him how she loved each heather stalk and pebble of Glendessary – more so than Alan ever would, though he would be the laird one day and she never – and her father would smile with indulgent understanding. He loved his land as she did.

She turned her head briefly to look back the way they had come. This way came the cattle in the summer months and the clansmen with them; this way came the pedlar's garron at fair-time from the neighbouring glen. But in the winter of short days and stormy darknesses, the only travellers were arctic hare, wild cat or fox, the only watcher the eagle on Fraoch Bheinn. The burn was gorged now with clotted foam, and wherever the gully widened to form a pool, the water churned green as her mother's peppermint cordial, and thick with bobbing ice. Eastward, Glendessary stood bleak and proud at the western tip of Loch Arkaig with the loch stretching grey as a sword blade towards Achnacarry. To the south, hills soared, layer on layer, proud and secret, snow-wrapped; to the north the same. In the valley at the loch's head stood the square block of her home, and beside it the lower, squatter shapes of steadings and dairy where hung the salt fish and what remained of the winter beef. Her mother would be still abed, or sitting swathed in her plaid in the windowseat, staring eastward. Her sisters would be...what? Squabbling? Copying passages from the Bible in blotched script? While her brothers, except Alan of course, teased that ineffectual tutor, Mr Graham; and in his library her father read.

She felt a mild twinge of conscience about Alan. Hugh was Alan's foster-brother and they had shared the same breast, though not at the same time, for Alan was five years younger; but the milk which had firmed Hugh's muscles and made his limbs grow straight and strong had not done the same for her brother Alan, though he had shared Hugh's home on the shores of Loch Arkaig for five years, eating the same kale and oatmeal, sleeping on the same bed of gathered heather stalks and running barefoot wherever Hugh and Jenny led. For Jenny had known Hugh since they were infants: how could she not, when Hugh's father Alexander was her own father's haunchman? Jenny had grown long-limbed and strong and promised to be tall as her father, but Alan remained puny, and Glendessary decided the

14

boy's native training was complete. He must return to his own home and the tutor they found for him.

But even when younger brothers and sisters joined him in the schoolroom, Alan persisted in following Hugh and Jenny whenever they would let him and Alan was a nuisance. For one thing, he cried. Jenny never cried, even when she fell from her horse and broke her collar bone and the bone-setter was sent for all the way from Inverness. Alan was nervous-footed and clumsy. Today when Hugh had promised to take them into the hills to look for arctic hare, for stores were running low, Jenny had deliberately eluded Alan, telling him to wait for her in the dairy and then creeping out another way. But he would have been frightened, she told her conscience now. He would have wept for the hare and felt sick.

She glanced down at her girthstrap, at the white feet, bunched together under the leather thong, at lolling head and blood-streaked muzzle. She smiled at the thought of what her mother would say if she knew who had contributed to the family pot. But her mother thought her safe in the school-room and Mr Graham would not tell. Nor Alan, though he would be red-eyed and reproachful and come into her bed after dark for comfort.

They were at the falls of Dearg Allt when they heard the skirling of distant pipes.

'Who?' asked Jenny, her voice taut with excitement. Side by side they looked eastward along the valley from their vantage point above Glendessary. As they searched the emptiness of loch and hillside the noise of pipes grew stronger on the wind and Jenny's face lit up with recognition.

'It is Uncle Ewen!' Twisting one hand into the wiry mane she heeled her horse into a slithering descent. Spray drenched horse and rider, but Jenny's voice was sweet with laughter as she called over her shoulder, 'Ride faster, haunchman! We go to meet Lochiel!'

Margaret Cameron sat at the window embrasure in the upper drawing room at Glendessary, the embroidery frame untouched in her lap. It was the same motif she had begun to sew a year or more ago and though it was to form the front panel of a formal petticoat, she could not find the energy to complete it. What was the use? Who would there be to see her but her husband and her children? No one made the sixty-mile trek from Inverness but the pedlars at fair-time; and as for Edinburgh . . . Margaret Cameron's face fell into the familiar lines of melancholy. Once, as a young girl, she had spent a winter in Edinburgh and it had been the brightest part of all her life. She had lived with an aunt in the Lawnmarket, had been to evening parties, travelling in her aunt's sedan chair with a servant running behind and another in front to clear the way. She had been to musical gatherings, called on influential ladies. In memory that Edinburgh period was a brilliance of candlelight and satins, of lute and harpsichord and the slow elegance of the dance. If she closed her eyes she could hear the rustle of silks over polished floorboards, smell pomander, orris root, and powdered wigs. But Hugh Cameron of Glendessary had seen her and claimed her from her father. Though she loved Hugh – who could not, with his affectionate nature and gentle ways? – she hated Glendessary with a cankerous, draining hatred which owed as much to fear as to loneliness. She feared the darkness and the silences, the summer lightnings and the water. Especially the water, from the endless grey blade of the loch which concealed who knew what terrors beneath its treacherous surface and which was whipped to a fury of lashing waves whenever the wind funnelled, howling, down the glen, to those cataracts which screamed at her endlessly from every hillside till she thought her head would burst apart. But when she had mentioned it that first year, her husband said only, 'What noise, dear? I hear nothing.' And her daughter actually liked it.

But Jenny was a changeling. How could any woman have produced such a daughter except through witchcraft from the glen itself? Margaret shivered. She had heard them talking when they thought her out of earshot – of cats and witches and monsters rising, weed-wrapped and oozing, from the deep. Margaret knew now why there were so many cataracts. They were feeding the loch with blood, white-flecked and foaming, and green as every monster's blood was green; the loch which haunted her days and terrified her nights ... the loch beyond which lay Achnacarry and Lochaber, Loch Lochy and Lochiel, the wild and secret territory of their chief.

She too was a Cameron now and must forget her upbringing, but when the talk was of old battles and clan triumphs or, later over the winecup and never before strangers, of James their exiled King, waiting in France until the time should come for him to be restored, her Lowland heart melted with terror. Lochiel's own son, they said, was in the Stuart king's confidence, had attended at his French court. When the call came and the *crosh-tarie* was lit, how could any Cameron stand apart? Her husband and her sons would be killed, her house burnt and her daughters raped. She could see the flames leaping, hear the screams ...

Behind her, in the well of the dark-panelled room, hung oil paintings of Glendessary's father and grandfather, uncle of

16

Ewen Dubh of Lochiel who was seventeenth chief of the Camerons and at seventy-eight years of age their nearest neighbour, at Achnacarry.

He, too, frightened her. Ewen Dubh was big and bearded, his eyes black as rock pools with glinting lights that hid his thoughts. Her daughter Jenny had eyes like that and hair as dark as Lochiel's had been, though now his was grizzled grey as a hoodie's breast feathers. Jenny was not fair as her parents were – Glendessary sandy-haired, pale-eyed and freckled, his wife blonde as a Viking with porcelain skin and eyes clear as the mountain blue-bell. Jenny, they said, took after Lochiel, who had the second sight. They said he had killed a wolf with his bare hands. He was well-named 'the black'. Margaret shuddered at the memory of Lochiel's last visit. A year ago he had drunk their cellars dry. The side of salt beef they had been saving against the springtime had gone on the first night, to the accompaniment of roaring laughter, and all the fowls Glendessary could provide had gone the same way in the days that followed . . .

She shifted awkwardly to redistribute the weight of yet another unborn child, with the last dead scarce a month and the ground so thick with snow they could not make the journey to the church at Kilmalie and must bury the child on the hillside behind the house, with only Mr Graham to administer the rites.

Poor Mr Graham. He was unhappy as she was in this Highland wilderness, for he, like she, had known a gentler upbringing. But he was a good man, living a Christian life according to true Episcopalian principles. Without his prayers to sustain them in the long winter bleakness, she knew her spirits would have quite deserted her: he had read the burial service as solemnly as any minister and with compassionate understanding. It was a pity he was not a sterner dominie.

From the room above came a sudden scuffle, the creak of floorboards and a high laugh, but the boys were Mr Graham's concern and the girls were quiet enough. She glanced back into the shadows beyond the fire and saw them sitting where she had directed, stitching samplers, the Lord's Prayer for Catherine, the alphabet for little Meg. But where was Jenny? There was another loud thump from above, then silence. Margaret Cameron sighed. Her eldest daughter was no doubt with her brothers, as usual preferring their activities to her own, but what could her mother do? Glendessary did not seem to care if his daughter grew up an untamed hoyden and she had not the strength to combat Jenny's spirits.

Wearily she picked up the embroidery frame, drew the thread tight and bent her head over the delicate pattern of twined

17

acanthus and fleurs-de-lis, while the peat stirred in the wide hearth, and the murmur of distant waterfalls filled her ears. She did not hear the shouting till the door burst open and Alexander, her husband's haunchman, stood huge in the doorway.

'The master says to make ready, Ma'am, and quickly. Lochiel is moving up the glen with piper, bard and many gillies. It is clear he comes to us and comes to stay.'

'Uncle Ewen!'

Jenny kneed her horse to a splashing gallop along the shore as the procession rounded a shoulder of screening hillside and the piper came into view, his own gilly at his side and his plaid streaming while the wail of bagpipe lingered mournfully over the water and echoed in the hills.

'Uncle Ewen!' She leapt from her horse and ran barefoot among the threading horses to where her uncle sat high on his sturdy mount, his haunchman at his side, and strung out on foot behind him his gillies, his deer-hounds, and his clansmen, cut off from view as yet by the curving track. All were cheerful-faced and smiling. Her uncle, for all his years, leant from the saddle, seized her waist in his huge hands and swung her high and laughing.

'Well, Miss Jenny, still lithe and spry as ever? Still as quick of tongue?' He turned to a gilly and roared, 'Fetch the lady's horse.' When it came he dropped her neatly on to the animal's back. 'Ride with me, lass, and tell me what's afoot that brings you hoodless into the hills when you should be at your spinet or your woman's silks.'

Jenny looked in open adoration at the old man who was head of her clan and, next to Hugh, the finest, bravest man she knew. He wore the *brechan-feill*, pinned by a brooch of silver on the shoulder, Highland bonnet, good brogues and homespun stockings tied with leather below the knee. He carried a pistol at his belt as well as a dirk, while behind him came the gillie-more with his broadsword, musket and targe.

Hugh, son of Alexander, watching from a distance, felt his chest swell at the sight of so much weaponry, though he knew Lochiel came on a family visit and the guns would be used only on moorfowl or stag. Unless the King across the water came back to claim his own – for had he not heard his father talk with Glendessary of such a possibility?

'Boy!' roared Lochiel as Hugh still hung back in shyness on the edge of the company. 'Have you no greeting for your chief and father of your clan?'

'Sir, I . . .'

'Sir? I come among friends, not servants! Come boy, embrace me as one Cameron does another.'

Awkward and blushing before the laughter of the company, Hugh took the old man's outstretched hand and when Sir Ewen leant from the saddle and kissed him on the cheek Hugh could not speak for pride.

'Now mount, boy, and attend Miss Jenny. Look at the laddie,' he called back over his shoulder to his crowding followers. 'And look hard. One day he'll make a haunchman fit for a chief.'

Straight-backed and proud, his face glowing and his head high, Hugh rode beside his chief's own haunchman, the rest of the party strung out behind them along the lip of the water as they accompanied Sir Ewen and Miss Jenny on the last stretch of the road, while hounds loped scenting over the unfamiliar pathway and the wind whipped top spray from the loch.

'Tell us how you fought the English officer in the river, Uncle Ewen,' clamoured the children.

'It was not a river, silly, but a burn, so narrow that his shoulders were wedged tight, was it not so, Uncle?'

'What did it *taste* like when you bit him, Uncle? Was his windpipe tough?'

'I am going to be sick.'

Alan would spoil everything, thought Jenny in disgust as Mr Graham hurried the heir to Glendessary, retching, from the room. Now we will all be sent to bed.

The hall was packed and steaming as the peat fire quivered with scarlet heat and the moisture dried out of plaid and breeches and bonnet. For they were all there now, from Sir Ewen to the lowest gillie, gathered to greet their chief and hear the tales his bard and the Laird himself would tell until the piper took over with reel or jig and set their feet dancing.

They were in the great hall of Glendessary, for Sir Ewen refused to eat in Lady Margaret's first-floor dining-room, or to countenance namby-pamby affectations of dinner-napkins and polished silver. When Sir Ewen came, the master ordered the trestle tables to be set up in the great hall. There was a great to-ing and fro-ing between kitchen and outbuildings as fires were lit, spitted chickens set to roast and baste, moorfowl plucked and potted, barrels of oatmeal formed into bannocks and baked, or curled on a gridiron over the fire.

Sir Ewen dined with his haunchman at his shoulder, just as Hugh's father stood behind Glendessary, and all available servants waited at table, including, Jenny noted with a giggle, Hugh himself. There was claret and best ale and the room was bright with candles from Margaret Cameron's precious store. The children and Mr Graham ate at a side-table, and Jenny loved it, though it was clear from her mother's strained expression that she did not. Jenny loved to see the shadows move over the massive stone walls with their dusty tapestries, to see candlelight reflected in drinking-cup and platter and in the huge bossed brooches of the men. She loved the smell of wet wool drying, the aroma of roasting venison and spattering fat which wafted in from the kitchen with every scurrying servant. She loved the tang of male sweat, of dog-hide, of claret and brandy, and of the *uisge beathe* which the clansmen drank. She loved the noise, the companionship, the knowledge that they were all equal in the eyes of their chief, Lochiel.

Why must it be Alan who inherits this? she thought with genuine puzzlement. It should be *me*.

'You must teach that son of yours to have a stronger stomach, Glendessary,' said the old man now. 'I swear young Jenny here has twice his spirit, and she a mere maid. But I tell my son that Donald will go the same way if he be not checked.'

Ewen Dubh's son John, Younger of Lochiel, had stayed behind in Achnacarry, and his son Donald with him. 'Aye,' sighed Sir Ewen, 'Donald is too much inclined to music and book learning. Such things sit well enough upon a gentleman, but only when allied with strength and skill at arms. What good will books be when we are called to answer the *crosh-tarie*, the cross of fire and shame? As we will be soon and surely.' He looked around with quick caution. 'But we are all Camerons here ... If Queensberry's plans are carried and Scotland is sold to England for nought but the promise of a *Hanoverian* succession, there are many who will flock to our cause. John has letters newly come from France ...'

'It is late,' interposed Lady Margaret quickly. 'The children grow weary. You must excuse them now, for Mr Graham waits above to say evening prayers.'

'Nonsense, woman, the night is not yet begun.'

'Please Mama ...'

'The stories ...'

'Go to bed, as your mother tells you,' said Glendessary, seeing the strain on his wife's face. Jacobite talk was guaranteed to make her nervous. She would wake in the night sobbing, or on a nightmare scream, and in her present state it was not wise. But it was a pity: the children did not often have the chance to meet their chief. 'Sir Ewen will still be here tomorrow,' he reassured them, 'and, we hope, for many days.' He tried to keep the strain from his own voice. He was a Jacobite – what Cameron was not? – and eager for news. His guests were welcome. But though

Glendessary was a prosperous enough estate in a good year of long summer sun and a safe harvest, no one could guarantee a good year in advance and the winter had been unusually severe. If Sir Ewen stayed long, they would be forced to send to every cottar on the estate to ask for poultry or for meal, and Glendessary was a compassionate man. He would not have his tenants suffer if there was help.

'Go!' he ordered, loosing his irritation on the children who lingered, hoping for reprieve. Dutifully they lined up to bid their visitor good-night, but Jenny hung behind. 'Must I go too, Papa?' she pleaded as she reached up to receive Sir Ewen's kiss. The old man put his arm about her waist and drew her close.

'Nay, Jenny, you shall stay. Shall she not, Glendessary? Miss Jenny has spirit enough for Alan and my Donald both, and I would swear upon my dirk she loves Glendessary more than any man.'

'And why not,' retorted Jenny, 'when I can ride and shoot and trap a hare as well as any? And wield a sword too, if I must.'

'A sword?' Sir Ewen raised one bristling eyebrow in teasing disbelief. He had a soft spot for this great-niece of his who had the grace and bearing of a thoroughbred, and a heart as strong and true, he swore, as his own. It was good to know there was one Cameron at Glendessary who would not fail him when the time came, for her father, he knew, was not war-like, nor her brother, and when the loyal army rose to set the true King back upon his throne there would be need of every Cameron in the glen. 'What has a mere maid to do with swords?'

'A mere maid has surely more need of swords, Uncle, than a man such as you. For if a grown man can draw the breath from an Englishman's windpipe with his teeth alone, then a mere girl, whose teeth are not so strong, may surely be allowed to do the same with steel?'

'A good answer. Glendessary, you have a maid of stature who will do the Camerons credit. You must wed her well.'

'I shall not wed,' declared Jenny, 'unless I find a man to pair his stature with my own.'

'There's many a man I know would pair with you and willingly . . .'

'Yet he must be a Cameron and of the glen,' retorted Jenny, her eyes seeking Hugh's in the glimmering edges of the company, 'or I shall remain a maid.'

Glendessary regarded his daughter with amused indulgence. Naïve still, untaught in the ways of the world outside his glen, she had the arrogant beauty of a stag in its own domain. Her sisters were well enough, meek, docile, undemanding, and his sons healthy, but it was Jenny who filled his heart with pride.

She was a girl fit for a chief: marriage and its cares would come upon her soon enough without his choosing. Meanwhile, he liked to watch her, free and joyous as she was now, and so, he knew, did old Lochiel.

'I'd wed her myself,' went on the old man, 'and gladly, were I not her grand-uncle.'

'And I you, Sir Ewen.' Jenny dipped a demure curtsey, then dropped her bantering and turned ingenuous and pleading eyes upon her uncle. 'Take me with you when you hunt the stag! For how can I know how such things must be done if I do not see? Take me with you, and Hugh too?'

'Enough, girl.' Lochiel waved a dismissive hand, but his voice was genial as he added, 'We will see. But I was telling you, Glendessary, of letters newly come from France, from our King's court in St Germain. They are preparing. With matters as they are in our Scottish Parliament, there is no other course. When that traitor Hamilton moved that the *English Queen* should nominate our Commissioners, it was the beginning of Scotland's ruin.'

'Aye,' agreed Glendessary. 'September first was an ill day, and an ill judgement that recommended the choice be left all to one side. The Queen will surely elect only men favourable to her course.'

'And Union will be foisted upon us,' growled Lochiel, 'by our own doing.'

'And what of Andrew Fletcher?' Fletcher of Saltoun, though not a Jacobite, was a fervent nationalist and the most eloquent and zealous spokesman for the anti-Unionist cause.

'Fletcher spoke well as ever and with bitter vehemence. We had all thought, like Fletcher, that Hamilton wanted a federal union, for the benefit of both countries, not *incorporation*. *Incorporation* with a country which has passed an Act declaring all Scotsmen aliens until they accept the Hanoverian succession. Aliens in our own land!'

'It is certainly an odd approach to friendship,' agreed Glendessary as he refilled Sir Ewen's goblet and his own. 'To propose a treaty which will bind England and Scotland in amity and at the same time to threaten vengeance and economic ruin if we do not comply. It is unpolitic, to say the least.'

'It is downright insolent!' cried Jenny who had been following the conversation with close attention. 'Were it in my hands I would tear their Treaty to shreds and trample upon the pieces.'

'Well said,' laughed Sir Ewen. 'You have a proper pride in your nation. And Miss Jenny is right.' The old man fixed the company with dark and burning eyes, under brows thick as thorn hedges.

'Mark me well. It was an ill step to declare us aliens and it will be an ill step to insist we accept their German kings. If Queensberry and Seafield and the rest of the Queen's lackeys foist their Union upon us, with their Hanoverian succession, we have the remedy in our own hands.' He touched the jewelled dirk which he wore always at his belt. 'And our own King at the court of St Germain ... But enough of such talk. More wine, Glendessary, and tell my piper to make ready. Meanwhile, did I ever tell you of ...' He looked slowly round the assembled company. 'Of the day I stalked a beast deep into the hills of Lochaber and found an English soldier?'

Jenny curled at his feet in breathless anticipation. She had heard the story many times, as they all had, but could not hear it often enough. A happy hush fell on the company as Lochiel began the tale of how he had grappled with his English soldier in a fissure in the hills, his back on the rocks of a mountain burn in torrent, his shoulders imprisoned by the boulders on either side.

'... so I spat the water from my mouth and seized his arm, raised at that moment to drive out my life. The sun struck stars from the blade of his upraised dirk and burnt his eyes with fire ... I saw the pulse beat thick as a tree-root in his throat ... I made a last defiant effort and sank my teeth into his wind-pipe ...'

The hush of held breath gripped the hall. Jenny's hand felt instinctively into the gloom at her back where Hugh found and held it tight in his, and her heart beat hard with fear and expectation. The old man's voice rose till it shook the roof-beams with reverberating triumph.

'The blood gushed hot upon my face as I tugged and tore ... the flesh came away ... the man fell dead.' As the echo died, every breath in the hall was loosed on a sigh of proud content.

There were more tales after that, of victory and escape, of legend, witchcraft or ancient love, while the drinking cups were filled and emptied until men slept where they lay, plaid-wrapped, content in the warmth of the fire and their clansmen's company. And Jenny slept, forgotten, with the menfolk, one arm across a hound-dog's sleeping shoulders, her head cradled on Hugh Cameron's knees.

Young Hugh sat wide-eyed and watchful in the hall of sleepers, as the fire settled to a glimmer, and the candles guttered one by one. His back was against the hard oak settle, his bare feet flat on the stone floor, but he would not adjust the plaid about his shoulders for fear of waking her.

He looked down in wondering pride at her sleeping face. Were he to search the whole world, from Inverness to Edinburgh, he would not find her match. But she was the Laird's daughter: his heart turned with misgiving. The Highlands held no hope for young men of promise, his mother told him, and she urged him often to leave in search of better fortune. His mother was embittered by too many mouths to feed and little comfort, but Glendessary held all Hugh loved and ever hoped for. His ambition was simple: to hunt, to fish, to drive the cattle, to range unhindered over every hill and glen of Cameron country and to serve his chief, if necessary to the death. And he wanted Jenny.

Hugh looked down at the tumbled shadow of her hair, her paler cheek and the curve of her lifeless arm across the deer-hound's back, and his young breast swelled with pride that she should lay her head against his thigh and sleep. He would be her self-appointed haunchman until the day when she saw him as he saw himself, and he won her father's consent. He looked deep into the dying fire and the ashes formed a pattern of battle and glory, ranks of horsemen and marching columns, and Jenny herself in splendid livery at the head of them, high on a prancing horse, while he rode in full battle-armour at her side . . .

Morag, one of Lady Margaret's women, found them sleeping when she came to tend the fire in the first light.

'That girl', she muttered dourly, 'will come to no good.' She woke her with scant ceremony and sent her skipping upstairs with a jug of icy water and instructions to 'wash the drunken sleep from your sinful e'en and pray the good Lord for forgiveness'. As for Alexander's laddie, that overgrown stirk of a Hugh, he got a blow on the head from her besom and orders to fetch peats for the kitchen fire.

But one day the hall was empty once more, Lochiel gone. Jenny missed the company and the noise. She missed the piper under her window in the morning, piping Lochiel's toilet to its conclusion while the loch shimmered under the pale sunlight and on the hills the laverocks sang. She missed the barking of his hounds as he loosed them on the mountains; missed the wind in her hair as she followed on her garron, through cloud and sunlight, where her grand-uncle and her father led. She missed Lochiel's voice, loud in the great hall, his laughter and the endless tales over the wine-cup, late into the night. Glendessary seemed empty and colourless without him.

But the men were already ploughing in the valley: four horses teamed together while the cottar walked backwards ahead of them, his eyes on the precious wooden plough blade lest it snag,

24

or crack against a hidden stone. When the soil was too shallow for the plough or the glen too steep with rock, they dug the ground with wooden spades while the clouds scurried fast from the west on a squall of sudden rain. Then the rain passed, a rainbow spanned the valley and the ground steamed under the returning sun.

Hugh worked among them and where Hugh went, so went Jenny. Some days her mother kept her at her side, making her card thread or spin the yarn for worsted, but Jenny submitted only when her father ordered it, which he did from time to time and usually after a tearful interlude with his wife. For the rest, she did as she chose.

She went fishing for the yellow trout with Hugh. She shot hare and moorcock, rode the hills in search of deer, and killed a hooded crow which had stolen one of Hugh's mother's hens. She grew taller and fuller-breasted above a narrow waist and long, lithe limbs, until the skirts of her last year's dress were almost at her knees, and no one noticed, least of all herself, that she was a girl no longer. Or almost no one. For with a sweet, increasing torment Hugh saw the change; so did Morag, Lady Margaret's woman, and the plain face closed with enmity.

When the planting was finished, it was time to take the cattle to the hills. The first herds were gathered and moved slowly up the glen.

'We go to *A Chiel*,' said Hugh one morning. 'My father stays here, with Glendessary, but I must go.'

'Then I go too.'

Jenny lay on her stomach above the little lochan watching for the ripple and splash which would tell her the salmon were moving, while further upstream a dipper, neat in black and white, bobbed on a glistening stone. On either side the hills rose, smooth and green with young grass, and the heather had lost its brown anonymity in a prickle of bursting buds. 'When do we leave, Hugh?'

Hugh looked uneasy. He had not touched Jenny since that day in the hills, but every day it became more difficult as he saw her grow more womanly and his own body lost its boyhood innocence. In the turf-walled shieling with a shared bed of heather stalks, or cocooned in a plaid under stars, how would he bear it? His big hands twisted awkwardly about the stem of the whittled spear. When the fish leapt and he loosed the spear, he missed his aim. Jenny laughed.

'It is well there is meal still in the tub, for we'll not grow fat on your fishing.'

His face flushed with mortification and a rising anger that she should mock him, unchecked. When she scrambled to her feet and ran into the water to retrieve the spear, calling over her shoulder, 'I will show you how it should be done,' he plunged after her in sudden fury, seized her shoulders and wrenched her back.

'I will fetch it', he said through clenched teeth as she struggled, but Jenny was strong: they both lost their footing and fell.

Margaret Cameron's woman, scrubbing linen with the others at the loch-side, heard the commotion and opened her mouth to cry out for help ... then closed it again as she saw what followed. For that overgrown laddie Hugh, son of Alexander, lifted Miss Jenny kicking in his arms as if she were no more than a twig and waded back with her to the shore ... when he set her on her feet again, and Miss clouted him and they fell to the ground, wrestling, she could hear the laughter from where she stood, knee-deep in the suds of the wash-tub, then the silence and a moment later, more and different laughter from Miss Jenny.

'If I had not shouted, Madam, to part them,' she told her mistress, 'Miss would have lost her most precious possession on the heath there, in full view of all the valley.'

'Hardly,' commented Glendessary with some asperity, for he had been summoned to the drawing-room at his wife's urgent, and apparently trivial, request. 'They are but children, and high-spirited. They were merely romping as all young things like to do when there is the surge of spring in the valley.'

'But Jenny is no longer a child,' protested his wife. 'She should be learning womanly accomplishments as her sisters do, not ranging like a tinker's daughter in the hills.'

'You know my theories of liberal education. How can a gentleman run his estate with understanding if he has no knowledge of how his tenants live? And it is as important for Jenny, who will one day marry a chieftain, as it is for Alan who I hope will succeed me here. It breeds only discontent to set one's children apart from those whose lives they must always share in the closest sense. When the children live, as ours do, with their tenants' children, a bond is formed which cannot be broken.'

'That is what I fear ...' began his wife, but Glendessary silenced her with a raised hand.

'Let me finish. If a child is pampered, how can that child hope to combat adversity in later life or triumph over privation? When the child is grown to a sufficient age, as you know yourself my dear, his natural education is balanced with a gentleman's accomplishments. Mr Graham tells me that Alan is already ...'

'But it is *Jenny* we talk of,' interrupted Lady Margaret in exasperation. 'She should be here, with me, learning *ladylike* accomplishments, not running wild as an untamed horse! She is a *woman*, Hugh! Why can you not see it? Sometimes I declare you see nothing until it is penned in the best India ink on the best vellum and unfurled under your bespectacled nose!'

Glendessary looked at his wife in surprise. It was rarely that she raised her voice against him, for he truly believed she loved him as unquestioningly as he loved her. It was the sure comfort of his life to know his delicate-featured Margaret with her soft hair and porcelain skin sat dutiful and loving in his drawing-room. She was the ornament and comfort of his days. To hear her criticize him as she was doing now was rare indeed.

'What can you mean?' he said with unaccustomed sternness. 'If I choose not to see evil where no evil exists, is that blindness? I will not be a party to baseless suspicion and', he cast a shrewd glance at his wife's servant, 'malicious, jealous lies.'

Morag's eyes were hard as granite as she said, 'There's nae pleasin' some folk. Ye ken fine ye'd be after my head gin Miss Jenny fell. Miss Jenny may be a quinie in years, but her body is old enough to bear children – I can testify to that – and the lad is man enough, and willing too, I'll vow, to father them.'

'His father shall hear you repeat that,' said Glendessary quietly. 'I will vow upon my sword that Alexander's son is as loyal to me as Alexander himself, and no daughter of mine is in danger at his hands.'

'Maybe, sir,' retorted the woman who was used to speak her mind. 'But there's provocation even the most loyal canna fight, and when a lass romps wi' a laddie and flaunts hersel' half-naked...'

'Quiet, woman!' thundered Glendessary in a voice that would have credited Lochiel. 'I will hear no baseless slander of any woman, least of all my daughter. Go!'

As the woman scurried from the room 'afore the master took completely fou'', as she told them in the kitchen, Lady Margaret dissolved into helpless weeping.

'Oh my darling husband, do not frown so. I cannot bear it. But what am I to do with Jenny? She will not wear shoes nor stockings and I gave her such a pretty pair like mine, see, with clocked ankles and sheer as silk, with shoes of blue satin ... but she prefers to run ragged as any vagabond, her legs quite caked with mud and her skin dark as an Egyptian's with the sun and wind. Her breasts are near full grown and should be laced, yet she refuses quite to be measured for her stays. She will not do one thing I say.'

'Hush, my little linnet,' soothed Glendessary as he cradled his

27

wife's head against his breast and stroked her silken hair, which gleamed pale as milk against the dark green worsted of his coat. But his eyes were sombre as he stared over her head through the narrow window embrasure and across the waters of the loch. The list of his daughter's misdemeanours was a familiar one, but for the unlaced breasts . . .

Grey as steel, the loch stretched into the distance like a sword blade parting the hills. He had an aunt in Edinburgh. . . Lochiel himself had mentioned the possibility of sending Jenny there. 'Aunt Cameron would be a match for any girl,' he had chuckled, 'and Jenny would liven up those Edinburgh fools, I'll warrant.'

Lochiel's half-jocular suggestion had lodged itself in a corner of Glendessary's mind and he thought about it now with a sinking heart. One day, he realized, he would have to send his daughter away, if only to advertise her in the marriage market. But not yet . . .

He gave his wife a final reassuring pat. 'Do not worry, Margaret. Jenny is innocent. She is wild at times, but she is loving-hearted. She will do nothing to hurt us.' When his wife still looked unconvinced, he added, 'If it will set your heart at rest, I will confine her to the house for a while. It will be punishment enough for her to stay indoors now that the weather brightens and summer comes.'

Jenny heard them from the bedchamber: the lowing of faraway cattle and the faint shouts of men. In a trice she was awake, coverlet and bed-curtain pushed back: siblings and nurse slept on, undisturbed. She sped to the window embrasure, eased open the wooden shutter and thrust out her head, heedless of her own nakedness and the chill of the early morning air.

The sun was not yet up, but there was a pale light in the east, enough to touch the surface of Loch Arkaig with an eerie sheen. On either side the hills rose soft with daybreak, their rocks still masked in shadow; the only sounds the curlew and, from somewhere close at hand, a laverock. For a moment Jenny thought she had been mistaken until, far away, low at the water's edge, she saw the shapes, men and cattle and panniered horses. There would be babies in some of the creels, their mothers walking beside them with milking utensils, plaids and bags of meal.

They were taking the cattle to the summer shieling.

Swift and silent, she tugged her brown dress over her head, looped the girdle tight at the waist and snatched up her tunag. She ran combing fingers once through her hair, but in the dim

28

light of the bedchamber could not find the band which kept it from her face. No matter. She stood a moment straining for any sound of watchful life.

On the sward below Glendessary rabbits loped, grazing. A coracle lay upended in the shallows, a bird preening morning feathers on its keel. But in the room where she stood there was only the regular breathing of sleep . . . .

She moved to the door, lifted the heavy latch, and slipped outside on to the stone-wedged, spiral stair. A whispered 'Jenny!' stopped her in mid-step. Alan, white-faced and frightened in his night shift, tumbled down the steps to fling thin arms about her waist and bury his face in her chest.

'I had a nightmare, Jenny,' he managed through his tears. 'I was coming to find you.'

'Find Mr Graham instead,' she whispered fiercely. 'I am in a hurry.'

'Where are you going, Jenny? I thought Papa said . . .'

'That is no business of yours.' She pushed him away from her and held his thin shoulders tight in her hands. 'If you tell,' she went on in a voice whose whispered faintness lost none of its threat, 'I will call the bogles to haunt you in your bed.'

Alan's eyes grew wider still with terror and his whole frame shook. 'I will not tell, Jenny. Honest I will not.'

'Then go back to your bed . . . and do not be afraid,' she finished, more kindly. 'The cock crew half an hour ago. The bogles cannot get you now.' But he still clung to her, pleading, 'Stay with me, Jenny.'

'Let go of my dress!' She wrenched the folds from his clutching hands. 'The servants will be up soon . . .' Then she leapt down the spiral steps two at a time. At the foot, at the door to the great hall, she paused. No sound. No rattle of morning pails. No calling from the yard. She eased back the bolt of the little postern – when they found it open they would each think another had done it – and slipped out into the rainwashed cleanliness of early morning.

Under her bare feet, moisture sprayed up from laden turf as she sped across grassland to drop safe into the gully of the nearest stream. It was only when she crouched, regaining her breath and planning which route to take to join the drovers, that she remembered she had come empty-handed. But it was too late now. She would borrow a knife, catch fish or game as Hugh did and be no burden. As for Hugh, how dare he set off to the summer shieling without her?

In the cleft beside her was a stunted tree, branches lichened grey with moss. Jenny snapped off a small branch and flexed it over her hand. With Hugh's knife it would make a perfect fish-spear. She touched the switch lightly against her thigh and her eyes danced with mischief. She would show Hugh that she might be only a lassie, but not one to stay at home at a mere man's bidding!

With a carefree heart, Jenny Cameron shook the moisture from her hair and set off along the gully of the stream.

In the valley behind her the woman stood motionless in the shadow of Glendessary's walls. Her eyes were shrewd. She would tell no one. Yet. Not till the girl had had full time to condemn herself beyond excusing...

'Where is Miss Jenny?' The cry went up an hour later when the board was set for breakfast and her place empty. Normally no one would have heeded her absence, for Miss Jenny often helped herself early to broze from the pot over the kitchen fire or creamed her upper lip at the milk crock in the dairy. But the household knew Miss Jenny was confined indoors and ordered, for once, to conform.

From turret to cellar, every closet, clothes-press, kist and bed was searched before the Laird conceded that his daughter had disobeyed him. Only then did Morag remember that she had seen someone early, on the home paddock, but had thought it one of the cottars' girls. Horses and search parties were ordered immediately into the hills.

It was Glendessary himself who found her, late in the afternoon and his eyes were bleak behind the anger and anxiety. She did not hear his horse's approach; the men in the space around the shieling gave no sign. Later, she realized it was embarrassment that kept one man's eyes on the hare-hide he was scraping, another's on the whittled stick which was to spear a mountain trout or salmon. But at the time she abused them for their lack of watchfulness, used anger to hide the apprehension which grew as she saw no understanding in her father's face.

'Suppose it had not been my father,' she demanded, turning on the nearest, 'but Macdonald's men come to steal our cattle? Would you have seen *them* before the dirk ripped your throat?'

'Enough, Jenny,' warned her father.

'Poltroons!' cried the girl, close to despair. 'Lily-livered Lowlanders! 'Tis well you have a tolerant chieftain in my father or you would see your heads on your own peat-spades and...'

'*Enough*!' Glendessary thundered at his daughter who stood now at his horse's head, her hand on the animal's neck. She was taller than he had realized and, with her cheeks flushed as they

30

were now, her thick hair dishevelled but gleaming black as a raven's breast, and her eyes wary behind their spirit, she was astonishingly beautiful – not with the conventional beauty of his wife, but with the wild, unconscious beauty of the hills behind her. His heart was wrenched with the pain of what he knew he must do.

'Come home.'

'Papa, I am sorry,' said Jenny propitiatingly, 'and I should have asked, but when you confined me to the house you did not specify . . . "for a while" you said, and it has been so long. When I heard them passing on their way to the shieling, you were still sleeping and I knew you would not mind. I have not been to the hills. You said yourself that I must learn whatever . . .' Her voice faltered to a stop in the face of her father's unbending silence. She said, in a different voice, 'I will come to no harm, Papa. Hugh is with me and . . .' She stopped again, but this time it was not her father's anger which dried her words. For the first time she looked at the men who had come with her father and there, beside Alexander at her father's heels, was Alexander's son.

Hugh had betrayed her! She had thought him gone further into the hills to find pasture, but instead he had gone back to Glendessary. It was as if the earth had split under her, or the hills burst apart. She had no words to protest when her father summoned a horse for her and bade her mount. She said nothing as they made their way back down the long valley in the fading light of evening, the horse's feet silent on the springing turf. She hardly spoke in the weeks that followed as clothes were found and altered, travelling boxes packed.

Hugh had betrayed her. It was a fact she could not assimilate, however much she turned it over in her mind. To be sure, he had been surprised when she came upon them in the shieling and caught him unprepared. He had looked angry for a moment and had told her to go back. But when she refused, facing him in defiance and flexing the rowan switch in her hands, he had, she thought, submitted. When he had moved further up the stream-bed and out of sight, she had thought nothing of it. The men were gone, someone told her, to see if there was better pasture in the next glen, and she had settled happily to her task of whittling fish-hooks, while all around her the work of the little settlement went on.

She had been turning a pair of spitted trout over a fire of heather stalks when her father came upon her and now, a lifetime later, the scent of smoke still lingered in her hair, in spite of Morag's cruel scrubbing with icy water from the loch and a handful of lye.

'For ye'll no' go to Edinburgh unkempt and reekin' o' the byre,

31

Miss, if I can help it, though they say yon toon has a reek o' its own fit to choke the breath i' your mou', and maybe naebody to mind ain reek from anither. But ye'll smell sweet when ye leave Glendessary, if I have to scrub the hair from your scalp. So hold still and cease yon wriggling.'

To her mother's satisfaction and her father's bafflement, Jenny submitted. She submitted when they measured her for petticoats and stays; when they forced her feet into unfamiliar stockings and, worse, shoes. She submitted not from obedience, as her mother thought, but because she was oblivious of what was happening about her. Her mind was wrestling still with the momentous fact that Hugh had betrayed her. Hugh who, when she was but five or six had sealed a bond of eternal friendship on a solemn oath of wetted thumbs. Hugh who had sworn on his drawn dirk to make a *creach* for her and who, she knew, would die rather than betray one member of the clan for *tascal* money. Hugh, her lifelong friend and haunchman and, since springtime, her declared gallant, had turned her over to her father and inevitable exile.

She would never forgive him for it. She had not seen him since that terrible evening at the shieling and was glad, for if she had, she would have flown at him with tooth, claw and dagger; a traitor in the Cameron clan must be punished with death.

Her father, watching her unaware, saw her spirits dwindle as a candle-flame when the wax runs low, and his heart swelled painfully with compassion. If there was any way he could have done it, he would have kept his daughter in Glendessary, but what his wife said was true: Jenny was no longer a child. And though heart, mind and spirit soared free, her body bound her to convention as surely as a jess fettered a hawk. Why could not Jenny be more shrewd and niggardly with her affections, as other unmarried maidens were? But the instinct which guided most young virgins safely to the marriage-bed was an instinct born of generations of watchful chaperons and mothers – and Jenny's instincts were untouched by artificial restraints. It was a fact which had delighted him till now, but he had no weapon against convention and no other defence for his daughter's innocence than to send her to Great-aunt Margaret Cameron, in Edinburgh.

They set out on a morning of light rain and fitful sunshine; her father and Alexander, followed by gillies leading packhorses, and Morag's daughter Bess who was to go to Edinburgh with them and then return: a doe-eyed, placid girl but well chosen to keep Miss Jenny under close surveillance on the week-long journey, for she had a private reason for wishing to escort the young lady safely out of Glendessary and Hugh Cameron's eyes.

As they drew away from the eastern end of Loch Arkaig where the falls of Cia-aig thundered their final contribution to the waters before they narrowed through the dark mile to Loch Lochy, the noise filled Jenny's head till she thought her skull would split apart.

She knew the falls well, though they were twelve miles from her home, and closed her eyes tight on the tears which threatened to disgrace her. Behind the lids she could see the tiny, climbing path, narrow as a foot-span and knotted with tree-roots. She could feel the oak-leaves soft under her feet, smell the scent of resin and damp rock. Hugh and she had played there often in summers past, but had not ventured further eastwards than those falls, which, with the little bridge at their feet, marked the boundary of Glendessary. Now, as her father's horse moved on to the single arch of the bridge, the column following after, the waters thundered to a climax in her head and her silence burst on an animal cry of despair. She leapt from her horse, darted between startled riders and ran like a hunted hare for the trees and the cliff path at the falls.

Jenny was awkwardly clad in yellow petticoats and damask, but she kilted her skirts high and would have outstripped her pursuers had not her unaccustomed shoes slipped on the mossy rock. She kicked against her captors, bit Alexander deep in the hand. When he held her helpless as a rolled blanket under his arm, she screamed her anguish high above the roaring of the falls. But even as her screams echoed, fading in the tree-tops, she knew defeat, and when she stood before her father on the bridge, he saw it in her face and turned away lest his heart betray him.

'Give me your word,' he said, more harshly than he intended, 'that you will not run away again.'

When she gave it, he said, 'And that you will go to Edinburgh as I require you to do; that you will obey my wishes and your aunt's wishes in every way.'

He waited, unmoving, in the long silence which followed until Jenny, in a voice parched as drifting leaves, gave him her promise. Glendessary released his held breath on a sigh of relief. 'Ride with me, Jenny,' he said more kindly. 'Do not leave my side.'

As the cavalcade moved off again in silence along the first stretch of the dark mile he added quietly, 'Remember Jenny, a Cameron never breaks his word.'

They followed the river eastward between narrow, tree-thick

hills which seemed to Jenny dark as prison walls. As the thunder of Cia-aig dwindled into the far distance with Loch Arkaig, Glendessary, Hugh, and all that she had ever loved, Jenny turned her face away lest her father see the tears which she could no longer hold in check.

2

When Miss Jenny came to her Aunt in Edinburgh, she was a wild, uncultivated Hoydon, who did not want Sense and had a surprising ready Wit, which was buried in a violent passionate Temper, impatient to the last Degree of Contradiction; but the Regard her Aunt had for the Family made her undertake the taming her . . .

They reached Edinburgh late on the fifth day. Though Jenny still fretted against her capture and grew more wan with every ell that separated them from Glendessary, she was stirred to unwilling interest by the prospect of the city.

Jenny had never seen a city, and was equally unprepared for the terrifying space of water which must be crossed before they reached that castle on the rock. She had thought Loch Arkaig limitless, but this water was grey as a pewter dish and to both east and west, where the hills should have been, was a great hole in the air so that sky and water mingled. Jenny could not understand why it did not drain away entirely, for where were the cataracts to keep it full? But the water, her father said, was salt and deeper than any loch, for it flowed straight to the sea. To Jenny it appeared uneasy, with no end and no beginning . . . for the first time she had an inkling of the fear which her brother Alan must feel in nightmare when confronted by the unknown.

At the little harbour men spoke in Lowland Scots, not in the Gaelic of her hills, and they smelled different. Jenny was surprised the garrons did not shy in terror when Alexander led them away to be stabled against their return. When she saw the ferryboat draw up on the shingle and the great breadth of water to be crossed to reach that other bank, she was afraid to climb into it lest it whisk her away to the Devil, or the bottom of the sea. But when her father stepped in and ordered her to follow, she did so with a high head and unfaltering step. When the boat pulled away from the shore and she closed her eyes for terror, she let it be thought she closed them for the *mal de mer*.

They entered Edinburgh by the West Port and the Grassmarket an hour before sundown, and Jenny could not comprehend the crowds. And the houses! She had thought her own house large, but here the street was battlemented either side with buildings, eight or ten stories high. Noise overwhelmed her: dogs, children, drunken songs from subterranean taverns, pedlars crying their wares, clogged feet ... and everywhere the noise of hammering from the white-smiths' shops and the silver-smiths' in the Bow. When they reached the top and turned right into the chief street, the noise was even greater in density, the houses spattered thick with signs – wigmakers, goldsmiths, tailors ... Tunnels burrowed either side of the street, with arched roofs and sides as steep as Cia-aig, beyond which were courtyards, steps, more buildings, deep in cavernous shadow.

For the light was fading. Already there were flambeaux in some of the closes, footmen carried smoking torches held like cudgels head-high, while behind them hurried figures muffled in velvet or silks. Four men pushed past them, trotting, poles across their shoulders, between them a swaying contraption of painted wood and curtains.

'A sedan chair,' explained her father, seeing her mouth drop open in wonder. 'The street is steep and crowded as you see. It is hazardous for horse and coach alike.'

Jenny remembered tales she had heard at home of the little rooms on wheels which horses pulled as they pulled the plough in Glendessary's pastures. There had been no coach in the stable-yard where they had left their hired horses on entering the town. After that Jenny and her father had gone on foot, with Alexander and Bess close behind them and the gillies, proud and wary, hand on sword, the dirks at their belts glinting in the passing light of torch or lantern.

Alexander, close at Glendessary's back, wore pistols as well as broadsword and dirk, and the close-knit group caused many heads to turn as they made their way along the centre of the street past stall, luckenbooth, tavern, eyes alert in constant watch.

Everywhere were people shouting in the Lowland tongue, women loud-voiced and cheerful, children shrill. Once they passed a lord, as Jenny thought, or a prince ... for who else would dress in such a splendour of sky-blue silk, white lace, powdered wig and high-heeled buckled shoes to walk on a street that was filthier than the midden at home? And his haunchman as ill-dressed as himself in pink velvet, and *shoes*. The lackey who walked ahead of them to light the way was the only sensible one amongst them, in his brown breeches and homespun shirt, and if his hair was unkempt, at least it was his own.

'Lord Belhaven,' said her father. 'A good man and one of us.'

36

'One of us?' echoed Jenny in surprise. How could such a womanish fop be any kin of theirs?

'An anti-Union man who has done much for Scotland's cause. 'Tis well he is in town.'

Before Jenny could ask why, a boy pushed past them, running.

'Caddie!' called her father and the boy slithered to a stop, spun round and ran back to them with hardly a pause in motion. Bare-foot and dirty, his clothes a collection of assorted rags, his eyes were sharp and wary.

'What is your name, boy?'

'Boy, an' ye say so,' said the lad, with a wink at Jenny. 'Though it wasna' "Boy" ten minutes past when Belhaven thankit me wi' a bawbee and a "weel done, Wattie". But "Boy" it is, if ye've anither bawbee to match.'

'I may have, if your wits are quick as your tongue,' replied Glendessary, with a warning hand on Alexander's arm. 'Do you know Mistress Cameron's in Geddes Close?'

'Third stair? Merchant Brodie's Land? An old body wi' a hookit neb?'

'Mistress *Margaret* Cameron,' said her father, reproving. 'Cousin of Lochiel. Of Parliament Close, Lord Crossrig's Land till the conflagration there; now moved to new lodgings.'

'Aye. That's hersel'.' He caught Jenny staring and when she continued to look at him in unblushing wonder, he said, 'Ye'll no' forget me in a hurry – or are ye plannin' to tak' my likeness in oils?'

Jenny's hearing was not yet attuned to the Lowland tongue and she made no answer, but Alexander, her father's haunch-man did with a blow to the lad's ear.

'Ye'll keep a civil tongue in your head, if you want to keep your head on your shoulders and earn good silver for your pains.'

'I'm engaged,' said the lad, 'wi' this,' and he held up a sealed note. 'And if it isna' in the hand o' Master Fletcher by sundown my lugs'll be filled so full o' holes I'll sell 'em for Flanders lace.'

'Sundown is a while away,' said her father, 'and I will give you this – ' he held up a coin between finger and thumb, 'to direct us to Mistress Cameron's – now.'

Jenny felt the first smile of many weeks lift her mouth when the lad turned them round and pointed at an entrance at their back.

'Yon's the close ye're seekin' – yon casement at the turn o' the stair is Mistress Cameron's – and her own ill-visaged spying servant-fellow at it,' he added in an undertone to Jenny. 'I'll gladly see ye safely to the door, sir, and rasp the tirl for ye.'

'We will not be needing . . .' began Alexander, but Glendessary raised a hand. 'Thank you, Wattie. A good caddie is beyond price,' he added *sotto voce* to his haunchman. 'Mark him well. You too, Jenny, against future need.'

They moved along the dark tunnel of the wynd, the walls scarce an arm's breadth apart, the roof so low that Alexander had to stoop his head, while underfoot the path was slippery with moisture. A dark shape burst from the shadows and scuttled past their feet.

'A rat,' explained her father. Jenny had never seen a rat. 'You will see a superfluity before the week is out, my dear. The city is full of them.'

The tunnel disgorged them into the close and there was sky again overhead. But what a small sky. The walls rose high as cliffs on every side with windows, jutting stories, balustrades, all in shadow now and sinister. Woodsmoke choked the air with undertones of boiling kale, burnt fat, and, like the sludge in a stagnant pond, the pervasive stench of excrement. There was no wind. Jenny clapped a hand against her mouth and involuntarily retched.

A flight of stone steps mounted to a darker, dirtier flight inside the building, winding up past closed doors and muffled voices to the third landing and a heavy door with an iron tirling-pin and ring which Wattie rasped vigorously up and down. The door was wrenched open and Wattie yanked half across the threshold at the feet of a pink-faced youth in footman's clothing of dark worsted jacket, breeches and ruched linen, the edges of which, Jenny noticed, were none too white. The young man's eyes gleamed with satisfaction as he looked down at the caddie. 'Awa' wi' ye, Wattie. The party is in good hands and has no more need o' the likes o' you to clutter the stair wi' filth.'

'I can see that, wi' the like o' yersel' to spread the stink o' ten.'

'Here, boy,' said Glendessary quickly, thrusting a coin into the caddie's hand. 'My thanks to you.'

'And mine to you, sir,' said the boy with a grin as he saw the size of the payment. 'My commiserations to the wee folk i' yer periwig,' he called to the footman as he skipped out of reach, 'wi' a' yon dry rot to contend wi'.'

Jenny would have laughed were it not for her father and Alexander at her side, for the footman's expression was aboil with as many ingredients as a pot of cock-a-leekie on the fire at home – fury, frustration, shame at being ridiculed before strangers and, surprisingly, an ill-concealed and private grin.

Jenny turned to the casement behind her to catch another glimpse of the extraordinary caddie who looked as if he had lived all his short life homeless in the same few rags, yet moved among the Edinburgh gentry as proud as any clansman on the hillside, at home.

Home . . . she spun swiftly away from the memory lest it lead her on to Hugh, and turned instead to a perusal of the young footman who apparently waged private battle with Wattie.

Older than Hugh, though not by many years, he was as tall, but where Hugh was knotted with muscle, the footman's limbs were thin as willow twigs so that his head in its powdered wig looked precarious as a seed-head of foxtail grass which she could send flying with one flick of finger and thumb. His face was set now in a pompous expression which made Jenny want to laugh, especially when he caught her looking at him and, flushing, averted his eyes.

Her father propelled her across the hall into a dark-panelled room with painted ceiling and polished floor, a small fire in a large hearth, and, in a heavy chair beside it, a white-haired old lady with surprisingly dark eyes. She was thin as a besom, in a gown of black brocade cut so low that it showed the fleshless ridge of breastbone and ribs. Diamonds hung about her skinny throat and in the white mound of hair were scraps of black lace and more diamonds. Her face, thought Jenny in astonishment, had been dipped in the flour tub!

'Don't stare, girl! Curtsey your respect. Here!' the old woman indicated a square of floorboard at her feet, 'where I can see ye!' She took an eyeglass from a string at her neck and held it over her nose which was hooked white as a rabbit's jaw-bone. 'So *this* is Miss Jean Cameron. Stand still, girl, while I study ye! And ye wish her "fashioned" is it, Glendessary?'

Glendessary flushed at the word. If he had his heart's wish he would keep his daughter as guileless as she was now, but his head and his wife dictated otherwise. He looked uneasily at Jenny, who was behaving quietly enough, thank God, but her face was unusually pale, her hands clasped tight together at her back.

'Whatever education you find necessary, Aunt Cameron,' he said, 'to supply her deficiencies.'

'It is obvious she has no deficiency of impudence,' said the old lady as Jenny continued to look her full in the face. 'What have you to say for yourself, girl?'

Jenny took courage from her fear and said clearly, in the quaintly accented tongue of the Gaelic-speaker speaking English, 'That if I had such a deficiency, you would supply it, Ma'am, for I do but take my cue from you.'

'Hoots toots! A pert Miss!'

'Not pert,' corrected Jenny, two red spots on her cheeks now. 'Merely accurate.'

'Jenny,' warned her father, 'you are not in Glendessary. You must not speak to your aunt so.'

'And why not, Papa? Am I to be looked over like a drover's beast at market and be grateful for it? If Aunt Cameron wishes to study me that she may know me again, surely I may do the same by her? What is correct for one must by all logic be correct for the other.'

'Logic? What logic can there be between an old woman and a child?'

'I was brought to Edinburgh,' flashed Jenny, 'because it was universally agreed that I was *not* a child.'

'Nor an old woman either, so hold your tongue, girl.'

'Aunt Cameron, Jenny does not mean to . . .'

'You too, Glendessary! I'll decide for myself what Miss "means" or does not mean in my own house. Andrew!' The door opened and the young footman entered, an expression on his face which told Jenny instantly that he had heard every word and enjoyed it. 'Fetch Mackie! Tell her she is needed. With a switch.'

'You will not beat the girl,' said Glendessary. His voice was quiet, but firm. 'The tawse is a barbaric curb to natural development, a humiliation to the spirit, and an instrument of deliberate cruelty which I abhor, as I abhor all unnecessary infliction of pain.'

'You may abhor what you choose,' retorted Mistress Cameron. 'But you have given your daughter into my care – and not before time, I see. If I decide a curb is necessary, then I shall give it.'

'I have given my daughter, as you put it, into your care, to be taught the refinements of life, not its most primitive practices. You cannot beat wisdom into a child.'

'At home,' said Jenny, 'when we train a garron, we use a switch only when all other methods fail.'

'Well ye're not at home and ye're not a garron, whatever that might be, and the first lesson you'll learn, Miss, is to hold your tongue when told to do so. Mackie, show Miss Jenny to her bed. See yon Bess, or whatever her name is, unpacks her mistress's box before she leaves, then give Miss Jenny gruel and a tot o' second ale. See she is up for her lesson at six sharp. Say good-bye to your father, Miss, and take that sullen look off your face.'

But it was not sullenness which set Jenny's mouth in a hard, tight line. It was the knowledge that by next day her father would be gone and with him all connection with the home, the glen, the people that she loved – and the determination not to let this bone-beaked, black-eyed woman see the despair which rose like a rock in her throat to choke her with unshed tears.

'Good-bye, Papa. My duty to Uncle John.' Glendessary was to spend the night at the house of Sir Ewen's son John, Younger of Lochiel, where he had business concerning cattle for the estate. 'And to Mama and Alan and the others,' she finished, 'when you are safe home again.' She dipped a curtsey, eyes downcast, then looked up and saw her father's sorrowful face. Pride and imagined injury fled: she flung her arms round his neck and clasped him so tight against her that he caught his breath.

'There, child,' he said, soothing, 'it will not be long before we meet again. No doubt Aunt Cameron will spare you a while in the summer months, or I will have business again to bring me south.' But he clasped her just as tightly before he kissed her on the brow and untwined her arms from his neck. 'Go now with Mackie. And Jenny, remember your promise.'

'What promise was that?' demanded Mistress Cameron when the girl had gone.

'A private bond between my daughter and myself,' said Glendessary stiffly.

'Then I'd best not ask the details lest it go against my plans. Awa' wi' ye, Andrew, and bring the claret. Well, Glendessary, ye'll have time to tell me what Lochiel and his brother are up to wi' you-know-who, and what the news is from St Germain.'

'Little enough,' said Glendessary, looking up as the footman hovered, decanter in hand.

'Never mind him. He may be thick as a plank o' Finland pine, but he'll keep a careful tongue in his head – or I'll have it clipped afore he knows it, eh Andrew?'

'You can rely upon me, Ma'am,' said Andrew with incongruous dignity.

'I knew his father,' smiled the old lady, for the first time showing a ray of human warmth. 'He was a fine man, and true as your own Lochaber axe. But you were telling me of the Chevalier. How does he regard this Union of Parliaments which daft folk seem set on thrusting upon us?'

'I know not at first hand, but it can only be a spur to fortune. On this issue I understand Cavalier and Country are united. Lord Queensberry's support of Union with the English Parliament can only add strength to our cause, for Union inevitably involves acceptance of the Hanoverian succession. No true Scot could accept that, and every Jacobite will be spurred to arms for his King.'

As she lay in the box bed in the wall of the adjoining room which she was to share with her aunt and, on a pallet bed, the woman Mackie, Jenny heard the voices drone on ... Lord Queensberry, Tweeddale, Andrew Fletcher of Saltoun, more names, and always Lochiel: Sir Ewen or John Younger, or Sir Ewen's brother Allan at the French court ... Jenny listened as she listened at Glendessary to the adult talk of drovers and cattle prices, of borrowing and lending money, and, lately, of the threat to Scotland's nationhood from the English plan to unite the Parliaments: Sir Ewen she knew was against it, as he was against Queen Anne and the Hanoverian succession – and whatever Lochiel decreed, in Jenny's eyes was right. The thought of Sir Ewen reminded her of home and of her promise to her father. She had promised to obey her aunt's wishes in every way and she could not break her word. Yet the thought that she had bound herself in obedience to that crow of an old lady in the adjoining room almost choked her with frustration and despair.

She heard the scrape of wood on wood, the opening and closing of a door, then voices on the stair. Her father was leaving. Jenny bit her lip hard to stop the trembling. Her father's wishes for her were known; but not those of her aunt. If she took care to remain in ignorance of them, could she be expected to obey?

With this Jesuitical comfort, Jenny curled under the unfamiliar plaid and slept.

'Jenny sends you her duty,' said Glendessary as Sir Ewen's son John Cameron, Younger of Lochiel, rose to greet him. 'I have come straight from Margaret Cameron's where she is to lodge.'

'They will be two of a kind, I fancy,' chuckled John Cameron, a man of middle-years, fresh-faced and cheerful. 'Glendessary's daughter,' he explained to the company at large. 'A lass of spirit, come to be tamed by Aunt Cameron – though if the tales I hear be true, Cousin, she'll be a garron long in the breaking.'

'What tales?' bristled Glendessary.

John Cameron laughed. 'Come, Cousin, you are too quick to take offence. The tales are of the best kind, such as my father's bard sings of an evening. In fact, 'twas he who told us of your daughter's prowess. "Skill and spirit fit to deck a chieftain" I believe he sang, and more about quickness of wit and eye, not to mention beauty.'

Glendessary looked gratified. 'Aye, Jenny is a fine lass.'

'I know my father thinks so. You must marry her well.'

'I intend to do so, when the time comes.'

'The time will come for more than a maid's wedding,' said a

voice from the fireside, and all eyes turned towards the plain-dressed, country-faced man who sat straight-backed in a carved oak chair, a pewter goblet in his hands.

'How goes it, Fletcher?' asked Glendessary. 'I am newly come from Lochaber and out of touch. Is our country to be sold, as Queensberry plans, to England?'

Fletcher, Presbyterian though he was, was a champion of Scottish nationalism, and welcome in the Jacobite ranks whenever the threat of Union of the Parliaments seemed close. His speeches in Parliament were retailed throughout the drawing-rooms of Edinburgh, and distributed in broadsheets and pamphlets in the streets. It was Fletcher who united 'Cavalier' and 'Country' parties: but many suspected that Fletcher was defending a cause already lost.

'Seafield and Queensberry are busy as ever,' Fletcher explained with sombre gravity. 'They argue and promise, they hold out the titillating bait of recompense for the Darien disaster, of flourishing and profitable trade links, of positions of State in Westminster . . . they talk of expedience and economic sense, and forget their country's sovereignty is at stake.'

'And is it?' asked a neat-clad wine-merchant of middle age. 'I have heard it said that the Union might after all bring nought but benefit.'

'Then you hear strange tales, Baillie, and a man of your intelligence should know better than to listen to them. Do you forget what we are offered? Forty-three members at Westminster to their 513? Sixteen of our peers to 190 English Lords? What hope have we but to be swamped among so many?'

'But there is the Equivalent. There are many here who welcome any means of redress for the terrible losses sustained in the Darien enterprise.'

'Money! Always it comes down to money. Would you have Scotland sold to pay a few business debts?'

The talk turned naturally to matters of trade, of herring shipments to Ireland, of the price of French wines and, of course, of cattle. Then as the evening progressed, as the wine flowed and hired sedan chairs were forgotten, the talk veered to lighter matters.

'There is cock-fighting I hear in Leith links,' said Glendessary, and his cousin Cameron was quick to recognize the wistfulness behind the slurred and slowing words.

'Aye, and excellent sport it is. Shall we hire a coach and go, Cousin, tomorrow?'

'My Jenny would like fine to ride in a coach, and I am guilty that I left her where I did. If I could give her one pleasure before I return to Glendessary – a coach-ride and a cock-fight would delight her heart . . .' His eyes blurred with sentiment and wine. 'But tomorrow I go home.'

'Cousin, I fear cock-fighting would not delight Aunt Cameron, however much it pleased Miss Jenny; and as for a hackney! Remember the scandal when a coach ran down a woman in the very street of Leith?'

'And on the Sabbath, too,' put in the Baillie, 'and all of them drunk.'

'These are troubled times,' said Fletcher, with careful diction. 'Treachery and oath-breaking in our Parliament. Sabbath-breaking and debauchery in our city's streets. What hope is there for our nation but shame? I fear you chose an ill time, Glendessary, to bring your daughter to Edinburgh for her education. What can she learn but to sacrifice liberty to licence and sovereignty to servitude?'

'You will learn to obey me, Miss, for you'll get no sustenance till you do.'

'I did not disobey you, Aunt. You told me to go to bed and I went. You did not tell me to stay there.'

'The Lord give me patience! No, I did not: because it did not enter my head that you would choose to vague abroad at dawn with every caddie and scavenger in the town. How dare you, Miss? Have you no decorum?'

'I went abroad, Madam, because I was stifled by the closeness of the walls and the stink of my bedchamber. At Glendessary the air is clean and fresh. There is an abundance for everyone. Here one has to fight for air to fill one's lungs.'

Jenny still could not assimilate the smothering fact that her aunt's house consisted of a mere three rooms – the parlour, the bedroom, and the kitchen where the kitchen-maid slept under the dresser. There was also the hallway which was all the space allotted to the footman – he was considered fortunate, though Jenny did not know it, for many of his acquaintances were put outdoors at night to sleep on the common stair. But this constriction was an unforeseen torture to Jenny, accustomed to the stone warren of Glendessary and the unlimited hills. She would have burst with suffocation had she stayed a moment longer in that airless prison.

'So you went out of the house, down the common stair, into the close and thence to the *High Street*?' Aunt Cameron's bony frame quivered with outrage.

'Aye, Ma'am. To look about me.'

'To look about you,' repeated her aunt with ominous calm.

'The town is new to me. I must learn my bearings if I am to

44

go about with ease and not lose myself like Papa lost us all last night . . .'

'Silence! Have you no conception of the enormity of your conduct?'

'But I merely walked abroad.' Jenny was genuinely surprised at her aunt's reaction.

'You merely walked abroad,' quivered her aunt between tight-drawn, painted lips.

Jenny began to wonder if the old woman was afflicted in her hearing, or slow of wit. Why else should she repeat each sentence on a question?

'I merely walked abroad,' repeated Jenny, more slowly and with raised voice, 'to see the town.'

'I am not deaf, Miss! God help me, if this wean is not the Devil's own child!'

'I am sorry, Ma'am. I thought as you repeated all I said that your hearing might be impaired.'

'Faugh!' The woman struck the floor with her stick. 'I will not have such impudence in my own house.'

Jenny dipped a swift, propitiatory curtsey – the woman was obviously touched in the head. 'I did not mean to be impertinent, Aunt. I merely pointed out the reason for my action. Is it not important always to know a person's reasons? I went abroad not to disobey you, but to satisfy my own curiosity. And the reason you are angry with me is that I did so without your knowledge, is it not? Next time I will leave a note to tell you where I am. Will that be . . .'

'Hold your tongue! The reason I am angry with you, Miss, is that you regard your will as master in my house. You will please to remember, Miss, that you are in my charge. Like the rest of my household.' Here she directed a fierce glance at Andrew who stood chastened in a corner by the door. 'Stand up straight, ye dolt. Shut your mou' and open your e'en, or I'll have ye thrown i' the horse trough. To let a country lass trample ye and wrench the bolt back and slam the door again in your flapping ear, and not stir a mite to stop her.'

Andrew shifted his feet and looked uncomfortable, his eyes fixed on a green painted bird on the ceiling, but when her aunt looked away from him, Jenny caught his eye and was surprised to see accusation and resentment. 'It is not his fault, Aunt,' she said quickly. 'No footman, however alert, would wake, for I am skilled by long practice.'

'So I see, Miss.' Her black eyes glared into Jenny's unsuspecting brown ones which, however, did not waver. 'And where are your stays?'

Jenny looked down at her front in quick surprise and then

laughed. 'I cannot bear them, Aunt, and now that I am delivered safe to you, there is surely no more need? The whalebone digs into my flesh and the laces constrict my ribs.'

'And your shoes?' said her aunt through closed teeth, her stick tapping on the wooden floor with ominous regularity.

'Do not worry, Aunt, they are not lost or spoilt. I never wear shoes. Hugh says the only use for shoes is to polish the floor of the kirk, and it is not Sunday.'

'Andrew,' said Aunt Cameron with deceptive quiet, 'fetch Agnes Mackie.'

They waited and, as Aunt Cameron made no attempt to speak, Jenny moved over to the window and looked down on to the street which was thronged now with people and with stalls from which rose a cacophony of creaking wood, the ring of brass and copper pots, the shrill argument of countrywomen vending cheeses and pot-herbs and horn spoons. Somewhere a knife-grinder was already singing his custom and the flesher's stall was heavy with meat and flies.

'Is it market day, Aunt?' she asked, but when she met only silence, she turned her attention back to the horses and the crowds until Agnes Mackie arrived at the run and with the same nervous expression the footman had worn. Aunt Cameron dismissed Andrew and, to Jenny's surprise, turned the key in the lock.

'Mackie. Miss Jenny informs me she does not like her stays nor her stockings nor her shoes. Nor anything, apparently, that a young lady is required to like. Moreover, she does not like to obey any will but her own. It is time, I think, for her first lesson.' She brought out a switch from its concealment behind her back. 'Bend over, Miss, and lift your skirt.'

Jenny whirled round from the window and looked from one woman to the other in astonished outrage. 'I will not! I have never been beaten in my life and I will not now.'

'We will see about that, Miss. Bend over when I tell you or you will have twice the punishment.'

But Jenny remained defiant, though her eyes were big now with fear. 'I will not. My father forbade it and so do I!'

'*You* forbid it, Miss? Hold her, Mackie.' But Agnes Mackie was a small woman of middle years, thin-chested and frail. When the woman attempted to grip Jenny by the forearm, the girl wrenched free with such vigour that Mackie lost her footing on the polished floor and had to clutch the table for support.

'Up again, Mackie, and take her!' shouted Aunt Cameron, her eyes afire with battle. '*Will you bend*, child?'

'I will not!' cried Jenny Cameron, equally defiant. 'Unlock the door and let me free. My father shall hear of this.'

46

Woman and girl glared, each unyielding. Then the older woman turned on her servant. 'Stop your snivelling, Mackie. She's only a wean, not the Wolf of Badenoch! But ye'd best fetch Andrew after all.'

Jenny's eyes darted from mistress to servant and then to the switch in Aunt Cameron's hand, and her natural instincts, born of her native hills, came rushing into their own. When Agnes Mackie opened the door, went out and closed it behind her, Jenny leapt across the room, turned the key in the lock, withdrew it and concealed it in the placket of her gown before her aunt could take one step to prevent it.

'If you have anything to discuss with me, Aunt Cameron,' she said, her back against the door, 'discuss it with me alone.'

'I will not *discuss* it, Miss! Move away from that door!' She brought the switch down in fury on the table-top so that the crash reverberated through the room. Jenny remained where she was, looking back at her aunt with eyes equally determined, though behind the anger was a surging exultation in the conflict and a steadfast conviction that she was in the right.

'Do you defy me?'

'I do. I will not be ill-treated and for no reason. My father forbade it.'

With a cry of impotent rage, Mistress Cameron launched herself at Jenny, bringing the switch down hard across her face. Jenny screamed with shock and fury, wrenched the weapon from her aunt and in the same movement lashed back at her across the thigh. 'How do you like to be struck?' she cried. 'Is it not painful? And *I* had the grace not to strike you where you struck me, in the face! Though I swear I will do so,' she added as Margaret Cameron fell back a step, gasping, and in her turn sought the table in support, 'if you do not give me your solemn word that you will obey my father's wishes and banish the rod.'

Aunt Cameron did not answer, but continued to lean against the table, breathing deep. Her eyes gave nothing away. In the stillness between them, Jenny saw the ageing bones and sagging skin – Aunt Cameron was closer to Sir Ewen's age than to her father's – and the exultation of her victory ebbed on a stab of shame. 'There, Aunt,' she said with a conciliatory smile, 'I am glad we agree, for I wish you no harm, truly . . .' But something in her aunt's eye made her add, 'And you will swear?'

Mistress Cameron seemed at a loss, as if rage choked her words. Then on an instant, she capitulated.

'You are right, child, and I was wrong. I see it now. Unlock the door and we will forget the matter.'

'And do you promise to forget the rod, too? Do you give your solemn word never again to strike me?'

'I do.'

'Then there's an end to it,' said Jenny laughing with relief, 'and let us now be friends.' She kissed her aunt on both cheeks, tossed the switch into a corner, extracted the key from her placket and unlocked the door. Agnes Mackie and Andrew stood open-mouthed on the other side.

'Come in, both of you,' said Aunt Cameron with slow calm. But when they were inside the door, she turned the key again in the lock and this time pocketed it herself. 'And now,' she said, looking slowly round the assembled company – Jenny, Agnes Mackie, Andrew – 'let there be an end to this farce.' She motioned Andrew to one side of Jenny, Mackie to the other, while Jenny, unsuspecting, waited smiling to see what reconciliation ceremony her aunt was about to perform.

'Hold her between you!' ordered her aunt and before Jenny realized what was happening she was pinioned over the table and held there by Mackie on the one side and the footman on the other while Margaret Cameron brought the switch down hard, again and again, on her unprotected behind and Jenny fought and struggled and screamed at the top of her young lungs entirely in vain.

When her aunt at last ceased on an exhalation of triumph, Jenny wrenched free and whirled on her tormentor, her eyes blazing with fury.

'You broke your word! A Cameron and you broke your word! You should be hanged!'

'Tush, girl. A word given under duress. Perhaps now you will do as you are told.'

'You broke your solemn oath.' Jenny stood uncowed, the red weal clear as a sword-cut across her cheek, and looked her aunt full in the face. 'There is not a Cameron in Glendessary who would do as you have done. If this is your Edinburgh "education" I spit upon it. I despise you, Ma'am. I shall never trust your word again.' She walked with dignity from the room and at least one of the company looked after her with awe and a new respect.

But in the secrecy of the box-bed which was to be her room, Jenny remembered home and the reason for her leaving it and knew that she, too, had lied. She had found treachery in Glendessary, just as she had found it here. Yet Hugh had only betrayed her to her father, his own liege lord; Aunt Cameron had beaten her against her given word and her own father's command. She took paper and pen, to tell her father of it before he left Edinburgh, for when he knew how little store Aunt Cameron set upon his wishes, surely he would take her home?

When Agnes Mackie arrived, plainly nervous of this untamed Highlander, to dress her in the ordered stays and stockings, Jenny ignored her. She stood coldly aloof as Ben Nevis under snow while the woman fumbled her into shape. She walked with dignity to her indicated place in the parlour and took up the indicated book, under her aunt's exulting eye. Aunt Cameron thought she had won and Jenny would not disabuse her. She was content to wait for retribution to fall, as assuredly it must.

The moment the chance came, she seized the footman's arm between digging fingers, pressed a folded note into his hand and ordered, 'Give this to Wattie, for my father. If you do me this service, I will overlook the other. You will be well rewarded,' she finished – 'wi' a' the air o' a Heelan' chieftain,' as Andrew reported later over an ale-jar in Lucky Spence's tavern.

Jenny's spirit remained deceptively quiet as she awaited her father's answer. She had no doubt that when it came she would be free to send her aunt and her aunt's household straight to the Devil, where they belonged. Meanwhile, she would show her aunt that she, too, could be canny. Her father would receive her note tonight, or at the latest tomorrow early, and he would not hesitate. Tomorrow forenoon should bring her release.

But Glendessary had left, his droving business done. Though John Cameron sent the letter after him, by the hill post, reported Wattie, Jenny waited in vain for a reply while the town filled steadily with people from all over Scotland – Highland chiefs with their pipers and bristling weaponry; Lowland lairds with their fashionable silks; even, it was rumoured, an English spy sent by the Queen herself and disguised as a glassworker or a fishmonger – no one knew which – all come for the opening on 3 October of what might prove to be the last Session Scotland's Parliament would ever see.

Still Glendessary's answer did not come, and while Jenny waited, she relied increasingly on Wattie. Though she did not venture out again unaccompanied, she became adept at lingering in the hall when the house door was open and more so at snatching a moment's talk with the ragged caddie who lived, it transpired, on the seventh step.

'Do you have no family?' she had asked, aghast, when he claimed that step as his home.

'None.' Wattie spat airily into the stair well. 'But as long as I keep in wi' the constable o' the caddies I'll do well enough. I mean to be Baillie o' the town one day.'

Jenny regarded the ragged urchin with a mixture of awe and

compassion. From his size he must be two years at the least her junior – the same age as her brother Alan who crept into her bed at night for fear! She could not imagine this lad afraid of anything. His eyes were old and shrewd. He knew everyone and everything of importance that happened in the city.

'Then it is not your family who lives in all those other rooms above and below?'

'Mine?' Wattie laughed. 'I am all the family I need. But let me see, there's the candlemaker and the tailor, the wee scaffie-mannie, the Master o' Baillis and his family, your ain Aunt Neb and above that, Sir Patrick Johnston – he's a Writer to the Signet and she a laird's daughter, like yersel', and there's Merchant Thom, his lodger and apprentices and a brood o' weans.'

'All in one house?'

'On our stair,' corrected Wattie. 'Each man's place is his hoose.'

'And yours is a . . . step?'

'Aye, and every inch o' it my ain.'

'I'll bring you bread,' said Jenny in quick concern. 'And ale. I know my aunt will have plenty. Wait here till I fetch it.'

Wattie tipped back his head and roared with a laugh fit for two grown men. 'Ye'll fetch it!' he gasped at last, his eyes streaming. 'Do ye nae ken you Neb is the meanest hussife i' the whole o' Edinburgh? If ye so much as tak a crumb from a bannock, she'll know it. If ye think to take aught, ye'd best think again or she'll skelp the skin from your hide.'

Remembering her betrayal, Jenny was silenced, but as the days dragged past and the nights lengthened with no word from home, she came to regard Wattie as her only friend in a city of traitors. When ten days had passed, her endurance snapped.

Jenny heard the noise from the parlour where she sat sullenly copying a metrical psalm 'to perfect your vile, ill-shapen letters'. From the window and a height of three stories, she looked down on to a thronged and surging street. There were horsemen, drummers, and more velvets, laces and plumes together than Jenny had thought it possible to see. Dogs barked, children screamed and pushed, men shouted, as the procession came steadily onward – gentlemen in periwigs on sidestepping horses, lairds, Highland chieftains and their followers, French-dressed gentlemen with footmen, trades and guildsmen, and hordes of townsfolk shouting, though she could not make out the words for the din . . .

'They are riding to the Parliament,' said her aunt. 'That is all. Attend to your work.'

'That is *all*?' Jenny shot to her feet, scattering quill, ink and sand. Before her aunt could move to stop her, she looped her skirts high in one hand and ran from the room, knocking over a chair in her passage. Then she had torn back the bolt on the door to the stairs and was leaping down them, two at a time.

She did not hear her aunt's furious order to 'Come back this instant, Miss!' nor Andrew's shout as he came running after her. She was oblivious of everything but that black-bearded, bonneted figure in plaid sitting head and shoulders above the rest of them as the procession moved in slow and noisy splendour towards Parliament Close.

'Uncle Ewen!' she cried, pushing her way through the throng. Uncle Ewen would have word of her father; and if not, he was her friend and would rescue her. 'Uncle Ewen! *Uncle Ewen Dubh!*'

'Are you gone daft?' shouted a voice in her ear and she looked round to see Andrew, red-faced and anxious. 'Come home!'

'I wish to speak to my uncle. I may do that, surely, without let from you?'

'Not in the street. Come home, Miss, and send to see him later. The mistress orders it.'

Andrew grabbed her arm and tugged. Jenny instantly struck him, screaming, 'Help! Assault!' Andrew dropped her arm in horror and ran.

'Ye saw yon birkie nicely awa',' said Wattie cheerfully. 'Are ye playin' hooky again?'

But Jenny wasn't listening. The procession had moved on during her altercation with Andrew and she pushed hastily through the crowd shouting, 'Uncle Ewen!'

Wattie stuck close. 'He canna' hear ye – and nor could you wi' the din o' yon drummers in your lugs, and the pipin' an' a'. He'll not hear a'thing till he's in yon Parliament wi' the Queen's Commissioner – that's him i' the yaller gownie at the front – an' the Chancellor an' a'. Ye'd best bide yer time till he come oot agin, the night.'

'I can't.'

'Then that's an end o' it. Come awa',' and he led her to the back of the crowd, close under the overhanging eaves where the press was less dense and they could move fast, till they had overtaken the bulk of the procession and were close at its head. Then they pushed to the forefront.

'Which is the Chancellor,' asked Jenny, on tiptoe.

'Seafield? Yon thin chappie on the grey – wi' a chain round his neck and the sly grin on his mou'. Tho' he'd be better to rin awa' wi' a' that clobber and sell it quick for profit while he can.'

51

'Why?' shouted Jenny above the din. She clutched the back of the lad's ragged coat so as not to lose him.

'Why, because the Parliament's sold to the English as any fool knows, that's why. Crossrig knows it – see yon look on his face, like a man at his own wake – and Belhaven too, yon feller i' red; and there's the twa-faced Duke o' Hamilton aye looking both ways to keep 'em guessing. An' there's Carnwarth and Saltoun – ' a great cheer greeted these two in which Wattie joined, 'an' yon's the Lord Provost and the Burgesses.'

Jenny forgot Andrew, her aunt, everything in the general excitement as she and the little caddie were swept with the cheering, jeering crowd to the steps of Parliament House. Then men were dismounting, horses were being led away and there was her uncle, huge and imposing in his Highland plaid and bonnet, already mounting the step.

With a cry, Jenny thrust past the guard and flung herself after Lochiel.

'God's wounds, girl! Get home where you belong!' Sir Ewen's face was dark with a fury Jenny had not expected, softened by none of the indulgent affection she had been used to see.

'But Uncle, I want news of . . .'

'Away with you, Miss, before you disgrace us entirely.' He motioned to his followers. 'See her home and quickly. Mistress Cameron's, Geddes Close.' Then he was gone, caught up in the throng which filled the entry to the Parliament chamber.

Jenny stared dumbfounded. Uncle Ewen had spoken to her as if she were nothing. Worse than nothing. A mere female embarrassment. She had expected welcome; he had seen only disgrace.

'Come away, Miss,' grunted the gilly who had been detailed to escort her. 'Show me to your home.'

'I'll lead ye,' piped Wattie, nimble as ever to spot custom. 'I'll tak' the lass mysel' if ye prefer.' But the gilly had his chief's orders.

'I will follow,' he said, and with Jenny's forearm in his firm grip, they made their way back along the High Street against the flow of the crowd.

'Why was Sir Ewen angry?' asked Jenny, less imperious now and touchingly anxious. 'He did not use to treat me so.'

'There is much work afoot,' said Sir Ewen's man, 'some good, some bad. Lochiel needs his wits about him. I doubt ye upset him by your open approach.'

'Tell him . . .' Jenny hesitated. 'Tell him I beg his pardon if I offended, and I implore him, if he has the time, to give me word of home.'

But they had reached the close. 'Please,' she added, with a

52

look from the limpid brown eyes which touched the fellow's heart, 'beg my uncle at the least to send to me, or call.'

They were on the stair now and the man did not answer, for Wattie had rasped the door for them, then took his bawbee and scurried away to watch proceedings from the turn of the stair. The door opened to reveal Aunt Cameron herself.

'I am home, Aunt Cameron, as you wished,' said Jenny, but there was a note of despair behind the bravado. 'My uncle's gilly kindly accompanied me through the press. Perhaps he could be refreshed before he returns?'

Aunt Cameron looked sharply from Cameron to girl, and was trapped. 'Come in,' she said with scant courtesy, 'and wet your throat wi' ale.'

But the Highlander excused himself. 'Lochiel awaits my return. Good-bye, Miss, and I'll not forget.'

'Well?' said Aunt Cameron with ominous quiet, when he had gone. 'What was your reason this time? Curiosity? Asphyxia? Or did you plan to join the Parliament and speak against the Union yourself?'

'I wished to speak with my uncle.' Jenny's voice was steady enough, but her eyes moved swift with anxiety over entrance-way and parlour. Agnes Mackie hovered nervously in the shadows behind her mistress, but there was no sign of Andrew.

'And did he wish to speak with you?' The girl did not answer. 'Of course not. I could have told ye so myself and saved your feet, for what man would acknowledge an ill-clad, ill-mannered hoyden such as you before the assembled nobility of Scotland? You disgrace your uncle! You disgrace the Cameron clan. But what I will not tolerate is that *you disgrace me*. Hold her, Mackie!'

But Jenny did not wait to be held. She had the house door open in a flash and leapt for the steps – and the arms of the returning Andrew. 'Let me free!' she screamed, clawing and kicking.

'Hold her, Andrew!' cried his mistress as the stair miraculously filled with people, drawn from the window and the Parliament procession by this rival entertainment inside. From the merchant on the top floor to the tailor in the basement, they were all there. Jenny hated their hostile, predatory faces. She would have kicked out at them, too, but Andrew swung her feet from the ground and, holding her pinioned, managed somehow to stagger back up the stairs towards her aunt's house while Jenny screamed imprecations in Gaelic at the top of her healthy lungs.

'It's the Cameron girl ... a wild one ... Lochiel's grand-niece.'

At the mention of Lochiel, Jenny had a flash of memory – her uncle in the great hall at Glendessary telling tales – and sank her teeth deep into her captor's shoulder. If she could have reached his neck she would cheerfully have bitten out his windpipe. Andrew bellowed in pain and dropped her. She scrambled to her feet again and turned to run – to find her way on all sides blocked. Only her aunt's house door stood open: it was inevitable that she would be driven back inside.

Wattie, sitting on the seventh step, heard the scuffling, the crash of furniture and the screams – always of fury, he noted with satisfaction, and in two voices, old and young – and often with oaths that even Wattie had not heard before. At least, he assumed they were oaths, for when Missie lapsed into the Gaelic there was no saying what cursing she was about.

But it was a shame for a spirited lassie to be broken, as she must inevitably be, by such as the Neb. As for yon stuck-up, opinionated Andrew, the lassie was the best thing that could have happened to him. Wattie chuckled at the memory of Andrew's public humiliation – to be bitten by a half-grown lassie and to scream! Nevertheless, he hoped Lochiel would find the time to send the lass a message. She had little enough to pleasure her in Geddes Close.

'A letter has come from Lochiel,' announced Aunt Cameron the next morning. Jenny would not stoop to ask her aunt what it contained, though her heart quickened with hope. 'He is to call here at the four hours. After your disgraceful conduct – no, do not protest – you are not fit company for the byre, let alone the parlour and a gentleman. You will remain in your closet.'

'I will not.'

'You will so.'

'Then I will scream and kick until the walls break and the neighbours call the magistrates.'

'And do you think that will win your uncle's company? He comes to see me, not an ill-bred Highland wean.'

Jenny was silenced and, for the moment, baffled. If Uncle Ewen was coming to see her aunt, it must be out of family duty. There could be no other reason: surely, then, he would wish also to see her? But the memory of that scene outside Parliament house shook her confidence. Had her uncle forgiven her? Or was he come to make a formal complaint to her aunt? As she bent her head once more over the odious sampler she had been ordered to stitch, her mind worried at the problem like a rabbit at a tightening snare. But one thing she knew, whether Sir Ewen saw her or not: somehow she would escape, and go home again

54

to Glendessary where life was uncomplicated and honour understood.

Jenny, locked in, heard the voices through the walls of her bed-closet and laid her ear unashamedly against the wood. But her aunt and Sir Ewen talked low and intimately: she could make out little but an occasional name – Hamilton, Atholl, St Germain and, repeatedly, 'the Colonel' – the rustle of papers, and once, she was sure, mention of a battering cannon. Then, as the conversation proceeded in the same conspiratorial tones, she gave up all attempt to overhear, and returned to the problem of how best to take the chance offered and secure a meeting with Sir Ewen.

She became aware of a suspension of speech in the adjoining room, the scrape of wood on wood and then her uncle's voice, suddenly loud. 'Then that is settled, Cousin.' She heard his step on the floorboards. Surely he was not leaving? Jenny put her mouth close to the closet wall and called clearly, 'Uncle Ewen, I am a prisoner here and may not speak with you face to face, but I humbly beg your pardon if I have caused you any offence. I wished only for news from home, which is denied me. If you have any such, I pray you let me have it before you leave.'

For a moment there was silence, then a roar of laughter and the crash of fist on panelled wall. 'Away out wi' ye, lass, and let me see your impudent face!'

Jenny heard the bolt drawn back from the outside, and shot out from her incarceration past the gawping Agnes Mackie and the cringing Andrew. She had paid back one at least of the many injuries he had done her, and in a manner Sir Ewen must surely approve.

'Uncle Ewen!' Jenny burst into the parlour and flung herself at Lochiel.

'There, lass, that's enough,' he said when he had kissed her on both cheeks. 'Let me look at you. You are paler than I remember.'

'Have you news of my father?' interrupted Jenny eagerly. 'When am I to go home?'

'Home? Is your education finished already, Miss? Are you so speedily fluent in the French and Italian tongue?'

Jenny looked from uncle to aunt. Her aunt stood beside the centre table, the fingertips of one thin hand just touching the polished surface. The candlelight tinted her white hair with warmth, shot the black brocade of her gown with light and shadow. But her face was expressionless, her black eyes bright and still. Sir Ewen stood, back to the fire, his face flushed dark with health and heat. Jenny's chin lifted an inch and she said, 'I have not yet been instructed in either – only in incarceration and the tyranny of the rod. Neither, I know, are my father's wishes, and I expect hourly to be summoned home.'

'Hmmm . . .' Sir Ewen rocked slowly on his brogue-clad feet which he appeared to study with drawn brow.

'I have been beaten and tormented,' went on Jenny, giving her indignation full rein, 'I have been cruelly held by servants and demeaned before them while my aunt chastised me, *against her given word*. I am glad to say I gave them *some* payment for their pains.'

'She bit Andrew almost to the shoulder-bone,' said her aunt, without expression, 'and raised a bruise the size of a medlar on my own thigh.'

'Did she, by Jove?' Unexpectedly, Sir Ewen laughed, but his face was swiftly grave again. 'What's this, Miss Jenny? Disobedience?'

'But I am not to be allowed to go abroad or to look about me or to do anything I choose to do,' she continued heatedly. 'I am to do nothing but stay indoors and sit. I cannot abide to be inert.'

'And what did you expect, Jenny? To be allowed to run free? To learn when you choose to do so, and play when you do not, as you did at home? Is that why your father sent you, like a cow to the shieling, so that you could be irresponsible and ignorant in fresh pastures and grow fat, before being driven to the marriage market and sold?'

'I will not marry,' declared Jenny, 'except when *I* choose.'

'You'll get no chance, Miss,' snapped her aunt, 'unless you mend your ways. No man will bid for an untamed wildcat not worth her keep in porridge!'

'Then I will stay unwed,' retorted Jenny, 'like yourself.'

The old man's eyes were creased with glee: there had not been such a clash of wills, he thought, since his own childhood. He remembered a particularly domineering tutor with private satisfaction. But if the girl was to be any good to them, she must be schooled, if only in discretion. 'You can safely leave the lass wi' me a minute, Cousin,' he said before Aunt Cameron could reply. 'If you had a mutton pie or a cold fowl I would welcome it, for 'tis many a long hour since my stomach dined.'

'I will see to it,' said Aunt Cameron with a glare at Jenny. 'Mind and behave, Miss, while I am gone.'

'Did Father send word?' asked Jenny the moment the door closed.

'Were you expecting any?'

'He must have received my letter. When he does, I know he will send for me.'

'Do you now.' He put a hand inside his jacket and withdrew a packet superscribed in a familiar hand *Miss Jenny Cameron*. 'From all of them, I think,' he said as he handed it to her with a smile.

Jenny tore open the wrapper, leafed agitatedly through the enclosed papers – her mother's hand, Alan's, even one from Catherine and little Meg – till she found what she sought. But as she read her father's letter which was full of affection – *'we miss your company and your laughter . . . we pray daily for your happiness and well-being . . . my dearest daughter, much loved and sorely missed . . . '* her face lost its animation.

'But he does not send for me,' she faltered, and her hands trembled as she refolded the letter to be read, with the others, again and again in the winter weeks to follow. *'Why?'*

Her uncle regarded her steadily and when he spoke his voice was quiet but firm. 'He asked me as chief of your clan to remind you to keep your word.'

'But why should I, uncle,' cried Jenny, 'when others do not?'

'Because your word is your own and to break it is to sully yourself,' snapped Lochiel. 'But tell me,' he went on more kindly as Jenny looked down at her hands in silence, 'what would you like best in the world to do?'

'Live at Glendessary,' she said without hesitation, 'and run my estate. Alan does not want it, and besides, I know that I could do it better than he.'

'And would you expect obedience from your tenants as from anyone subservient to someone in authority?'

'Of course.' Her voice was subdued as she realized the direction of her uncle's questioning. 'But why must I do always what someone else decides? At home I . . .'

'At home you were a child and free,' interrupted Sir Ewen. 'Now you must learn new skills in order to fill the role I have in mind for you.'

Jenny looked at him in surprise. 'What role? I thought . . .'

'You will know when the time comes. But *think*, girl. How does a captain become a general but by obedience?'

'And leadership, and the power to order others.'

'Anyone can order a maidservant or a gilly, but could you order, say, a regiment of the French army in Flanders? Or report to St Germain on the state of the Scottish nation? Can you speak the language of our own King's court in exile? Or write it?'

'No uncle, but I could learn soon enough at home, from my father.'

'You have lived at home all your life.'

Jenny was silenced. She spoke only Gaelic in Glendessary and, remembering her uncle's visits and her own ignorance, was ashamed. 'When I return,' she said after a moment and seriously, 'things will be different.'

'They will,' agreed the old man with a twinkle, 'because you will not return until they are.'

Jenny looked at him in horror. 'But uncle, I cannot stay in this faithless, stinking city. I will *die*!'

'You will not die of discipline and learning,' said her uncle drily. 'French is not yet a disease, though it may well sound like one on some pupils' tongues.'

This final comment convinced Jenny that her uncle was not to be moved, and the spirit went out of her, leaving her small and very cold. 'Then I may not go home?'

'No.' He looked at her in long silence and something in his gaze made her catch her breath, for his eyes had darkened and he looked through her as if into some distant country. When he spoke it was in a voice she did not recognize.

'*You will speak a foreign tongue in a foreign land before you ride in glory to your King . . .*'

Jenny dared not speak, but her eyes looked deep into her uncle's until the darkness in them cleared and he saw her again. With a small shake of the head he said, 'At the moment you are fit mate for no one but a drover . . . when you marry – and there have been offers enough already – it will be to one of *us* who will assuredly need a wife as strong as you are, but well-taught, too.'

Jenny kept silence. When she married it would be to Hugh, for in spite of his small betrayal were they not pledged? Her uncle would know one day, but now was not the time. And Hugh would wait for her. Lochiel misunderstood her silence.

'If you do not marry,' he said calmly, refilling his glass, 'I hope you will at least have the grace to earn your keep.'

'When Glendessary is mine I . . .'

'It will never be yours. You have brothers and cousins enough for Glendessary, Dungallon, Torcastle and Fassefern, so you can put that idea out of your head. If you want an estate, Jenny, you must buy it with your marriage *tocher* and a husband.'

Jenny paid no heed. Her uncle did not understand. When she married Hugh they would live at Glendessary as they had always done. She and Hugh would range the hills above Arkaig, hunt and ride together and fish in the mountain streams. Glendessary would be theirs as wholly as if by legal charter. She clasped the thought to her for strength, but said only, 'What would you have me do?'

'Stay here and learn what is required. You must become proficient in French and Italian and write a clear, firm hand. You must learn obedience, discretion, how to conduct yourself in company. You must learn all the social graces expected of a woman, for only then can you move freely in society and begin to be of value to your chief and to your King.'

Despair found release in flippancy. 'I would prefer to learn the *épée*.'

Sir Ewen threw back his head and roared in delight. 'You are incorrigible. You go in *skirts*, girl, and must learn to accept it.'

'And you can also learn to offer your uncle suitable hospitality, Miss,' interrupted her aunt from the doorway. 'Put the ashet on the table, Andrew, and fetch more wine.'

'Hand me a leg of that excellent fowl, Jenny,' said her uncle, 'and tell me what you make of this hurly-burly that is breaking all around us.'

That day the Queen's Commissioner had introduced the Treaty of Union to the assembled Parliament. Andrew Fletcher and others with him had vowed to dispute every one of the twenty-five articles, yet Lochiel was worried. Though the mob was restive and Unionist supporters in increasing danger, Lochiel knew how little a mob could be relied upon.

'Do you mean the opening of the Parliament, Uncle?'

Lochiel looked at her eager, innocent face and inwardly sighed. What was to be her future?

'The opening will do for a start, Jenny,' he said with sadness, 'but it is the closing of it which I dread. If something is not done to prevent it, I fear it will bring us the end of an old, old song.'

As she lay in the stifling closeness of her box bed, with that odious Agnes Mackie snoring on a pallet in the corner, Jenny knew she herself had come to the end of a song: the sweet freedom of Glendessary was lost to her and she was condemned, by Sir Ewen himself, to the prison of her aunt's house in Edinburgh, and the inquisition of her aunt's reign. She felt suddenly old and sad . . .

Footman Andrew shifted weight from foot to tired foot. He had been waiting now for two hours and still they talked, yet he dared not lie down and sleep. His mistress had told him to wait in the hall outside the door 'lest I need you for anything', and wait he must or he'd have his wages docked – and two pounds sterling was little enough. Besides, if he crossed the old woman he'd not get a 'character' when he moved on to better things, as he intended to do. The footman upstairs at Sir Patrick's was old as Methuselah and doddering as a duck with one leg. He'd not last the winter out, and when Sir Patrick's daughter said, 'Papa, we must have that handsome young man from Mistress Cameron's, I have always thought him too good for her,' Sir Patrick would say, 'By Jove, Charlotte, the very man. A finer, better set up young fellow I could not ask for. My own tailor shall measure him for his livery. Do you think the young man will deign to come to us for five pounds a year?' 'Seven, Papa,' she would plead and her blue eyes would fill with tears of anxiety. 'For he will not come for less.' 'Then I will give him ten, my dear, and gladly. An honour to have him...' Miss Charlotte would laugh and catch her bottom lip with her teeth, such pretty little teeth, not like that vixen Miss Jenny's – he rubbed his shoulder in painful memory – and the dimples would come and go in her cheeks. 'Oh Andrew,' she would whisper, when her Papa was not looking, 'I am so glad you came.' Her little dimpled hand would steal into his. 'You are so fine and handsome...' Andrew's own eyes misted over as he drifted into the familiar reverie ... till the door opened behind his leaning head and precipitated him in a bony heap at his mistress's feet.

'Get up, ye great dolt.' She dug him hard in the ribs with her stick. 'Or I will sell ye at the next fee-ing mart for a scarecrow!'

'Caddie, sir?' said Wattie cheerfully from the doorway, but Sir Ewen's own men had materialized from the shadows. A broadsword glinted in the lamplight which spilled on to the stair from Mistress Cameron's open doorway, and there was a sudden odour of unwashed wool and sweat. 'He will not be needing...' began one of them with a threatening move of the hand and Wattie slipped prudently back.

'Whisht, Donald,' said Sir Ewen. 'He is a good lad. I know him well. He can go ahead of us and light us to the street. Ye'll hae a groat for your pains ... and silver too, if ye serve me well and secret,' he added, low in the boy's ear, when they reached the High Street. 'Come to my lodging in the forenoon, early.'

'Gladly, sir – and God go wi' ye.'

But though he had been dismissed, the boy followed Sir Ewen to the door of his lodging, moving swift and silent as a rat in the shadow of overhanging eave and arched close. Wattie liked to know who dealt with whom and which way blew the wind. The Duke of Hamilton's men, he knew, were against the Treaty with England, Breadalbin and Atholl too; but that Presbyterian Fletcher and his followers were also against the Treaty, and Piscies and Kirkmen side by side was a rare wonder. Then folk said the West Coast Covenanters – called 'Cameronians' though as different from Sir Ewen's Cameron men as caddie from king – had offered to take up arms and march to stop the Parliament. The Treaty, they said, would surely go against the Covenant and threaten the security of the Kirk o' Scotland. But the Highlandmen, though they did not say so outright, wanted to restore James Stuart who everyone knew was a papist; and all of them took wine with old Lochiel, whose grand-niece lived with the Neb who was thick as thieves with Sir Patrick up the stair, and he as plain and honest a Treator as ye could find.

It was the same mixter-maxter all over the city, with some afraid of peace, others of war, not knowing which cause to follow for the best. The boy was astute as any – years of surviving on nothing but his wits had taught him early to watch, weigh and ponder – but Edinburgh now was a clouded pool. It was impossible to predict from one day to the next which way what fish would jump. But if there was one thing in all this muddle that was clear as day, it was that there would be trouble, and a lad would need all his wits about him to survive – and to prosper, as Wattie meant to do.

Lochiel passed safely into the entrance to the close, his men beside him, lantern light swaying over glistening stone. The windows of his house glowed with welcoming candlelight. One by one the visitors arrived. Still Wattie, in the deeper shadow of a goldsmith's sign, kept silent watch, while from a tavern close at hand came the noise of laughter and singing, and from the Castle, the steady throb of the evening drum.

Hugh Cameron lay so still he could hear the beat of his own heart. In the gully below him, the animal moved, slow and ruminant, its jaws working rhythmically over gobbets of torn grass. Hugh heard the crunch of flat teeth on padded stalk, the dribble of juices, the regular sigh of breathing flank and swishing tail. It was the beast he had waited for all summer – a fine bullock, glistening black with the health of summer pasturing, its neck and shoulders solid with flesh. A beast like that was a *creach* fit for a chief.

Carefully, Hugh eased his body forward over the flattened heather till he could see deep into the gully and eastward where it opened into the wider basin of the glen. The rest of the herd grazed quietly at the river's edge with, beyond them, the shieling, peat-walled and heather-roofed, where the Macdonald drovers rested after the day-long march.

A heron blew, quiet-winged, from nowhere across the evening sky and dropped, long feet outstretched, into the shallows: Hugh heard the brief flurry of thrashing waters, saw the flash of fin and beak. With infinite patience he inched his way closer to where a trodden track of deer or hare threaded the heather downwards, towards his prey.

The other Cameron men were lower down the valley, waiting in ambush to take the whole herd, if they could, but Hugh moved alone after his single, chosen beast. It was his first *creach* and promised by a solemn bond to Glendessary's daughter. Now that she was gone, he could not drive it to her in her father's house, as he had hoped to do; but he would see she got it just the same. It was the more important now she had left, and left despising him for what in bounden duty to his chieftain he had had to do. Had not her father and his own father charged him to protect and guard her, and to tell them if she went astray?

It had not been easy, especially when he saw her running, barefoot and eager-faced, to the shieling. It had not been easy when she had thrown her arms around his neck, kissed him, laughed aloud with happiness at her escape. It had not been easy to walk away from her on a pretext, to go back and tell her father, when all his young heart longed for was to lie with her, plaid-wrapped together, under the starlight of the high hills . . . But it was his duty to his chief and he had done it. Jenny, he knew, despised him for what she saw as a betrayal, but it had been the opposite. Had he not loved her as he did, he might have allowed her to walk her own way to damnation and to take him with her. But the *creach* would put everything right . . .

The sun had set two hours ago. The northern sky was still pale as watered silk behind the dark bulk of the hill. But in the valley shadows lay black with tightening frost. The beast's breath hung about its muzzle in small, pale clouds . . . Hugh watched, intent, his own breath evanescent in the gathering twilight, until there was nothing in the vast world of hill and glen and silent star-specked sky, but Hugh Cameron and the stirk he meant to take.

A distant bellow shot Jenny suddenly awake with the clamour of cows, lowing their discontent. In an instant Jenny was at home, in her room in Glendessary, with her sisters sleeping in their curtained bed, and outside her window the cows moving slowly along the shores of Loch Arkaig in the half-light of morning, on their way to the summer shieling.

On a rush of homesickness too violent to resist, she tossed back the plaid and padded to the window. The bottom half was closed tight with the wooden half-shutter: she dared not open it for fear the light and the increased noise would arouse her aunt. But out of the upper glass-paned window, tiny though it was, she could see a little: stalls, awnings, the tumbled brightness of the pedlar's tray flashing gaudy ribbons and glass beads, the noisy, bustling fringe of the market.

She could slip out through the sleeping household, as she had done once before: could lose herself in that market crowd, find the drovers who had brought those lowing cows and, the market over, go home with them to the hills.

She glanced swiftly over her shoulder towards the bed. Today she was to have a French lesson with Miss Simpering Charlotte upstairs and then there would be sewing with Agnes Turnkey Mackie under her aunt's glaring gaolership, and then, if she were lucky, a trip to take tea with a cousin of her aunt's, a Miss Campbell who lived in the Canongate. The only luck in the whole affair was that it necessitated a journey between the Campbell house and the Camerons', for there could be no other pleasure in it. Argyll was a Campbell and no friend to the Camerons or to Scotland. Yet she was expected to be polite to them all, while out there, in the cattle market, was freedom . . . .

Behind the closed curtains of the four-poster, Margaret Cameron lay wide-eyed and motionless, every sense alert. For the camlet hangings of the bed were threadbare and against the square of light the girl's head was plainly outlined. The old woman too had heard the stirk and, as she watched that shadowy outline, she knew exactly what went through the girl's head.

For Aunt Cameron had once lived, like Jenny, free in the hills, and the wild girl from Glendessary had revived forgotten memories, stirred buried longings and, most surprising of all, breathed life into a long-withered heart. In Jenny, Aunt Cameron saw herself an empty lifetime ago and, with a fierceness which surprised her, did not want Jenny to be wasted as she herself had been. The girl was intelligent, fine-looking; she would not let her throw away her chances through ignorance or headstrong pride. Not for her the despised years of spinsterhood and parsimony, of teaching empty-headed girls. Jenny would make a brilliant marriage, not waste herself loving where there was no hope . . .

Margaret Cameron felt the old bitterness. There was no place for love in any girl's life, least of all in the marriage-stakes. She would see this girl got the best available bargain, and one day, perhaps, though she did not yet acknowledge the thought, Jenny would offer her affection, and gratitude. But Jenny herself must take the first step. So Aunt Cameron did not call out, but continued motionless, waiting for Miss Jenny to decide.

63

The girl stood a long time at the window while the argument tossed to and fro inside her head. Uncle Ewen had ordered her to stay and learn. He was her chief. Yet how could she learn in this constriction? Her father would find her a better tutor at home. He missed her, they all did, and it would surely please them to have her home and save him expense. Yet she was a Cameron, and Lochiel's word was law. In spite of argument and all longing, she knew where her course lay.

Aunt Cameron saw the figure move aside, the window square emerge again, unbroken; but no floorboards, no muffled latch. Only the soft creak of the panelling on the girl's bed.

The old woman loosed her pent breath on a slow sigh of relief. The first battle had been fought. And won.

Already the first link-boys were moving in the crowd when Aunt Cameron and Jenny set out for home – on foot, for from the Canongate to their own lodging was 'nobbut a step and no cause to line other folks' pockets wi' siller for want o' a pair o' feet'. Jenny did not mind. Any excuse to walk in the open street was welcome and it soon became apparent that tonight the journey would be slow, for in spite of the hour, the street was crowded.

'Stay close, girl,' warned Aunt Cameron 'and keep your wits about ye. There's trouble afoot and the sooner we're hame the better.'

Close at hand a voice said something incomprehensible in French. Another answered. Even through the confusing babble of sound Jenny recognized the voice of sedition.

'What did he say, Aunt?' Jenny tugged at her aunt's arm in impatience, but Margaret Cameron pushed ahead unheeding. The girl's arrival had stirred memories, and now the unaccustomed crowds brought one in particular too sharply to the surface: Edinburgh in her own childhood. The exhumation of the long-dead, mutilated hero, Montrose. The cheers and singing. And so soon after as to seem in memory the same occasion, the execution of Argyll and the same crowd cheering. She felt again her childhood puzzlement and horror – the long-dead, decomposing remnants and the new, still-bleeding corpse, the lust and laughter of the crowd. The same crowd which roared now, all about her, with the same cruel expectation . . . For the first time for many years Margaret Cameron was afraid, and was grateful for Jenny's strong and fearless company.

But when the girl repeated her question, the old woman loosed her agitation in annoyance. 'No concern of yours. And if ye think it is, listen for yoursel'. Keep hold of my arm, girl, or we'll both be felled. Where's that dolt of an Andrew? He was told to fetch us a half hour ago.'

'Trampled in the press,' called Jenny cheerfully above the noise and added to herself, 'with luck!' But she did as her aunt advised and kept close, as much from a wish to protect the old woman, who seemed unusually agitated, as herself, for the crowd grew denser with every step they took towards the castle.

Suddenly, from the direction of Parliament House there came a roar of 'Hamilton!' On an instant taverns spilled a crowd of querulous men into the street, where they were joined by more from close and wynd and alley until the Canongate was filled. Before they could find refuge, Jenny and her aunt were caught up in the swell and carried with them up the hill to the entrance to Parliament Close. Here hundreds jammed so tight that egress was impossible. Through the swaying crowd Jenny glimpsed the painted wooden top of a sedan and another cheer of 'God bless the Duke!' and 'Scotland's Champion!' deafened the air as the crowd milled, moved, changed course like the waters in the pool at Cia-aig.

Jenny was tall for her age, tall as many of the men, and could see where her aunt could not: to that sedan, with its liveried bearers, and, through looped curtains, the wigged head and scarlet robes of the Duke himself.

'It's Hamilton, Aunt!' she cried. 'Huzzah!'

'Silence, for God's sake girl. Hold your tongue!' But Jenny did not hear; as the crowd roared and swayed and they were wedged inescapably in the press.

'He looks for a' the world like a king,' cried someone beside them. 'And why not?' shouted another. 'He'd be better for Scotland than yon Queen Anne.'

'We have a King!' Jenny glared her indignation, unafraid. 'When he comes, we'll need no other.'

'If he comes, lass. Hamilton's a Stuart, too, and *here*.'

'For pity's sake, girl, be quiet! Do you want the world to know your inclinations?' But Aunt Cameron's words were lost in the general roar of delight as the chair turned, not downhill for the Abbey, but left towards the Lawnmarket with the castle at its head.

'He's for Atholl's house!' The murmur spread to a roar. 'For Atholl's!' The crowd surged around St Giles and spread from luckenbooth to overhanging eave as they marched with purpose now, beside the Duke of Hamilton's chair. Some had staves, others pikes, even a matchlock or two, and Jenny felt the mounting excitement fill her own breast till her fingers itched to carry arms for her country's cause.

'Oh Aunt, is it not exciting? Are you not glad we came when we did?' For that this rabble was her country's loyal army, Jenny had no doubt. But her aunt had pulled them both into a backwater beside St Giles and held tight to Jenny's arm while the crowd moved on without them. She was white-faced and shaking.

'Use your wits, girl!' she managed at last. 'And hold that babbling tongue.'

'But they're for Hamilton, Aunt. Where is the harm?'

'They are for Hamilton, as you say.' Her aunt mopped her brow with a kerchief and straightened her plaid with hands that still shook. 'And tomorrow they'll be for Queensberry or anyone else they're told to follow. Never trust a crowd, girl, and keep your own counsel. Remember that.' She paused on a catch of labouring breath and Jenny realized with surprise and concern that her aunt was not after all invulnerable. But before she could offer solicitude, the old woman had recovered.

'And now, as the pack is baying ahead of us and young breath is better than old, perhaps you'll be kind enough to see me home.'

'Yes, Aunt, and I am sorry.' Jenny was instantly contrite. 'Take my arm. Lean on me if you feel the need. But Aunt Cameron, was it not exciting? Do you think there will be a Rising?'

'What I think and what you think had best be left unsaid. Keep your breath for the road.'

The crowd had gone ahead of them now. They could hear the chanting from higher up the hill where the company had reached the entrance to Atholl's lodging. They cheered the Duke to the forestair, the outer door, the inner door, and cheered him again when he stood in the candle-flooded window on the third floor. But when he stepped back out of sight, deflation turned to mischief.

'The Treators . . . stone the Treators . . .' The murmur gathered momentum until the crowd swirled on a rush of venom and roared back down the Lawnmarket.

The two women heard the sound as of a tidal wave approaching and drew into the doorway of a bookbinder's till it should pass. But it did not pass. Instead it gathered at the foot of a high and lighted building across the street and Jenny realized, with anger and astonishment, that it was her aunt's close which was filling now with shoving, shouting men; her aunt's stair up which they stumbled in the crowded darkness, roaring obscenities.

A stone crashed through glass and Jenny's fervour turned to rage. 'Not that one!' she cried, shaking off her aunt's restraining hand. 'She's for Hamilton.'

'I know that, ye vixen! The stone fell short.' It was not her aunt's window they were aiming at, after all, but those of the house above, Sir Patrick Johnston's, a well-loved and much respected citizen until he had opted to speak out for Union.

'Treator!' yelled the rabble and the building rang with the thud of sledge-hammer on wood. At the window above her aunt's appeared a woman, a candle held high in each hand.

'For God's sake,' she cried piteously, 'someone fetch the Guard!'

Another stone flew, this time with better aim and the window shattered on a scream of 'Help us!' In the roar of triumph which followed, no one but Jenny noticed the little caddie slip out of the close and across the cobbles to the apothecary's shop, nor the apothecary himself as they set off together at the run for the castle hill and the Lord Provost's house. Then Jenny forgot all else in the desperate business of keeping the press from crushing them both, which she did by a judicious mixture of Gaelic oaths and strength – 'Like Horatio holding the brig',' the old woman reported later, with querulous admiration.

From the street came a warning shout: 'The Guard!', and the sound of drums and marching feet. Miraculously, the hammering ceased, the close emptied on a rush of fleeing men and the staircase was cleared of all but half a dozen of the Town Guard and their captives, the hammermen from the top landing who had had least time to escape.

'And now,' said Aunt Cameron, stepping out of her refuge and dusting down her skirts, 'perhaps we will be allowed to go home.'

But when Jenny had helped her up the many stairs and rasped the tirl of their own door, a high voice, quivering with terror, called 'Go away or we'll call the Guard.'

'Hold your tongue, Andrew, you drivelling idiot, and let us in.'

'Who's wi' ye?'

'I am, ye dolt.' Her aunt's vigour had returned on her own threshhold and she hammered on the door with her fist.

There was the noise of bolts being drawn back and the door opened a careful crack on to darkness. Jenny pushed impatiently inside to where Andrew crouched, white-faced and trembling, behind the door. 'Can't you see my aunt is exhausted? Fetch brandy. Light the candles. Then root out that Mackie woman from wherever she's hiding to come and be of use to her mistress!'

That evening's events marked a turning point in the relationship between Jenny and her aunt. Though the latter's harsh regime continued, apparently untempered by any concession to her father's wishes, Jenny noted that the switch made fewer appearances and instead of dismissing her questions out of hand with a 'Hold your tongue till you're asked to use it,' her aunt occasionally conceded an explanation. For instance when Jenny asked whether the Frenchmen they had overheard on the evening of the rioting were spies from King James's court of St Germain, her aunt retorted, 'More likely merchants, seeking to make a quick profit on their brandy and Bordeaux before the Treaty adds a tax to Scottish imports.'

'But they said *ce soir* aunt and I know they talked of insurrection, not of wine. I am learning French as fast as I can, but it is so frustrating, especially when the Rising is imminent.'

'And who tells you there is to be a Rising, Miss? I know of none.'

'I thought my uncle told you? He and Atholl and Breadalbin are pledged to it, Belhaven and Gordon too, with a dozen others, and Hamilton at the head. But we must be wary, with a Treator on the story above. And all about us,' she added, remembering Wattie, 'even those we call our friends.'

'Sir Patrick is certainly a friend, as he is friend of many and will, I hope, remain so. But that is all he is. We do not talk of other matters, and nor should you. Andrew! Ye've disgraced yoursel' enough wi' your whimpering and cringing, without stretching your ears to the size o' bannocks to hear what's none o' your concern. Awa' wi' ye to bed.'

Andrew scurried from the room before he could be further shamed, to stretch on his blanket in the narrow hall and dream of softer, kinder women, like Miss Charlotte up the stair . . .

'And now, girl,' she turned to Jenny. 'Listen to me, and listen well.' Margaret Cameron paused, choosing her words with unaccustomed care; for the wild one they had sent her from Lochaber was not obstinate as she had once thought, nor vicious: she was the strangest mixture of naïveté, fearlessness and old-fashioned honesty that the old woman had met. Such guileless trust could lead her into a hundred dangers. 'About the Rising ye speak so freely of, ye'd best learn to hold your tongue. If there is to be such a thing, which I do not say there is, it will not be talked of wi' Government men everywhere and a deal o' tattling tongues to bring the armies hotfoot over the border.'

'But the rioting, Aunt? Surely that was a signal?'

'The rioting, as you call it, was too soon. I cannot think what they were at. The spring will be time enough, with the Highland winter past and the seas calm. But if you hope to be here to see it, ye'd best heed what I tell ye, Miss. Learn, watch and wait. And above all, keep your own counsel. The mob's a monstrous, fickle beast, full of ears to spy and tongues to tattle. I've seen it fawn on one man, savage another, and in a moment switch to the reverse. Too many young men dead . . . ' She paused, her old eyes for a moment young and anguished.

'But a Cameron, Aunt, is never a traitor, and we are for King James.'

'Aye, Lord help us.' Jenny looked up in surprise at the bitterness in her aunt's voice. 'But what good is a king without a country – or a country without its children? If the Rising succeeds, all well and good. If not . . .'

'It *will* succeed, Aunt. In the spring. And by then I will have mastered this cursed French enough to know what's what, when next I overhear a spy!'

That winter Edinburgh was seething with rumour and expectation. Hamilton's progress from Parliament Square to Atholl's house, with its resulting anti-Unionist riots, was seen variously as a bid on his part to win allegiance, to point the mob to violence, to escape that same mob's attentions to himself; and while the wrangle in the Parliament continued as each clause of the projected Union was fought and passed, secret talk in the Jacobite camp was increasingly of the Rising, of the imminent return of 'the Colonel', sent abroad to settle matters of men and munitions. Names were already subscribed, bonds sealed. Only the timing remained at issue: for in the softer distances of St Germain the considerations of a harsher climate were forgotten. For weeks Loch Arkaig was isolated so deep in snow that no one could reach the kirk, let alone Maryburgh or Inverness. Fervour could not triumph over snow-drifts. Plans of insurrection must wait upon the weather.

Meanwhile, the foot-soldiers set to keep order in the Edinburgh streets were seen as forerunners of the oppression Union would bring. It was sixty years since the city had seen troops on guard in their own streets, pointed out the Loyalists. Such a sight meant tyranny and war. On the contrary, countered the Unionists, they were necessary to ensure the public safety and public peace, sorely threatened by the anti-Unionist 'rabble'.

For a time it seemed the anti-Union faction would triumph. With two regiments of foot on constant duty in the city, the streets were quieter, though the townsfolk simmered with discontent. The Duke of Hamilton continued to be mobbed with cheering escorts and there were growing rumours of country tumults. The whole land should rise up, they said, and march to Edinburgh to free their country's Parliament by force.

In November 200 of the Protestant Cameronians of the West marched into Dumfries and burnt the Articles of Union on a midday bonfire in the market place. By the time the news reached Edinburgh, the number of reported rebels had swelled to 6,000 men-at-arms and 1,000 horsemen. Twelve thousand men in all were to march on Edinburgh to raise the Parliament and sacrifice the Treators as betrayers of their country. Hopes ran high among the anti-Union faction, for if the honest Protestant men of the West had joined the Jacobite Episcopalians, then who could stand against them?

But the church commissioners refused to be drawn into an anti-Union declaration, refused to rupture among themselves. Instead they declared a fast to pray for wisdom and guidance and the preservation of the true kirk. Dr Rule, Principal of the University at Edinburgh, declared that Union did not go against the Covenant, as many, and particularly the Western Cameronians, had feared. As a result, many of the Protestant protesters had second thoughts, preferring a limited Protestant freedom under Queen Anne to the company of those who aimed to restore the Popish James.

So the arguments went on and somehow, inch by inch, the Articles were fought and passed until – no one knew why or how – the fight died out of the opposition as economic considerations and the wish for peace prevailed.

But the Scottish Parliament was a long time a-dying and before the final death throes of a nation's independence, the promise of new life-blood came.

'The Duke has received a letter,' announced Lochiel to his assembled Loyalists, and his old eyes burned with impatience and battle-lust. 'In secret, from St Germain. The "Colonel" is on his way.'

3

When she had brought Miss to a ready Compliance, she applied herself to her Education, in which she advanced so surprisingly that in less than two years she was Mistress of the French and Italian, wrote a fine Hand, had learn'd to dance, could play upon the Spinet, and was a compleat Mistress at her Needle . . .

For Jenny the night of the Edinburgh rabble was the beginning of a new excitement. She threw as much energy into mastering the French language as she had been used to spend on catching and breaking the mountain garrons at home. She accompanied her aunt without complaint to church, and though the sermons were tedious beyond belief, she suffered them for the training they gave her in endurance and for Sir Ewen's sake. She had been brought up in the Episcopalian faith, but she recognized the politics of her aunt's compliance, and the forms of religious observance had never troubled her. She even submitted with tolerable grace to the sewing, handwriting and music lessons which her aunt insisted must balance the French. Miss Charlotte from upstairs joined her for the latter, and though Jenny despised her for her simpering helplessness and her yellow, bobbing curls, she tolerated her for diverting half her aunt's attention to herself.

Since that day in the Canongate when she had overheard the Frenchmen, Jenny had had one ambition: to learn the language of the French Court so that she, like the Cameron men and Hugh, might serve her true King. The only question was whether she could learn in time, for had not her aunt talked of the spring?

But the spring brought the voting of the Act of Union, the final dissolution of the Scottish Parliament and the end of an old, old song.

'We are betrayed, Aunt!' cried Jenny. 'If I had a sword, I would . . .'

'Run it through the nearest Unionist, get clapped into the Tolbooth and hanged. There is a better use for every sword than that. Be patient, girl.'

'Patience never won anything,' retorted Jenny. 'It is better to go boldly and take what you want.'

'If you have the means to do so. If you have not, then it is only prudent to wait until you have.'

'But I am weary of waiting! If you will not tell me when it is to be, then I will ask my uncle; and if he will not tell me, then I will ask the Duke of Hamilton himself!'

Her aunt looked at her without answer, but there was a gleam of mischief in her old eyes. She opened the outer door of the house. 'Wattie! Is Lochiel in town?'

'No, Ma'am. He left for the country as the others did, when Union was passed.'

'And the Duke of Hamilton?'

'In his bed, with a putrid fever, and none allowed near. Not that any call, for he is the only gentleman left in the city. Summer is a thin time, Ma'am, for the likes o' me, wi' the gentry gone and the Parliament closed and the sending o' messages at an end.'

'Well, well,' said the old woman hastily, 'I will bear you in mind for a letter, if I have one to send,' and she closed the door in his face. 'Perhaps now, Miss, you will see the wisdom of my words and wait. Or do you mean to accost Hamilton on his sick bed and extract an answer with his dying breath?'

'I shall wait,' said Jenny with dignity, 'for my own summons home.'

Behind the dignity, however, her heart beat fast with a mounting excitement. At Glendessary, in summer-time, her uncle would surely tell her everything. And there would be Hugh. She had forgiven him long ago for his betrayal: when she saw him again, he would explain and it would be as it always was between them. He would teach her swordsmanship, marksmanship too, and as the year moved towards high summer, they would ride endlessly together in the hills she longed for.

'It is a beautiful beast, Hugh,' breathed Bess, looking nervously at the black bullock in the pasture above Glendessary. 'You are brave to have captured it unaided and brought it all that way home.' She laid a soft hand on his bare forearm. 'You are so strong ... were you never afraid the Macdonald would catch you and take it back again?'

'They could not,' boasted Hugh, flattered in spite of himself by her attentions. For Bess was a comely enough lass, though not tall and well-proportioned like Miss Jenny. Bess was squat and square, with pudding breasts and round, cow-like eyes. But when she came close to him as she seemed always to be doing these days, he could smell the female warmth of her, sense the

softness of her flesh as vividly as if he had touched her, naked.
And now, as the fingers sent blood racing through his youthful
body, he drew hastily away.

'What is the matter, Hugh?' she murmured and her eyes grew
even rounder with perplexity and simulated hurt. 'Don't you
like me to touch you?'

'I have work to do,' he gulped and moved away towards the
higher track. 'There is a beast to be fetched home.'

'It is not the work! You are afraid *Miss Jenny* would not like
it! You behave as if she owned you.' Too late, Bess regretted her
words.

'No one owns me, except my God in heaven – and my King.'
He turned his back and strode for the hills.

Later as he paused on his way homeward to rest his burden,
Hugh looked again at the black bullock grazing on the high
pasture, its hide gleaming in the sunlight, its shoulders massive
with gathering strength, and his anger melted in pride and sweet
anticipation. Soon she would come home, for no one spent a
summer in the foetid rancour of the city. He would lead his
offering early on to the sward beneath her window and tether
the beast to a stake, that she might know he had fulfilled his
promise and made his first *creach* for her. Hugh swung the
new-shot, gutted roedeer across his shoulders with the ease of
strength and strode with a lighter step for home.

But it was not the daughter of the house who arrived in secret,
in early May . . . It was Colonel Hooke, the long-awaited envoy
of their King in France.

'In the circumstances,' wrote Glendessary, 'I feel it would be
wiser if my daughter Jenny spent the summer in Edinburgh,
with you. My wife is to visit cousins in Perthshire, with the
younger children . . . only the menfolk will remain . . .'

'So,' said Aunt Cameron, folding the letter slowly and setting
it aside. 'They are clearing the decks.'

'I should be there,' said Jenny with bleak despair. 'Not put
away with the women and children.'

'Your father will visit you, when next he is in town, and your
mother too.'

'I don't want to be *visited*. I want to be *there*!' She loosed her
frustration in a crashing fist which set the table rocking. 'I want
to sit at the table when they plan their strategy, blot the ink as
they sign their pledge of intent. Oh Aunt, I want to take part
as the men do, and share in the glory.'

'Glory? Faugh!' Margaret Cameron swept up the letters and
locked them away in her writing desk. 'There'll be little enough

73

o' that wi' Scotland poor as yon caddie friend o' yours. Who's to buy bread for the soldiers' bellies or bullets for their guns?'

'Our own King James of course, Aunt, and the King of France who..'

'Has troubles of his own, not least the threat to his native language of a stammering word-mangler in an Edinburgh "Land". Pray God you never fetch up in France or they'll think you a Hottentot and burn you alive! But it is past your lesson-time. Get out your grammar and show me what you have to offer in the way of mutilations today.'

'You ask what can we offer, Colonel?' Lochiel's brows gathered in fierce intent. 'You may tell His Majesty that the whole Scottish nation will rise upon the arrival of its King!'

Once more the great hall of Glendessary was decked and silent in the presence of its chief, though this time the entertainment was discreet, the visit secret. Lochiel had arrived with only his haunchman and the gillies necessary to lead horse and pack-horse for his companion, long known in whispers as 'the Colonel'. Colonel Nathaniel Hooke had been sent, with all possible secrecy, from France by Monsieur de Chamillart, Minister of War and Secretary of State, to assess the spirit of the Scottish nation and the likely success of any Rising to establish James, the exiled Chevalier de St George, upon his rightful throne. Glendessary had provided welcome for the chosen, trusted few. Negotiations must be secret between Colonel and each Highland chief in turn, for there were spies everywhere – and a chief's word was enough to bind his clan. Glendessary's haunchman Alexander stood at his shoulder, and Alexander's son, with some half-dozen Cameron men of probity and leadership, who when the time came would take command – but no more: the servants who had scurried in and out again bearing roast fowls and venison had orders to stay in the kitchen unless called.

At the long deal table, heads bent close and confidential across discarded platters and still-circulating wine. The Colonel drank slowly and with evident savour before replying, 'I welcome your assurance, Lochiel. Nevertheless, if we are to succeed in this venture I must be able to inform His Majesty of numbers, both of troops and ammunition. How many men can you raise?'

Lochiel glanced swiftly round the assembled company, Glendessary's men together with those few Lochiel had brought from Achnacarry, and said, 'Twenty-five thousand foot with 5,000 horse and dragoons.'

'But Cousin,' protested Glendessary, 'they will need arms and provisions. We have lead enough for no more than fifty and no powder at all. What of field-pieces and cannon?'

'The Great Marshall offers twenty-eight field-pieces and two battery cannons,' said Colonel Hooke. 'They are even now in his castle at Dunolgo.'

'But if we are to offer so many men, our King must bring extra provisions from France.'

'*Must?*' cried Lochiel. 'It is we who are bound in duty to His Majesty, not he to us.'

'But remember the years of famine, Cousin. And the Darien venture took most of our spare resources.'

'*Spare?*' Lochiel's roar shook cobwebs from the rafters. 'We do not offer what is *spare* to our sovereign. We offer all we have. Glendessary, you will raise 200; Atholl will raise 600, armed and regimented; Breadalbin, Drummond and Gordon more, and myself ... We pledge 25,000,' he repeated, turning to the Colonel, 'with accoutrements and provisions. And when the King comes to lead us, we will march to England, take Newcastle and its vital coal supplies, and then London.'

'But what of the English armies, Cousin?'

'All in Flanders,' said Lochiel with growing impatience. 'It is the scholar in you, Glendessary, that makes you see difficulties where none exist. It is rare in history for any king who marches on London with his army not to be swiftly crowned. James *will* succeed.'

It was the Colonel's turn for caution. 'We must proceed slowly and in secret,' he warned. 'We cannot hazard His Majesty's person until the Rising's success is assured.'

'Not slowly,' corrected Lochiel. 'We must act before the end of summer, or the seas and weather will prevent us. The tide of enmity to England will ebb on the winter's coming.'

'Nevertheless, preparations must be thorough and will require time. We cannot hope to move before ...'

'September,' interrupted Lochiel. 'At the latest. A frigate may sail from Dunkirk to Edinburgh in two days if the wind is favourable. The King will land at Leith and instantly be proclaimed in Edinburgh. The English will be forced to recall troops from abroad, the Dutch will not fight the Flanders War alone and will sue for peace, the commerce of London will crumble, and James will reign unchallenged.'

The Colonel had been wary throughout this meeting: with a price upon his head he was used to caution. But though his watchful eyes had moved ceaselessly from face to face in the flickering twilight of the great hall, even he was startled when a shape moved in the shadows and a clear voice said, 'The King himself must lead us.'

Hugh Cameron had listened enthralled to the plans which would set the rightful Stuart King upon his throne, but like Lochiel had grown impatient with the endless detail of provisioning and strategy. To the boy who had grown up in the freedom of Glendessary and the simplicity of its clan laws, the issue was clear as Luinne Bheinn in the frost of a spring morning.

'The King must come,' he repeated, self-conscious now with all eyes upon him, but he straightened his broadening shoulders and stood tall. 'The King alone must lead us so that all may see the Rising is an act of justice to restore our true liege lord.'

'Well spoken, lad,' roared Lochiel. 'Fill the boy's mug that he may drink with us to the Chevalier de St George, our rightful King!'

'Are ye not young Jenny's haunchman?' asked Lochiel later, when, at table with them, Hugh had drunk his share of the flagon. 'I mind ye well from yon meeting at the lochside, though you are a might taller now and so is she, and as fine looking a lass as ye'd find in all Edinburgh, eh Glendessary?'

Glendessary looked gratified. His daughter weighed heavy on his conscience, the more so since he had instructed Aunt Cameron to keep her in Edinburgh. He knew how much store she set by a summer in Glendessary, but it was out of the question that year. It reassured his conscience to know that she was flourishing.

'Aye, Lochiel, and if all I hear be true, has found some little favour.'

'Breadalbin's son?' Lochiel laughed. 'A pup! She'd be better matched with the old dog himself. He and I are of a rare vintage.'

'We'll drink to that,' and the Cameron men raised brimming glassed to their chief.

Hugh drank with the rest, but the clear eyes were troubled now with doubt. Breadalbin's son? Had Jenny not forgiven him after all? Had she taken the non-fulfilment of his vow to present his first *creach* to her as proof that the bond between them had been snapped? Did she think he had rejected, forgotten her? At the thought a slow flush mounted to suffuse his face with shame. He had known at the back of his mind that they would want to marry her to someone, someday, but she and he had been so close in understanding that it had seemed impossible. But Breadalbin's son! What hope had Hugh against Breadalbin's son? None but the strength of their given word, sealed with a dagger-vow and kiss.

Hugh listened to the talk around him, drank the wine when it came his way, while his mind worried at the problem, and his heart ached with the unshed anguish of his love.

Lochiel continued to insist on September, before hills were closed by winter snow, seas made dangerous by storms. The Colonel continued as obstinately to refuse to be pinned down. He had his orders, he must report to the French court and to St Germain. The dogged argument persisted late into the night, until the paper of intent was finally signed and, in the half-light of dawn, Lochiel's small cavalcade escorted the Colonel into the high hills and southward towards Glenfinnan.

Hugh Cameron went with them to the border of Glendessary's land and watched them out of sight beyond the snow-filled clefts of Sgurr Thuilm. Though it was mid-May already the April snows had not yet melted to string the valley with torrents, but soon the 'grey mare's tail' would once again begin to grow. He was reminded of that other April a year ago, of his promise to Jenny and their first kiss. The swelling of his heart at the call of his exiled King echoed and merged with his love for Jenny, his chieftain's daughter, till he was filled with a sweet, intolerable pain that made him cry aloud – an animal cry which echoed, anguished and jubilant, from crag and gully just as the sun burst above the horizon and lanced the dark lake with golden light.

'It is an omen,' thought Hugh in awe. 'When the *crosh-tarie* is carried through the mountains, our Rising surely will be blessed – and Jenny will come home.'

He moved in wonder down the stirring hillside. Before he reached the dyke of the home pasture, he heard the tearing of grass, the shifting weight as his bull grazed, restless in the gathering light. The animal was superb. Hugh looked on the rippling skin of neck and flank with a pride that held no element of fear. Soon Glendessary would want to put the beast among the cows at pasture. If only Jenny would come to see his *creach* before its strength was drained in mating and its hide worn threadbare; before the autumn, when the *crosh-tarie* would surely come and he like all the Cameron men, would answer the call.

But he knew now that Jenny would not come, and before September there would be the long summer and the shieling, then the drove-road to market.

At the thought of Colonel Hooke and the secret preparations that would already be in hand, the idea came to him, not slowly, piece by piece and cautiously, as most ideas did, but whole, clear-cut and blinding in its thunderbolt simplicity.

Wattie saw them first, coming up the curve from the West Port into the early morning sun, and already they had gathered a dancing crowd at their heels. The Highlander whose young, untroubled face belied his size, and the black bull, side-stepping, tossing its tethered head in a snort of frost-clouded breath. The boy walked barefoot and bare-headed, his plaid kilted at the waist with belt and dirk; the bull walked lightly on clean hooves, surprisingly small for its thick-muscled bulk. Both gave the impression of strength kept politely in check, of pride stilled out of courtesy to strangers, of a natural contempt for the pretensions of the city-dweller, which aroused antagonism, derision, or defensive laughter in any onlookers – and there were many.

'Hey, ye Heeland gype – the Cowgate's at yer back!' 'Wheesht, man. The laddie's awa' to tak' tea wi' the Governor's lady!' 'Whar's yer breeks? Ye canna show yer bum i' the Castle.'

But Hugh strode on, impervious. For if he heard, he did not understand, and if he had, would not have cared. He took no more notice of the gathering rabble than of a burn in spate, and as little heed of the noise. In spite of his natural scorn for the countryman, Wattie was impressed. The lad was six feet tall if he was an inch, with shoulders broad as a house door, and when he asked directions, in careful English, he spoke as a natural chieftain to a vassal. Even without the proffered coin, Wattie would have obeyed; for impudence was out of place. Moreover, Wattie had a quick eye for flesh on the hoof, and though that bullock would supply enough red meat for a garrison, it would also trample as many if aroused. Wattie was not alone in natural caution: even the Town Guard, after a tentative 'Ye canna go that way' had kept his distance. In consequence the crowd that assembled beneath Mistress Cameron's window in the High Street was unusually well-ordered, keeping a careful halo of no-man's-land between magnet and attracted. As the Highland lad and his bullock stood silent, heads raised towards the third-floor window, the crowd fell silent too, in anticipation.

It was the silence which attracted Jenny's attention before Wattie's rasp on the door and the sudden swell of voices in the hall.

'What is it, Andrew?' called Aunt Cameron. Before he could speak, Jenny answered for him.

'It is Hugh!' She flashed past her aunt in a swirl of looped skirts and laughter. Aunt Cameron witnessed their reunion from the window as Jenny threw her arms around the boy's neck, he in turn swung her off her feet and they kissed in the High Street, in full and public view of the Town Guard and what looked like the entire town population.

'Oh Hugh, you made your *creach*!'

'For you, Jenny, as I vowed I would.'

'But he is splendid,' and Jenny kissed Hugh again with all the overflowing ardour of her homesick heart.

'Jenny, forgive me that I told your father,' he managed, above the furious beating in his breast, 'but I was bound by a promise to him too, and he is my chief.'

'No matter,' cried Jenny, flushed and laughing. 'It is so good to see you, Hugh. But tell me how you caught him and where,' and she turned to the bull, laid a fearless hand on the animal's neck. But her aunt could bear no more.

'Come away in, you brazen hussy,' she cried from the window, and pandemonium broke loose. For when Hugh kissed her, he had slackened his grip on the rope which ran through the ring in the beast's nose. At the sudden noise from overhead, the animal struck the cobblestones with one anxious foot, then broke free and ran, scattering market stalls, produce and screaming indwellers in all directions, while Jenny and Hugh together laughed . . .

But only for a moment, then they were running as in the old days on the hills of home, down the High Street past the luckenbooths, St Giles, the Netherbow, and on, while the frightened animal turned and twisted, snorting, stamping, lashing its tasselled tail in a crescendo of shouting, and the frenzied barking of a score of dogs. But when the bullock took a wrong turn and headed into a close in the Canongate, Hugh and Jenny were at its heels. Together they had it instantly secured and a moment later were leading it back obediently up the hill, to the relieved cheers of the populace. At her aunt's house the Town Guard was waiting for them.

'I arrest you, boy, on a charge of disturbance, of bringing dangerous livestock into the public street and assaulting the young lady here with felonious intent.'

'She assaulted him!' called a wag from the crowd and there was general laughter, above which came the authoritative voice of Sir Patrick Johnston from up the stair.

'I will settle this, officer. If the young man will consent to sell me that beast, I will undertake there will be no more disturbance of any kind.' He slipped a coin into the man's hand and Jenny saw the glint of silver. 'I will pay a fair price,' he added as Hugh made no answer.

'It is not for me to be bargaining with you, sir,' said Hugh slowly, his eyes on Jenny's face which was flushed with running and happiness. 'The beast belongs to Miss Jenny.'

Jenny looked swiftly round the crowd – the overturned stalls, the trampled goods, the faces, some grasping and rebellious, some smiling, then at the Town Guard. In spite of the silver in his palm, there was an ominous glint in his eye and Jenny said swiftly, 'Thank you, Sir Patrick. If you will satisfy all these good people who have suffered from our runaway beast then we will gladly sell him to you.'

'But Jenny, the *creach* is for you.'

'And has been duly made.' Jenny's dark eyes shone with pride. 'Now our beast can go to better use, Hugh, *as can the money*.' Her eyes looked straight and calm into Hugh's own and the clear grey deepened with understanding. No word passed between them, but when Sir Patrick handed the pouch of silver coins to Hugh, he tied it at his waist without further protest as the beast was led away, and refused Sir Patrick's invitation to seal the bargain with a dram. Instead he turned on his heel and strode for the West Bow and his second task. With his oath fulfilled and her forgiveness, there was no need for parting. They were bonded true as man and wife. His heart was lighter than for months, as he marched towards the Grassmarket and that other business, with Jenny in his heart and money for the King's cause safe at his belt.

Jenny sang as she mounted the stair with Sir Patrick at her side, sang as he mollified her aunt and invited them both to sup that night upstairs with his wife, his daughter and himself. It had been a greeting, Sir Patrick said, to bring tears to the eyes – a chieftain's daughter and his son's blood-brother. In spite of her inner fury, Aunt Cameron was silenced. But she was not the only one to have witnessed the meeting of Hugh Cameron and Miss Jenny. So had young Wattie and the Town Guard, Andrew goggle-eyed beside his mistress at the window, and a hundred others ... It would have been better, though for differing reasons, if each one of them had been elsewhere.

Hugh sought out Lucky Spence's tavern as Glendessary had entrusted him to do, though only after days of insistent begging and, finally, an appeal to Lochiel himself. The bull he had taken without permission, for the bull was his to take. But the message when it came was inconclusive and disappointing. 'Not yet.'

In spite of pledges of intent from the highest in Scotland, of promises of men and arms, of the harvest of two years in the granaries, of meat, beer and brandy, a plentiful supply of woollen cloth, of shoes and bonnets, carriages for transport, in spite of a plea to 'come when you please and to what part you please, for if you do not come soon, the party will be broken and it will be too late', the King's advisers still hesitated.

'Tell them,' Hugh's contact looked swiftly to each side and lowered his voice, 'that we cannot risk failure by too hasty a move.'

'But if it be not now,' said Hugh, equally cautious, though his young face flushed ingenuously with angry disappointment, 'it cannot be till the spring! The snow imprisons us throughout the winter and the seas are treacherous with storms. *Tell them!*'

'The message is "not yet",' repeated the man, paid his account and swiftly left.

Hugh who had been buoyed up on a wave of fervour by his meeting with Jenny and Sir Patrick's unexpected bounty, felt suddenly weary and a long way from home. He finished his ale and stood up to leave.

It was evening now, the sky darkening, shadows cast by eave and forestair impenetrable. In the High Street, link-boys scurried about their business, their charges following close in pools of carried light, but here in the less salubrious territory of the Grassmarket there was only deepening murk blotted by patches of spilled candlelight from the tavern behind him. The boy scented the air, eyes wary, ears alert, as a stag on the hills would test the wind for treachery. He felt for the pouch at his waist; for his dirk. Both safe. With a tilt of the chin and a slow breath of resolve, he stepped forward into the darkness towards the lantern light of the West Port. If he walked fast, he could reach Cramond before darkness enveloped him, and the inn-keeper at Cramond barred the door.

Buildings crowded high on either side, smothering him with shadows. Bare feet silent on the muddied causeway, only the swish of moving kilt, the strong beat of his heart. He was in the midden of the city now, the stinking warren of hovels which lapped the foot of the hill with human scum. Nostrils pinched in distaste, lungs strained for the clean air of the hills. A rat leapt from a heap of refuse at his feet and fled; somewhere in the labyrinthine tenements an old woman laughed with the eerie horror of a screech owl, and Hugh felt the skin of his neck go cold as he remembered tales of witches. Hugh was afraid of no man, but the Evil One was a different matter ... He quickened his step, eager for the safety of the open sky.

He was at the foot of the Castle Rock when a twig snapped at his back on a hiss of indrawn breath, and in the second's warning this gave, he whirled round, dagger raised, and met the onslaught.

Five or six of them. He had no time to count in the thudding maelstrom of cudgels, knives and stifling breath. But Hugh was solid with muscle and Highland air. He smacked one man into the ditch with a backhanded swing of his targe arm, impaled a second on his dirk, lifted him, still pinioned, as a screaming shield against a third. He had his back against the rock when the next two came at him together, teeth bared and snarling. The stench of their clothes and breath combined all but overpowered him as the bare arms throttled, rags stank at his face, a sinewed leg hooked round his own and wrenched to topple him. Then nails clawed at his belt and he heard the thong snap. The King's silver! With a Highland war-cry that ricocheted from the rock at his back and echoed, bellowing, into the night, Hugh heaved his tormentors up and back, smashing one against the rock itself, another underfoot, while his dirk slashed a swath of blood and rags, till in a mêlée of muffled screams and frightened oaths, his assailants scrambled back into the murk which had spewed them. Hugh crouched alone and at bay, arms raised at once in attack and defence, ears alert to every sound, while the breath rasped in his throat and his chest heaved against the thumping fury of his heart.

Silence ... the settling of dust and debris ... a single whimpering exhalation from the ditch ... then nothing. In the dirt at his feet lay the glinting discs of his scattered silver. He dared not stoop to retrieve it, but kept watchful guard over his King's money, prepared to die, if necessary, in its defence, while he listened, every pore open to detect a threat. And threat was there, he knew it. Somewhere in the darkness was another, wary as he was, waiting too ...

Hugh remained motionless, breathing shallow now and silent, while his ears and eyes strained into the hostile darkness. The rock at his back was cold with gathering moisture. There was moisture on his cheek, too, and his thigh, but this time warm and trickling thick ... his mind leapt homeward to the Dessary burn and the cleansing coolness of its waters. Then a shadow moved and on the instant he was back on the defence, crouching, teeth bared, dirk raised to strike.

'Master Cameron, sir!' The voice was a cautious whisper, from the far shadows. 'It is me, the caddie, who showed you the way. May I come forward?'

Fractionally Hugh relaxed. 'Slowly,' he said. 'No further now. What do you want?'

'To help ... to see if you are hurt.' Wattie stood, a small shape against the murk of the tenements. 'See.' He spread his arms wide. 'I am unarmed and alone.'

'Where are they?' growled Hugh, eyes darting to the shadows on either side. Suppose the boy was a trap laid to catch him? To draw him off so that they could swoop and steal?

'Gone.' Wattie watched Hugh with wary respect. He had seen the fury of his fighting; seen him vanquish the toughest bunch of cut-throats in the Grassmarket. 'I swear it,' added the boy as the silence continued unchanged. 'I heard the noise, but dared not come till they were fled. Let me help you,' he added, moving forward, but with caution, having no wish to draw that deadly dirk upon himself.

'Stop. Stay where you are.' Hugh was not yet ready for trust. 'Why did you follow me, unless to take whatever that scum might have left you? Or are you their accomplice? The lookout boy who gives warning if a Guard approach?'

'No, I swear it, sir. I am no' but a caddie – Miss Jenny's caddie,' he added with inspiration, 'bid by Lochiel himself to watch her. I hoped to see you safely on your way so I could tell Miss Jenny and set her mind at rest.'

'If you are Lochiel's man, it is enough,' said Hugh with relief. 'Help me gather the King's silver so I may be swiftly on my way, lest they are gone merely to return with reinforcements.'

'They will not return,' grinned Wattie. 'I saw them. They'll be sousing their sore heads in Lucky Spence's ale, I'll warrant, and not set their noses out o' doors again till dawn.' He knelt and scratched in the dust of the path to collect a fistful of the scattered coins, which he tipped in a glinting stream into the open pouch.

'There is one more,' said Hugh when the boy at last stood up and brushed the dirt from his knees.

'Unless the villains took it?' suggested Wattie, turning the dirt with first one foot, then the other. 'And made off so quickly because they had at least something for their pains? I see nothing here.'

Hugh dropped to one knee to peer more closely at the shadowed earth and put a hand against the rock for balance as pain seared his thigh. His head swayed like a coracle in a high wind; and the caddie's voice came as from a great distance.

'Master Cameron, sir, are ye not weel?'

With slow deliberation, Hugh focused his blurred vision, felt for a hand-hold in the rock and raised himself, inch by inch, till he was once more upright, feet planted firm, a span apart, one hand on the leather pouch. Carefully, he took the other from the wall and stood alone.

'There is one coin still to come.' Like a wounded animal, he wanted only to be alone, but his King's work came first.

'I see none. I'll warrant yon vagabonds made off wi' it. And ye'd best be on your way, I'm thinking, before they send word ahead o' ye to their brothers on the road.'

Hugh hesitated, torn between obstinacy and prudence. He had lost the King's silver and ought to retrieve it. Yet the coins, which would buy much-needed armaments, were an unlooked-for bonus and it was a long way home to Loch Arkaig. If he hoped to reach the Glen with the remaining money intact, he could afford to waste no time.

'You are right. I take my leave of you,' and the Highlander turned westward into the darkening night.

Wattie stood immobile, watching the tall figure move down the track which led, through field and wooded copse, to Cramond. Only when Hugh Cameron's shoulders had dipped beyond the curve of the hill did Wattie move. Then, with a glance to either side and behind, he dropped to one knee, felt swiftly under a stone, and a moment later was running, nimble and silent-footed as a rat, back up the slope of the Castle hill to where smoking torches splashed the eaves with light.

Hugh did not reach Cramond. Instead he burrowed deep into a rowan copse, found a stream, plunged grateful hands into the gleaming water and doused face and swimming head with ice. Then, carefully, teeth clenched against inevitable pain, he washed and bound his wound, using a strip torn from his shirt to draw the ragged flesh together. That done, he dipped his hands again into the stream and drank, while he considered his position. He could not go to Cramond now. He dared not risk the company of others, not with the King's silver at his belt, his sword arm wrenched and bleeding in a dozen places, and his left thigh slit almost to the bone. Instead, he must move with the cunning of a wounded wildcat if he was to reach home in safety.

With infinite care, he eased his wounded body to lie full length on the bracken in the sheltering shadow of a dyke. Branches of rowan laced the sky overhead; through the berried tracery, stars prickled bright as candlelight. He would rest a while to gather strength, then walk till morning...

He felt light-headed, his body cumbersome with pain. His leg throbbed loud as a watchman's drum. But the silence of the star-lit sky enveloped him, the familiar murmuring of water soothed and reassured; and the night wind blew cool against his face. At last the boy submitted to the weariness of pain and drew memory close for comfort . . . Jenny loved him. Breadalbin's son, Glendessary, Aunt Cameron, all were nothing now, for Jenny had kissed him before a thousand witnesses . . . and had accepted his *creach*. She understood the meaning of that *creach* as he did: he was hers and she was his in plighted troth, for ever . . . He no longer noticed the ache nor the spreading warmth of blood as the starlight brightened to fill his head with singing.

The thud of galloping horses thrust him cruelly awake on a wave of pain. The high sun was warm on his face and from somewhere adjacent came the steady drone of flies. He raised his head enough to see that they were feeding close at hand: then saw the bloodstained rags and closed his eyes against the nauseous dread. For flies swathed his leg in a blue-black mesh of swollen bellies and quivering wings. In instant memory he saw the carcass of a deer, long dead, maggots in eye sockets and open mouth, while flies crawled slowly over rotting flesh in satiated ease.

By all the angels, he must rid himself of the creeping plague before he saw his own flesh eaten away! In one movement he rolled over and into the stream and lay there, gasping, in the shallow, racing water which froze the breath in his chest and gripped his body with healing ice. When he could no longer bear it, he clawed his slow way back on to the bank, discarded the sodden bandage and bound his leg afresh with another strip of shirt. Only then did he remember the pouch: the leather was slippery with moisture, but still closed, the coins intact. He dried his dirk on the bracken, honed it against a stone, cut himself a length of rowan to use as a support and turned his face towards the west. West first, then north, he told himself with careful planning. A hundred and fifty miles. Then west again along the secret cleft of Loch Arkaig. It was fortunate after all that the *crosh-tarie* would not go out before the spring. By springtime he would be healed. It was fortunate, too, that he was young and strong. An older wounded man might not achieve the journey with winter drawing close.

With the picture of Jenny to sustain him, he lengthened his halting stride in dogged resolution for the long road home.

Bess saw him first, meandering like a man asleep along the icy shore of Loch Arkaig. The first snow had fallen a week before and the land was piebald with snowdrift and protruding rock, the stream at the back of Glendessary choked green with tumbling ice. At first she did not recognize the skeletal, shambling form, the tattered plaid, the deep-socketed, feverish

85

eyes. Martinmas was long past and they had thought him lost, or dead.

From the sward below Glendessary where she had been drawing water for the clothes-tub, Bess watched, uncertain. But no one else stood tall as Hugh Cameron, Alexander's son – even now, bent as he was with pain and long endurance. As he drew towards the head of the loch, Bess dropped all caution and ran to him with welcome.

'Hugh! I thought you dead!' she cried, clasping her arms around him and laying her cheek against his chest. If he had stooped to greet her she would have kissed him, but he did not. He made no acknowledgement save a brushing away of her arms as he might an inconvenient branch or clawing bramble, and walked on.

Bess bit her lip, her eyes grew hot with tears – at first of mortification, then, as she saw the sunken cheeks, the fierce, unfocused eyes, of fear and of compassion.

'Hugh,' she said, taking his hand to lead him, though he moved without apparent bidding, like one possessed. 'Oh my dear one, you are ill. But now that you are home, I will tend you.'

His eyes did not swerve from the grey block of Glendessary on its knoll at the head of the loch. 'I go to my chief,' he said, in a voice rough as a corncrake's and scarce above a whisper. 'Jenny . . . lead me . . .'

Bess took his hand and did as he asked, though the tears flowed freely now. He did not care for her, while her own heart choked her throat with longing for him, even now, emaciated as he was, aged far beyond his years. She loved him and he did not even recognize her. The fever had left him no strength but for one fixed purpose – to go home – and, it seemed, one thought.

'Jenny, my Jenny . . .' He spoke her name often in the days that followed and Bess learnt to stop her ears against the hurt.

'It is the fever,' she told his mother and her own, and kept the nursing, jealously, to herself. For after his meeting with Glendessary when he had managed 'In the spring' and 'the King's silver' he had fallen insensible at his chieftain's feet. They had carried him to an alcove off the great hall where Bess gave him *uisge beatha* and, when he could lift his head enough to swallow, a dish of steaming broze. She fetched stones hot from the hearth for his feet and back, wrapped him warm inside a folded plaid. Glendessary himself sent cordials from the medicine chest and salves for the festering wound on the boy's thigh. The boy's father, Alexander, bade Bess watch him well, which she did, taking advantage of his delirium to kiss his eyes, his cheeks, his unresponsive lips and even, when no others were about, to lay her head on his chest and twine her arms about him, fondling. Sometimes he would stir in his sleep . . . once he laid a hand on her hair and held her close and she felt his lips briefly on her forehead. But all he ever said was 'Jenny . . .' Until the night the fever eased and he slept untroubled.

Bess sensed the change in him at once and knew she had little time. If she was ever to make Hugh Cameron hers, then she must take what she knew was the only possible course. And it must be now, before his mind grew clear again, and sharp . . .

Silently she took up her plaid and, swathed tight against the winter weather, slipped out into the darkness, the precious coin hot in the palm of her hand. It was to have bought her fine linen for her wedding kist, but if it bought her what she sought, it would be well spent. Shivering against the bitter wind, she hurried eastward, following the glinting shore-line and the whispering waters of the loch, then struck north towards Macdonald country and the turf-roofed hut which was her destination.

She was back before morning, and sitting watchful at Hugh's side when, still murmuring Miss Jenny's name, he woke to puzzled consciousness.

'Bess?' he said with awkward recognition as he took in his own apparent helplessness, the bed-closet, her air of proprietorial care. 'Am I then at home?'

'This three weeks past. You have been ill, my love. Drink this.' She held the goblet to his lips before he could protest. 'It is to strengthen your weakened limbs and give you vigour.'

'Is it?'

'Drink, my dear one . . . my sweet love.'

He had been going to ask her if it was springtime, but his head was unaccountably smothered in rose-pink velvet, his body languid with sunlight and longing, and his mind singing somewhere high above Glendessary . . . Jenny was there with him . . . he and she were birds together, love-birds, swooping and weaving in murmurous, soft-feathered wooing which grew suddenly fierce as a heath-fire, wind-blown and roaring, till it consumed him to a single, white-hot shaft of agony and longing . . . and, afterwards, to ashes . . .

4

She was now grown tall and well shaped, her Skin clear, and her Features agreeable; she had large sparkling Eyes, with a wanton Softness about them, that never fail'd to please if they designed to make a Conquest; so that if she might not be reckon'd a Beauty, at least she was very agreeable.

Edinburgh was a bleak place in that winter following Union. Her father visited her; her uncle John; and there were frequent letters from home – though none, by Glendessary's orders, mentioned Hugh's long disappearance and his illness. Glendessary had heard disturbing news from Aunt Cameron concerning the relationship between his daughter and the boy, and divined, rightly, that any mention of Hugh's trouble would bring Jenny racing home. Aunt Cameron kept similar silence, for Jenny's marriage was a matter of growing importance and, with such political uncertainty prevailing, of confusion. Neither she nor Glendessary wished to stake all on a Jacobite match which might prove worse than worthless – nor give the girl unnecessarily into the Union camp. Jenny herself remained ignorant of all such manoeuvres, thinking only of her King. For since Hugh's visit, she had been buoyed up with expectation of the Rising that must surely come; yet as the days grew shorter, the wind blew colder from the sea, and still the King did not set sail, Jenny became impatient beyond bearing.

'If only I had something useful to do!'

'It is fortunate, Miss, that you are called upon to do nothing more demanding than wait.' Aunt Cameron was worried. Breadalbin's son had seemed ideal, but should this threatened Rising fail there would be retribution, land confiscated, banishments, even executions. The Camerons would need friends in high places. There was one possibility, well-born, wealthy – if he could be tempted ... Aunt Cameron thumped stick on floorboard. 'Your French is minimal, girl. Your Italian no more than serves you to play *forte* or *pianissimo*. As for your manners, I despair.'

'And so do I,' thought Jenny, remembering the long months still to pass before the spring.

Yet her aunt had spoken with an automatic censure, now

outgrown. During those summer months when Edinburgh had emptied of every family of standing, gone to the hills for the country air, except for Jenny's brief and boring visit to her mother in Perthshire they had been thrown much together. Gradually Aunt Cameron had allowed her heart to open and enjoy the girl's company, had admitted Jenny's questions, answered them with increasing honesty, till Jenny had a grasp of political manoeuvring as competent as Aunt Cameron's own. That business in the autumn, with Hugh Cameron from Glendessary, had been an uncomfortable setback, but Sir Patrick had smoothed that over and the girl had shown no further wayward inclinations. When the time came, she would act as they wished her to act, if only for loyalty to Lochiel, and Aunt Cameron would see that the girl was well-matched and happy.

Jenny, however, had other plans: when the promised Rising had set their King upon his rightful throne, the Cameron men would march back to Glendessary, and Hugh and Jenny would go with them.

'Tush, child, stop your dreaming,' said Aunt Cameron briskly. 'I have told ye twice already to translate that passage of Corneille. How do you hope to pass as educated if you are fit for nought but making eyes at soldiers in the street?'

'It was not a soldier, Aunt,' said Jenny, turning back from the window. 'It was that caddie, Tom Watt.' She never called him Wattie now, and rarely saw him. Since the night of Hugh's visit, he had avoided her. Andrew said the lad was trying to apprentice himself to a trade, but he still ran messages and carried flambeaux, so perhaps no one would have him.

'Tom Watt? Have you nothing better to do than gawp at a common caddie?'

'I thought he might be bringing us a message, Aunt.'

'Even if he is, it will not be the news you wait for. Not in January with the seas rough enough to turn the toughest stomach inside out. We're nae looking for a king wi' legs like a jelly-pudding – nor for a fleet as full o' holes as a kitchen colander.'

'No Aunt. Yet if I were king, I could not bear this waiting.'

'Then I thank the Lord you are not, Miss, for you'd spoil any venture with your impatience.'

Aunt Cameron, too, would be glad when the waiting was over, for Jenny was past fifteen now and marriageable, and on the outcome of the King's venture depended who would have her. Somehow the right bargain must be sealed, before it was too late.

So aunt and niece waited in increasing impatience for what

must inevitably change the course of their lives, and Scotland's too. But when it came, it brought disaster.

In those last days of March, Edinburgh was in a ferment of expectation: the invasion fleet was gathering, taking on provisions, food, arms, men ... the King himself was in Dunkirk ... he had gone aboard ... in Edinburgh it was common knowledge that the Castle had no ammunition, nor had Stirling, and though there were English ships in the Firth of Forth and a Dutch East-Indiaman – 'waiting', it was officially explained, 'for a convoy to Holland' – there were also a hundred loyal fishing-vessels ready to put to sea the instant the invasion fleet was sighted, to aid the disembarkation. The sea was calm ... then treacherous with squally gusts ... then calm again ... and on the evening of 23 March the invasion fleet was sighted.

'It has begun!' cried Jenny as the news raced through the city. 'Why are the guns not firing? Where are the Highlandmen?'

'Peace, child, for discretion's sake! Do you want the whole town to know which side you support?'

'Yes! I am not ashamed. James is Scotland's King. And mine. I care not who knows it.'

'Well I do. The battle is not won, and until it is you will hold your fire. And your tongue.'

'But the King is there, Aunt, waiting for his people to rise up and carry him to the throne of Scotland.'

'He is waiting,' said her aunt with grim sarcasm, 'for the tide.'

But the tide turned in more ways than one. Afterwards the tale was of one long bungle – the French pilot missed the Firth of Forth and had reached Montrose before he found out his mistake. When the fleet turned back again, they had missed the tide and must drop anchor. While they waited in the darkness, the English fleet was able to assemble in overwhelming numbers, having raced after them from Dunkirk, all up the English coast. Dawn brought consternation as the King's fleet found its path to victory blocked by English warships, and as the guns boomed out from Edinburgh Castle, they turned tail and fled north. The English chased them. By afternoon, four of their best vessels had caught up, including one of seventy guns. The French resisted, drove them back. But when the cannon fired in Edinburgh for victory, it was a Government victory, sealed with the capture of the *Salisbury* and without a single invader setting foot on Scottish soil.

'At least the King escaped,' said Jenny, fighting bitter disappointment. 'The rest of the fleet will reassemble at

Peterhead. They will collect the clans' support and move southwards from there. We cannot give in now, when the campaign has just begun.'

'The campaign, as you call it,' said her aunt with bitterness, 'is already over. Bungled from start to finish. What did they expect when they left it to the French?'

'But the King . . .'

'Is back in Dunkirk, drowning his sorrows and his *mal de mer* in French brandy while his breeches steam before the French king's fire. Fools, all of them! Bungling, Frenchified *fools*!' Aunt Cameron loosed her anxiety and disappointment in vehement invective. She depended for her livelihood entirely on the young ladies good families sent to her – that, and the bounty she might expect from arranging a good match for her charges when their education was complete. She had no means of her own. If she had let her inclinations show too clearly in this latest disaster, she might find herself ostracized by the victors, left clientless by the vanquished. But it was the loss of the Breadalbin match which saddened her, for a Jacobite estate would have made Miss Jenny happy. The other would be harder to angle for, harder to present, considering the Cameron involvement in the latest débâcle. But *because* of that involvement it was now vital. And not impossible. The gentleman had seen the girl; admired her; he was the right age and wealthy, with a splendid estate. Most important of all, he had the affections and the ears of the ruling party, and with Jenny at his side would use them, if not to win advancement for her relatives, at least to win them leniency. Once she had accepted that marriage was inevitable, Miss Jenny would be happy. If her aunt had not thought so, she would have refused assent to the idea. As it was, there was no time to be lost.

'What are you goggling at, Miss? Sit up! Stop snivelling! Pull in your stomach and look alive. Have you forgot we take tea with Lady Johnston at the four hours? And mind ye say nothing of the King's fiasco. We are loyal Edinburgh citizens: remember that. Unless ye plan to give us all away.'

Jenny was silenced, though it was not easy to remain so when Sir Patrick joined them as the candles were lit, and talked affably of what he called 'most satisfactory developments'. The Government, it seemed, had sent out heralds to summon the principal nobility and gentry to appear before the Privy Council.

'Under pain of rebellion,' said Sir Patrick, 'for it is well known which names were foremost in the planning of the late and mercifully unsuccessful Rising.' Sir Patrick smiled genially and lifted his coat flap once or twice to warm his back.

'And have they appeared?' asked Jenny politely, but with a gleam in her eyes which set her aunt on instant guard.

'It takes time to ride in from the Highlands, Miss Jenny.'

'I doubt that many will undertake the journey,' she countered with deceptive sweetness. 'There is so much to attend to in the springtime and no time to spare for city visiting.'

'Unlike ourselves,' said Aunt Cameron quickly, 'who cram our schedule too tight with such affairs. I regret we must take our leave of you, Sir Patrick. We are expected at my cousin's.'

'I warn you, girl,' she said in a furious undertone as they descended the stair. 'Make no more such pert remarks or you will ruin us all.'

'Pert? How can you call me pert, Aunt, when I am merely loyal? Would you have me stand by silent and hear our King abused?'

'I would indeed – until you learn to practise diplomacy, as Sir Ewen wishes.'

The name of Sir Ewen brought instant sobriety, but could not dispel the resentment her aunt's words aroused. At the reception in the Canongate to which they proceeded via a hired sedan, Jenny behaved impeccably – and spoke not a word beyond the small requirements of convention, to Aunt Cameron's relief and the obvious approval of a square-set gentleman of thirty-five whom their hostess presented as Sir Roderick Campbell, first cousin to the Duke of Argyll. Even that hated name brought no embarrassing outburst, and Aunt Cameron allowed herself to relax as the rooms filled, the wine flowed, and later the ladies, one by one, performed at the spinet or sang. Aunt Cameron, looking from their ringleted, pale-complexioned frippery to her niece's statuesque and dark-haired beauty, felt the stirrings of an almost maternal pride. The girl had the air of a thoroughbred among cross-breeds, or a queen among serfs. She saw her own admiration reflected in the faces of at least one of the men, and knew that their King's débâcle had not, after all, destroyed all hope.

She wrote the following morning to Glendessary and when Miss Jenny, seeing the superscription, inquired as to the contents, refused to say.

Jenny did not find enlightenment for fifteen days, when news came that the King was safe in Dunkirk again and the Rising, for the present, over. The summoned Highland gentlemen appeared belatedly before the Privy Council, and with them came her Uncle John.

'There are urgent estate matters to be settled in the glen or your father would have come himself, my dear,' said John,

Younger of Lochiel. 'I bring his deep affection, and these.' He laid a packet of letters upon the table.

But Jenny's mind was still with the Highlanders, sent to England under guard for trial.

'No one will testify against them, Uncle. They cannot be proved traitors without witnesses of prosecution.'

'You had best leave politics aside, Jenny, and read your father's letter,' said her Uncle with a benign and puzzling smile.

'But I want to know what...'

'Read,' ordered her aunt, and watched the girl's face intently as she broke the seal and unfolded the stiff, close-written page.

Jenny did not at first understand. 'Sir Roderick Campbell.... Inverleary Castle ... 10,000 acres and a house at Holyrood. I understand you have met more than once with mutual approval ... a splendid match for all concerned ... your aunt has excelled herself on your behalf ... your mother overjoyed ... bless you, my dearest daughter ... I wish you both all happiness ...' The words danced like laughing demons on the page. Sir Roderick Campbell! That stiff-necked, self-satisfied fellow she had met at Miss Campbell's in the Canongate. *Mutual approval?* Jenny's eyes were huge first with disbelief, then with a dreadful, dawning horror. 'But he's a Union man! First cousin to Argyll!'

'And second to Breadalbin,' reminded her uncle, 'for whom we all have a high regard.'

'But *Argyll*! He is a Government man and a Treator.'

'You are not required to marry Argyll,' snapped Aunt Cameron. 'Merely his cousin, Inverleary, who does you *great honour*.'

'I will not! How dare you go behind my back and make my bargains for me. My word is not yours to give.' Jenny's eyes blazed now with a fury which made even her aunt's heart quail. She was reminded with disquieting suddenness of that incident two years ago with the switch, and this time Miss Jenny looked a stranger to all moderation.

'You will do as your father orders,' said John Cameron quietly, 'and before you throw further aspersions on the Campbell clan, remember that my wife was a Campbell,'

'*Was*!' cried Jenny in triumph. 'But she is a Cameron now, like her husband. You would have me give up my father's name in like wise. Because the King's cause is lost, the world lies in pieces! I had thought you a better patriot, Uncle John.'

'The King's cause is not lost, merely dormant. And because of that, you must marry as your father wishes.'

'I refuse. I will go to Sir Ewen. *He* will not allow it.'

'Lochiel gives his consent.'

She stared at him in disbelief, remembering Sir Ewen's promises. 'But Inverleary is not *one of us*.'

'He has relatives who are – and a large estate. Lochiel looks to you, Jenny, to be a lifeline for the Cameron clan, an ear in high places, a spy if you like...' but Jenny would not listen. Had they offered her Queensberry himself she could not have been more horrified. A Treator and a Unionist!

'Lochiel sees the wisdom of the match,' went on Sir John, 'as you must do.'

'Never!'

'That we will see,' said her aunt with ominous calm.

'Your father sends you his affection,' continued her uncle, 'and reminds you of your duty *and your promise*.'

'I promised to obey his wishes, and I have done so. I did not promise to marry any treating Campbell my aunt might find for me. It *was* your doing, was it not?' This time it was Aunt Cameron who received the full fury of her glare.

'Use your sense, girl. Breadalbin's son will be attainted: others with him. Lochiel himself bade me find a stop-gap should the Rising go ill. I have done so. Glendessary approves. *And orders it*!'

'Then I refuse. I am already pledged.'

'*Pledged*?' John Cameron was taken aback. 'And to whom, Miss, without your father's consent?'

'To Hugh Cameron,' replied Jenny, standing tall with dignity, 'on my father's estate.'

'Yon herdsman laddie who sold Sir Patrick a rogue stirk?' Her aunt gave a scornful laugh. 'Pshaw! Ye canna make a binding pledge wi' such as he.'

'*Rogue* stirk, did you say?' Jenny stamped her foot with rage. 'Did you not see his neck muscles? And his testicles big as cannon-shot? He was a fine-set bullock, fit to father a dynasty. Sir Patrick was *favoured* to be allowed to buy.'

'Ye may talk like a herdsman, Miss,' said Aunt Cameron with rising anger, 'but ye'll not marry one! And keep your voice down lest Sir Patrick and all Edinburgh hear ye.'

'I will marry whom I choose.' Jenny deliberately raised her voice to fill the building from roof to basement. 'And I choose Hugh Cameron, my father's *herdsman*, for Hugh and I are pledged.'

Aunt Cameron struck the girl hard across the face. It was a measure of Jenny's anguish that she did not immediately retaliate, but stood in quivering silence, one hand against the stinging cheek, while she looked from one enemy to the other.

Then she said, through clenched teeth, 'I vow to you Aunt Cameron and to you Uncle John that I will marry none but Hugh Cameron in Glendessary. You had best burn that marriage contract now, for I will have none of it.'

'And I swear to you, Miss, that you will not leave this house until you do.' The old woman's cheeks quivered with rage and frustration. She had expected opposition, though none that could not be reasoned away with good sense and affection, but the girl she had grown unwillingly to care for glared at her now in open hate. The old woman clutched the table edge to steady her trembling, and her clenched hand against the wood was bone-white. Jenny pushed past her without a word, out of the room and into the bedroom, where she slammed the door and locked it. Then, for the first time in her life, she threw herself face downwards on her bed and sobbed in a silent, draining anguish of fear and longing, with, beneath the tears, an enduring resolution.

Her brief capitulation over, she sat up, put her hair to rights, and opened her writing-desk. She took ink and quill and, after a moment's thought, wrote swiftly in a firm, round hand, folded and sealed the paper, and wrote the superscription: *To Hugh Cameron, Alexander's son, in Glendessary, Loch Arkaig.* She would forget her pride and pay the caddie Tom Watt to see her letter was delivered. And until Hugh came, as she knew beyond all doubting that he would do, she would treat her aunt's tirades with the dignity and scorn they warranted. Sir Roderick Campbell! She would sooner marry a Barbary ape!

'You will marry her,' said Glendessary, with cold anger. 'It is the law of church and clan and shall be obeyed.'

Hugh Cameron stood before his chieftain in the study at Glendessary and looked in bewilderment from his Laird to his father, then to Bess and her mother Morag and, her face averted behind a quivering fan, Lady Margaret herself.

'But I do not understand,' said the boy, and it was true. He had been a long time ill and a longer time in convalescing, but for a month past he had been fit again and as strong as before. His leg was healed and the scar no longer dragged. He could run and ride as well as ever, and since the winter grip had eased on the hills he had been busy with the horses and the harness, making ready what Glendessary's men would need when the call to rebellion came again.

'You understood well enough how to take advantage of the lass's kindness when she nursed you in your sickness.'

'She nursed me well, sir,' admitted Hugh, 'and I am grateful.'

'Do you deny you lay with her? Do you deny she is big with your child?' Glendessary's voice was stern, for he had no stomach for the business. He liked the lad, and thought him honest. If what that woman Morag said was true, it was as much her daughter's blame as Hugh's. But Kirk and clan decreed he carry the matter through and he would do it, if only to appease his wife who pleaded endlessly on her woman's behalf and would not be quieted. But the boy looked genuinely puzzled.

'Well?' Glendessary demanded. 'Do you deny it?'

'I do.' Hugh looked his chieftain straight in the eye and his own eyes did not waver, though his heart churned with shame that anyone should think such a thing possible, for there was only one girl in his heart. 'On my dirk, I swear it is not so.'

'And I swear it is!' cried Morag, Bess's mother, while Bess stood silent, eyes downcast. Her hands were trembling as she twisted them tight together at her back. Why would Hugh not look at her? She had not meant to make him angry, only to bind him to her so that he was hers to love and no one else's . . . She loved him as Miss Jenny never had and never would. They were meant for each other. Her mother said so, and her own heart knew it. She had only to touch him to feel the current race through his blood. She stole a look at Hugh's averted face, but it was aloof with righteousness. *He did not remember*. The hurt was unexpected and she felt her eyes sting with tears. In spite of the phial, how could he forget? But her mother was speaking.

'I swear they were together behind closed bed-curtains and that he took my daughter's maidenhead. She loves him, sir, and would deny him nothing. When the fever left him and he called for wine and comfort, he took her too. I found them together, sir, in the morning . . .'

Hugh's head swam with a black and stifling dread in which, for the first time, a worm-like memory stirred . . . a dream he had had long ago, a dream of flesh and ecstasy . . . he had thought it the delirium of fever for Jenny had been there . . . but Jenny was in Edinburgh. He was shaking now with a nightmare horror which choked the words in his throat so that he could not speak.

'Well, Hugh, what have you to say?' demanded his father.

Hugh now knew that nothing he said could change what must inevitably be, yet he said it. 'I may not marry Bess, Father. I am already pledged.'

'Pledged?' roared Glendessary. 'Why was I not told? Really

Alexander, this is too much. I might at least be kept informed.'

'The boy refers to a childhood bond he formed with Miss Jenny, that is all.'

Miss Jenny! Glendessary was shocked. Things were worse than he had thought. This matter must go through and quickly: for if what Hugh said was true, then Aunt Cameron had no conception of the trouble in store for her, in spite of the official blessing which Lochiel's son John would bring. Had he been able to go himself to tell Jenny, he might not have had the strength to resist her. Was it cowardice rather than duty which had made him plead estate matters as an obstacle to his leaving Glendessary? The disquieting suspicion sparked him to unaccustomed vigour.

'Tush boy, a childhood game. If that is all that prevents you, think no more of it.' Glendessary waved a dismissive hand, then frowned hard at Hugh. 'It did not prevent you fathering a child upon young Bess here and it need not stop you making her your wife. Why, Miss Jenny is herself betrothed. The contract is newly signed and she will be mistress of her own estate by Martinmas. You need not let a childhood game impede . . .'

Hugh ceased to listen. Jenny *betrothed*. He did not believe it. It was another trick to keep them apart. But . . . 'mistress of her own estate'. He knew how Jenny needed Glendessary, and if it was denied her, as it would be when her brothers married, might she not agree in order to win another such? Yet, 'It is not possible.' He heard his own words as from a far distance. 'She is pledged to me.'

'It is not only possible, Hugh, it is so,' said Glendessary, more kindly now that he had dealt the fatal blow. 'The pledge you speak of was nothing but a game. Jenny regards it so, and if you take it more seriously, you are the only one who does. Tush, boy, childhood pledges are cancelled by maturity. It is the natural order of things, and no shame. Your pledge is void,' he repeated as the boy did not seem to understand. 'You are free to marry Bess.'

'Which he *shall* do!' Hugh's father's brow was dark with anger, 'or he will be banished from Lochaber and the Cameron clan. I will not be shamed.'

'Mr Graham is entitled to officiate . . .'

Hugh no longer heard as the details were settled, the *tocher* discussed. Glendessary spoke the truth, for a chieftain could not do otherwise. Jenny was betrothed, and knowing Jenny as Hugh did, it could only be with her consent. Jenny had not understood: she had rejected his *creach* after all, and, with it, himself. She had taken the beast merely for money to give to the

97

King's cause. He had not thought it possible the world could hold so much treachery.

But in one thing Glendessary and his own father were wrong. He had made a dagger-vow. Others might regard that pledge as broken, but he did not. His honour was his to protect and preserve. He would show Miss Jenny – and all of them – that Hugh Cameron at least was capable of keeping faith.

The ceremony was soon over, in the chapel at Glendessary, with the Laird and his wife as witnesses, Alexander and Bess's mother too. Afterwards there was ale and feasting for everyone in the great hall, for Glendessary found such generosity a salve to his troublesome conscience, then dancing to the pipes which played till dawn.

Hugh heard them from the turf-roofed hut which was to be his home, for he had refused the Highland custom of bride and bridegroom bedding together in an outhouse while the wedding party warmed the house with jollity. They could keep their dancing to the great hall where it belonged and leave Hugh to his misery, alone.

But he was not alone. He looked sideways to where Bess was bending over the peat-fire, tending the quivering embers. Her face was soft in the fire-light, her hair lit with stars; her breasts were fuller now, with the thrusting life inside her, and when she stood up and came towards him, lips parted, he could see the nipples hard against the straining cloth. She laid a hand on his arm and murmured softly, 'Husband . . .?' But, as the blood raced hot with instant desire, he said through clenched teeth, 'Do not touch me!'

'But Hugh, we are married now. Give me at least a husband's kiss?' She reached up to put soft arms around his neck and he struck her roughly away so that she slipped on the trodden earth of the floor and would have fallen, but for the bed which she felt for with trembling hands. Hugh was ashamed of his violence, but it was necessary if they were to live together as he planned. She was feminine and helpless, full of winning female ways, and because of that she must understand, now, from the beginning.

'I am sorry, Bess,' he said, looking at her downcast head, 'but you did not listen. You say I bedded you and got you with child, and a Cameron does not lie. But if I did, it was through witchcraft and no wish of mine. Because my chieftain orders it, I will give the child my name and I will care for you both as a husband should. But *Air Malie tha*! I swear I will not lie with you again!' Hugh took up his plaid, tossed it across his shoulder, and his new wife felt the turf quiver under the thud of receding feet.

He was gone to sleep in the hills! Bess crept, weeping, into the bed she had made up so lovingly that morning with fresh heather stalks and sweet-smelling hay. She had hoped to woo him with her body, to spend her wedding night in new-taught love, and instead she must sleep rejected, alone. At the back of her weeping misery, hatred stirred. It was all that Cameron girl's doing...

'It is not my fault, Miss,' complained Andrew with what injured dignity he could manage in the whispered secrecy of the entrance hall. 'Wattie says he's bound apprentice now to a goldsmith at St Giles and he canna ... cannot take your letters.'

'Then find someone who can, you slow-witted dolt, and hurry or it will be summer and the men at the high shieling before we know it.' Jenny's voice rose on the edge of panic as she remembered Glendessary in summer with the menfolk all gone to the hills. If her letter did not reach Hugh soon, he would not get it till September, when they drove the cattle down again to the home pastures. But Andrew had not seen her fear: he was concerned only with his own dignity.

'It is not easy, Miss, since the attempted Rising. It is not politic to be seen sending messages to Highland gentlemen, especially with Sir Patrick up the stair a known Unionist.'

'And you are a known fool!' snapped Jenny. 'There are other caddies, and the post.'

'Not to Glendessary, Miss,' said Andrew, bristling. 'We'll need a pedlar or a fee'd horseman, and that needs money.'

'*Merde*!' said Jenny, too loud for caution. 'Can you not lend me some?'

'Miss Jenny!' called her aunt from the parlour. 'What business have you with Andrew that you cannot settle with me?'

'I'll pay you later,' said Jenny, giving the footman a warning push towards the outer door. 'Nothing, Aunt,' she called, 'except news of the Three Steps murder. I had thought you sleeping.'

'And when do I ever sleep?' retorted her aunt with an indignant thump of her stick. 'I leave that to my servants,' she raised her voice to reach the hall, 'who have nought better to do but gossip. Had you forgot the sempstress is due today to measure you for wedding linen?'

'I need none.'

'Mackie! Fetch Miss Jenny's clothes. As Miss refuses to be

measured we will take a copy from what clothes she has – and if she looks like a scarecrow in a turnip's skin, she has only herself to blame. As for you, Miss, you can stay in your room.'

Thank God Sir Roderick was out of town, gone to his country estate on business and kept there by a most opportune attack of the fever which was rife that summer. Aunt Cameron could, and did, dictate how Jenny replied to his letters, but she would have no such control over any meeting between them, so, until she had brought the silly girl to her senses, sickness and her own contrivance must keep them safely apart. It would be a long campaign, but Aunt Cameron meant to win.

The business of the sempstress set the pattern of the weeks that followed: orders, refusals, devious expedients by which her aunt pursued her marriage plans despite all the opposition Jenny could devise, and still the expected letter did not come. Until, at the end of June, Jenny's patience snapped.

'I wish to go home.'

'You may wish what you choose. You stay here.'

'I *will* go home. Everyone in Edinburgh goes to the country for the summer months and so will I!'

'Your father does not wish it. There is smallpox at Achnacarry, as you well know.'

'But not at Glendessary.'

'Too close, nonetheless. Your father values your health too highly to take the risk.'

'Why do you always cross me, Aunt? I have studied everything you told me – deny it if you can – yet I may do *nothing*. *Why*?'

'It is entirely your own fault, Miss. If you were tractable and obedient you would be treated differently. If you would accept that we wish only for your happiness, Jenny . . .' For a moment the old woman's voice faltered, torn between pleading and anger, but when Jenny turned her back, anger won. 'But you persist in your stupid obstinacy and think only of yourself. Very well,' she continued as Jenny deigned no reply, 'you cannot expect the privileges of a gentlewoman when you behave like a fishwife's wean! Mackie! Bar the door.'

Jenny's scream of anguished fury penetrated the entire building so that many an eyebrow was raised in expectation, but only silence followed. After the delicious luxury of that full-bodied scream, Jenny found it unexpectedly successful: and it gave her time to think. Andrew had taken the letter and disposed of it, but when would it reach Glendessary? It did not once occur to her that anyone but Hugh might open it . . . Hugh would get her letter somehow and, when he did, would send his answer. Or come for her himself.

So in silence she submitted to what measurements her aunt ordered. In silence she wrote letters at her aunt's dictation, to her parents, family well-wishers, her betrothed . . . In silence she ate, played the spinet, knelt in prayer, while her aunt's exasperation showed first in fury, then in bafflement and finally settled into a wary, tight-lipped patience which would have delighted Jenny in other circumstances. But in those foetid months of waiting in an Edinburgh emptied of gentlefolk and rotting with summer fevers, she had no thoughts but of Hugh and the letter which would set her free.

But when the letter came, it was from her father. Her aunt broke the seal and read it aloud. 'Were it not for the threat of smallpox, I would send for you, Jenny. I would have you with me, in Glendessary, so I might soothe your fears. But they are groundless. You will be happy, I promise you. Only remember your marriage to Sir Roderick is the dearest wish of both your mother and myself . . . dutiful obedience . . . a good and kindly man . . . a life of comfort on a prosperous estate . . . blessed, one day, with many children . . .' Jenny sat aloof and scarcely listening until a sentence jerked her to instant and appalled attention. 'Alexander's boy Hugh hopes to be a father by Martinmas. Your brother Alan will be godfather if it be a son . . .'

'Give me the letter!' Jenny, forgetting her vow of silence, snatched the paper from her aunt's hand. She ran to the window with it and turned her back. In the pale light from the fading sky she read her father's words for herself and there could be no mistake. Hugh was married. To whom, it did not matter. Hugh was married and had set their vow at nought. She felt hysteria rising till she could no longer keep it in check.

'He is *married*!' She tossed the letter fluttering into the air. 'Your herdsman is to be a father, Aunt. And Alan godfather. Alan!' She laughed then with derision and despair, in a crescendo of mirth so violent it could only end in tears. Yet when Jenny drew herself to a shuddering, breathless halt, her eyes were dry and hard. 'Thank you for opening my letter, Aunt,' she said with barbed calm. 'It was good of you to read it to me, your eyesight being what it is.' With that parting thrust she swept from the parlour into the bedroom, not this time to find relief in tears but to stand immobile, staring sightless into the gathering night. The sky was small, turquoise pale above the crowded roofs. Smoke clouds blotched the stars and from the distance came the ominous evening call which preceded the emptying of the city's waste.

At home, they would hear the curlew . . . The evening laverock, with a call like diamond water-drops, falling . . .

Cattle tearing the grass, chewing in rhythmic silence, their breath warm in the chill air as the cottars settled to their hill-side rest. Hugh would be at the shieling – with his wife. *'May I die by the blade of this same dirk,'* he had sworn, *'if I break my vow.'* She clenched her teeth so hard together that her skull sang with pain as she fought against the tears.

She was still motionless at the window when her aunt came early to bed, complaining of a headache and a chill. 'Brought on, no doubt,' she complained, 'by all these unnecessary tantrums.' Mackie busied herself refilling the warming-pan with ashes, hot from the kitchen fire; plunging a white-hot poker into the toddy can and mixing a soothing powder from the medicine chest. Jenny watched for an unconnected space of time, then picked up her plaid and walked from the room. In the hall Andrew stuttered into ineffectual life. 'Ye canna . . . cannot go abroad, Miss. Not so late . . . and alone.'

'Then come with me. Or I will find another to escort me, and what will my aunt say then?' With a terrified glance at the darkened bedroom, Andrew scrambled after her, pulling the door carefully closed behind them.

'Take my arm,' she ordered when they reached the High Street.

'But where are we going, Miss Jenny?'

'Anywhere . . . nowhere . . . what does it matter?' She searched her memory for a name and found one. 'To Lucky Spence's tavern.'

'But you can't, Miss.'

'And why not?'

'It is for whores and doxies, not respectable women.'

'I am weary of respectability. Take me to Lucky Spence's when I order you, or must I find the way myself?'

That evening was the first of many. Her aunt's chill fulfilled its early promise, rasped painfully into a putrid fever and then into pneumonia. Mackie was too concerned with nursing her mistress to notice what happened to Miss Jenny, and with Edinburgh emptied of gentlefolk there was no one else involved enough to note. So Jenny helped in the sick-room in the daytime and spent her evenings in the town. Andrew accompanied her, first because she ordered it and he did not know how to refuse, and then, when night followed night without detection, because he chose. Her company gave him status and he blossomed.

After that first night in the tavern, on Andrew's meagre savings for Jenny had none, they found a new intimacy in sharing each other's troubles. For Jenny was in the grip of a kind of madness. First, her King's invasion turned to ignominious

102

defeat; then her father's treachery, trading her in marriage to a Campbell; and finally Hugh . . . With Hugh's betrayal her past life had been cruelly shattered. Glendessary with its wind-blown freshness of hill and cataract was lost to her for ever, and she was condemned to the ordure-scented stiflement of Edinburgh, and Sir Roderick Campbell's bed. Hugh had left her, cast her aside for a wife and unborn child. She had thought herself his star, as he was hers, and found that she was . . . nothing. Her father was prepared to sell her for a satisfactory contract to a man who was neither Jacobite nor Cameron. Her life was an empty well which only mindless frenzy would hope to fill. And she sought it with the only companion left to her, her aunt's footman, Andrew.

For his part, he was at first cautious, then as he saw no sign of Miss Jenny's former scorn and no chance of detection, flattered, and as eager as she was to exchange confidences in lively company. Together they bemoaned the unfairness of a system which decreed that like could only marry social like . . . that Andrew might not have his Charlotte nor Jenny her Hugh . . . Jenny found the purse where her aunt kept the money Glendessary had sent for his daughter's trousseau. She took a coin, then another – for after all was it not money designed expressly for her use? And she and Andrew progressed from small ale to French claret and from Lucky Spence's to every tavern in the Grassmarket, then in the High Street itself. Till one night when they returned to the house on the third landing, they found Mackie as asleep as her mistress and both of them snoring, 'fit to shift the rafters' whispered Andrew, and Jenny laughed. But her laughter turned unexpectedly to tears which she could not stem and when Andrew attempted to dry them for her she put her arms around his neck and wept on his shoulder. 'Life is so terrible, Andrew,' she sobbed, 'and I have no one.' Andrew's own eyes blurred as he remembered Charlotte, remote and unattainable as ever. 'You have me,' he said and gulped at his own temerity, but Jenny did not scorn him. Instead she kissed him, full on the lips and went on kissing him with a hunger he could not satisfy, till she closed the door on her aunt's snoring and drew him down to the floor with her in the corner of the entrance hall he called his bed.

5

To her great Surprise, she found an uncommon Alteration in the State of her Health, and being ignorant of the Cause, applied to her Aunt for Advice, who to her Sorrow knew the Disease too well, but did not discover it to Miss, being resolved to find out the Author of her Misfortunes.

'I am sick, Aunt.' Aunt Cameron looked up sharply at the defiance in the girl's voice. 'Why do I feel so sick? I am never ill.'

'Perhaps you caught the fever from me?' But that was several weeks past and the girl would have succumbed long ago had she been susceptible. 'Or it is nerves at the thought of your wedding.'

But Jenny had no nerves. And since her father's letter and her aunt's illness, there had been no more talk of refusing Sir Roderick's offer. The contract was signed and witnessed, the arrangements made. She was to be wed at Martinmas in the church of St Giles. Jenny made no protest, because she felt nothing. She was dead, she told herself with a curious wonder, while her body went on living through no will of her own. Now, when even her body betrayed her, it seemed inevitable, and she welcomed the consternation it would cause. They had thought her life theirs to dispose of, like a parcelled gift. Let them deal, now, with this.

'Every morning I am sick, Aunt. I am surprised you do not hear me. Do you think I might be dying?'

She wished it were truly so. For since her aunt's recovery she had not even the solace of Andrew and a tavern's gaiety to ease her misery. She was fortunate no one had carried tales, but it was summer still, Aunt Cameron's contacts safely in the country, and Andrew would not tell. She felt a fondness for Andrew, as one might feel for a loyal, favoured hound, and for his part he behaved like one, following her every movement with yearning eyes. She was not to know that he had quite forgotten Charlotte. But since her aunt's return to querulous authority, they had hardly spoken. Aunt Cameron studied the girl now with a mixture of concern and dawning consternation. 'How long have you been sick?' She followed this with other questions, intimate and female. 'I do not record the natural functions of my body,' retorted Jenny when her aunt pressed her for dates. 'Why should I? They are of no interest.'

'Then they ought to be.' Her aunt clasped her hands across her chest to still the fear . . . In all the years she had been educating her young ladies, such a thing had never happened. If the news got about she would be finished. If Sir Roderick heard . . . Glendessary . . . Lochiel himself . . . and the wedding too far ahead for deception. She sat staring in silence at the cause of the disaster which threatened to wreck her life, while her mind raced round and round like a rat in a trap. But she kept hysteria firmly in check and said, with almost her usual acerbity, 'If you are suffering from what I suspect you are, Miss, then you are either incredibly naïve or the most brazen harlot in all Edinburgh.'

'But what ails me, Aunt?' asked Jenny innocently. 'Tell me, I pray you, that I might prepare myself.' She would not put words to the knowledge which had been with her now for several days and which had swept the blood from her aunt's face with such satisfactory speed.

Her aunt did not speak. Instead she wrote quickly on a paper and rang the bell for Mackie. 'Tell Andrew to fetch this from the apothecary with all haste. Here is money.' She unlocked a drawer of her desk and her mouth fell open in a travesty of shocked surprise. 'But the half of it is gone!'

'I took it,' said Jenny wearily, 'when you were ill, for ale for Andrew and myself. It is my father's money, after all.'

'Your father shall hear of this, girl, and quickly. *Mackie*! Where is the woman? Call Andrew back this instant – no, let him fetch the powders first. Go yourself and fetch that caddie Watt. I don't care who has apprenticed him, you fool. *Fetch him*.'

She drew another sheet of paper from her writing desk, dipped quill in ink and began to write with furious, ink-blotting haste.

Jenny stood unmoved by the tempest which had burst from nowhere to sweep the house with madness. Then as sickness gripped her, she sped for the closet and seclusion. When she returned, her aunt was sealing a folded paper with wax and her crested ring. She could not see the superscription.

'They say the Three Steps murderer has been caught,' said Jenny conversationally. 'Andrew heard it from a link-boy on the stair. He clubbed the servant girl to death to get the key and rob the house. A thousand pounds, Andrew says. He is to be hanged in the Grassmarket.'

There was the sound of running steps upon the stair and

105

Mackie fell panting into the room. A moment later a boy in neat brown jerkin and breeches, with shoes and stockings on his feet, stepped over the threshold and bowed.

'Wattie!' cried Jenny in astonishment. 'Are ye bewitched? Or was it you who robbed the poor maid at the steps to make your fortune?' Surprisingly Wattie had no answer, and kept his eyes averted. Had she not known better, Jenny would have said he blushed.

'I came, Ma'am,' Wattie addressed her aunt, 'for old time's sake, but I canna stay. My master needs me.'

'Your *master*?' said her aunt, incredulous.

'The goldsmith at the Luckenbooths, Ma'am. I am bound apprentice since Lammastide, by Sir Patrick's good offices on my behalf. How can I help you? Is it wedding spoons?' he asked, with returning spirits and a wink at Jenny.

'It is a letter,' snapped Aunt Cameron, 'to be delivered with all haste to Sir Ewen Cameron of Lochiel.'

'Sir Ewen!' Jenny's face brightened with hope. 'Then please to add a postscript, Aunt, on my behalf. Tell my uncle I am proficient, as he ordered, in both French and Italian, and am eager to serve him further. Tell him I remember his prophecy well and say that I await his further wishes.'

'Hold your tongue!' thundered Aunt Cameron. 'I have already asked Sir Ewen what he intends to do with you, Miss. As for you, Wattie, wi' gold dust on your fingers and the gentry's vowels on your tongue, you are no doubt above carrying aught as humble as a letter – but ye'll put it in the hands of one who can, and quickly. Here's money. Now away wi' you. And Mackie, see there's water boiling and, when yon Andrew returns, send him in here to me. It *is* Andrew, isn't it?' she said with deceptive quiet when Mackie had scurried from the parlour and Jenny and her aunt were alone.

'What do you mean, Aunt Cameron? I do not understand.'

'You will...'

Lochiel was in the great hall at Glendessary when the letter arrived. A six-pointer had been sighted in the hills above Arkaig and the chief had posted in all haste to join his kinsman for the hunt. But now Lochiel's roar of fury shook the dust from the rafters and set the glasses singing.

'I told you, Glendessary. You should have married her to old Breadalbin – even to young Hugh, your haunchman's son – instead of sending her to Edinburgh. *Education*!' He crashed a huge fist on the board, scattering plates and tankards wholesale. 'She could learn to fornicate at home! And I had such plans for

Jenny ...' To the consternation of his host and his assembled clan, Sir Ewen wept.

'Sir Roderick must be told,' he said later, when he and Glendessary had thrashed over every aspect of the sorry affair.

'Yet we must not move too hastily,' said Glendessary. 'If she miscarry and Sir Roderick remain in ignorance, it might still be possible to retrieve the situation.'

'Never!' cried his wife. 'Aunt Cameron writes that the measures may have no effect, and if they did, and by a miracle he were kept in ignorance, the girl would tell him herself. Ever since the marriage was arranged she has fought against it. It would not surprise me if she did what she did deliberately to confound us.'

'It is all my fault.' Glendessary shook his head endlessly to and fro. His eyes had lost their focus and his face was unnaturally grey. 'But I thought it for the best.'

'Of course you did, my love,' soothed his wife, alarmed by his appearance. 'And any other daughter would have complied, and thanked you for it.'

'Fornication,' intoned Lochiel without expression. 'Sir Roderick must be told. He made a bargain for a maid which we can no longer supply.'

'How could she do such a thing?' Lady Margaret's voice rose to a wail in which there was anxiety now for her husband as well as censure of her unnatural daughter. 'And with a common footman! The shame of it. If Alan were older, he would make him answer for it, would you not, Alan?' and she drew her son to her for comfort.

'Of course, Mama,' agreed young Alan, though his pale curls, small stature and white, unwhiskered cheeks denied such manly action. 'With his life.'

In the dim recesses of the hall, the shadows moved, firelight flared and died again on a sudden draught which tipped the candle flames in tongues of trailing smoke. A postern door closed, soundlessly, and the light settled again to a steady glow. No one noticed the vacant place at table, or the dark figure moving swiftly eastward through the glen, as Mr Graham was sent for and necessary plans made.

'I thought I saw her future clearly, Glendessary.' Lochiel's face was bleak with anguish. 'I saw her riding in triumph at a King's gathering. She was to be the jewel of our clan ...' The old man's eyes blurred again with tears. 'I loved her, Cousin.'

'And I ...' Of the two men, Glendessary looked the older as grief took hold of him and wrung his heart with a relentless pain which eventually choked the breath from his body, and with it, his life.

Wattie saw the figure from a distance and for reasons of his own stepped quickly into a sheltering doorway out of sight. The man was older, his face had lost the glow of youth and hope and he walked with an uneven stride, but Wattie would have known him anywhere. As the man drew closer, Wattie saw the expression of inflexible purpose and was glad he had hidden himself. But still he was drawn to follow, as he had followed in secret that autumn night a year ago. Along the Grassmarket ... pause ... into a tavern and swiftly out again ... pause ... Fishmongers Close ... another tavern ... then a straight, relentless path to a hovel at the foot of Castle Rock.

Wattie's flesh prickled at the memories the place called up, with the damp rising in noxious trails of mist from the nor' loch, the silent-footed rats, the threatening shadows. He stopped to remove shoes and stockings and tie them round his waist. His master was a stickler for a smart appearance. In five years time he himself would be a free man with an honourable trade; in another five as rich as anyone in Edinburgh, with money enough for frills on even his body garments if he chose. Meanwhile he'd take good care of the only brogues and stockings he possessed, for he did not intend to lose the apprenticeship he had worked so long and doggedly to win.

But even the call of his master's duty could not compel him now as, shrinking back into the cover of a nearby rock, his eyes followed that shape in the glimmering shadows. The figure melted into the murk at the hovel's door – appeared again, a second shape with him now, a thinner, propitiatory figure, awkward, nervous ... He heard the sibilance of whispered threat, a squeal choked short by terror, the snap of bone; then the black shadow-play of violence moved out of the concealing darkness into the gleam of open night. But even Wattie closed his eyes and averted his head to shut out the horror of slit flesh, of silent screaming terror, and that final, sickening mutilation ...

When he opened them again it was to see the sucking slime of the nor' loch's punctured surface slithering into place again around its newest jetsam, a crimson glint to the moisture on surface and pathway, and, for the rest, darkness.

Quaking with terror, Wattie strained to hear footfall or breath above the thudding of his guilty heart. He had witnessed vengeance, merciless, implacable ... if ever suspicion turned on him he knew he could expect the same. His back pressed against the rock as if beseeching it to open and swallow him into obscurity. Even the thought of the goldsmith's justifiable anger could not move him until he was convinced beyond all doubting that it was safe for him to emerge. Then he ran as though Old Nick and all his devils were at his heels, and did not stop until he reached the High Street and his own nook under the counter in the goldsmith's shop, his shoes still tied, unnoticed, at his waist.

'Where is Andrew, Aunt?' Andrew had not appeared since the day he returned from the apothecary's shop and had met with retribution.

'You dare to ask me that, Miss? Andrew is dismissed.'

'But why, Aunt? He did nothing wrong. It was I who took the money. It is unjust to punish a man for what he did not do.'

'He did enough – and more.'

'If you mean that he was wrong to lie with me, then say so. But that was no more his fault than the money. I made him lie with me, but not for fornication, Aunt. For friendship, and comfort.'

'*Friendship*! God give me patience!'

'Andrew was the only friend I had,' defended Jenny, 'since others were denied me. It is unjust that he should suffer for it.'

'He is lucky to be left alive! But you'll not see him again. He is *dismissed*.' And would have been turned over to the magistrates, Aunt Cameron made a point of telling everyone on the stair, if it were not for family connections. Taking advantage of her own illness to steal her niece's trousseau money, and the niece herself down with the sweating sickness!

But inside the house it was a different tale. Fornication, whoring, theft ... If Jenny had not felt so sickeningly ill, she would have put up more defence. As it was she spent her days in stomach-griping agony as her aunt dosed her with villainous potions 'to relieve the sickness' and immersed her regularly in a steaming bath which took poor Mackie half the day to prepare. Jenny had not the strength to question her aunt's motives or methods, had she wished to do so; but Jenny wished only to be dead.

As her aunt's ministrations failed to alleviate the vomiting but only increased it, Jenny began to think her wish would be granted, until the day when her aunt accepted the inevitable.

'I have tried all the remedies I know, and to no avail.' She spoke with a quietness which made the girl look up in surprise. 'Oh Jenny, Jenny! There is no help now for any of us. It is too late.'

'What do you mean, Aunt Cameron?' but her aunt had hurried from the room lest Jenny see the despair which threatened to engulf her: despair for herself and for the girl who was lost to her now, for ever.

It was not long before Jenny understood. She woke early one morning to the sound of voices in the hallway. Her aunt's and a man's voice, vaguely familiar. Could it be Papa? Then Mackie was at her bedside, urging her into the ritual of washing, fastening stays, binding up her hair, but to all Jenny's questions the woman answered nothing.

'Is it a message, Aunt, from Uncle Ewen?' demanded Jenny when she was marched into the parlour and found her aunt alone, an open letter in her hand, another on the table.

There was no answer, of antagonism or anger. Her aunt's face was white as a powdered mask, eyes black as pebbles in a stream, mouth a colourless split seamed tight under puckered skin. The old woman did not move: only the slack flesh of her neck quivered under a hidden pulse-beat and the diamonds at her throat flashed fitfully as the firelight caught them.

'You are to go to France.' The voice was almost soundless in the silence.

'To St Germain?' Jenny's face softened with delighted relief. 'I knew Lochiel would not desert me. He told me long ago that I would go on the King's business to a foreign land! When must I go, Aunt? Tell me, that I may make ready.'

But there was no reflected fervour in her aunt's face. Lochiel had written the unforgivable, and it was this girl's fault. 'You go today,' she said. 'To Paris. To a convent.'

'A *convent*?' Jenny was appalled. '*Why*?' Her aunt sat silent, implacable. 'But I am not a Catholic!'

'You will become one.'

'Never! I know the Camerons support King James, but he does not require his people to be papists, too.'

'Your instruction in the Catholic faith has already been arranged.'

'I should have known! First you try to sell me to the Hanoverians, now to the papists! It will be the Devil next.'

'You will find your own way there.' Still her aunt spoke in the flat and toneless voice which Jenny found so disconcerting and which drove her to put into words what had till then remained unspoken.

'But I am *with child*.'

'The convent has a convenient orphanage.'

'An *orphanage*? For a Cameron?'

'For a footman's bastard.'

It was Jenny's composure that broke. 'Oh Aunt Cameron, I

know I did wrong. But it was only a small wrong and it is over now. Father will forgive me. Let me go to him myself and ask his pardon. Please?'

'Your father is dead. The news of your behaviour killed him. It would have been better had it killed me, too. After the disgrace of this affair I am ruined. No family will entrust their daughters to me now.' Her voice quivered on the edge of breaking, but with conscious effort she drew herself straight. 'I hope you know, Miss, the extent of the evil you have done. Had not Lochiel a brother in the Roman church and another in the Court of France, I doubt we would have found even a convent that would take you. But the arrangements are made, thanks to Lochiel. Though it is distasteful to him, Mr Graham will escort you. He is gone to Leith to book passages.'

But Jenny did not hear. Her father dead. Hugh married. Her aunt implacable against her. Even Andrew gone. And Uncle Ewen, whose regard she most valued, had sold her and her unborn child to the papists and condemned her to a convent, for life.

But her father *dead*! It was not possible.

'Aunt Cameron, tell me it is not true!' She flung herself weeping on her aunt's shoulder, twined her arms about the wizened neck and clung sobbing to the only Cameron left to her. But her aunt sat unbending, her bone-white hands flat on the black silk of her knees, on her face the blankness of a death mask.

After a moment, Jenny, trembling, withdrew. She took up the letter from the table, read it in silence: '*Madam. Tell Jenny Cameron (no more my Daughter; unhappy for me that she ever was) that since she has preferr'd the Indulgence of an unlawful Appetite to the Peace and Honour of her Family, that Family will no longer have any Regard for her, but do cut her off as a Man would a troublesome and unsightly wen in his Flesh; she has brought the best of Fathers, as well as the best of Husbands, with sorrow to the Grave; and I am only left to curse the Remembrance, that I have nurs'd up a Serpent in my Bosom which has stung me to the Heart. The last Favour I request of her is that she will never pretend any Relation to me, for I shall never own that she has any of my Blood in her veins ... I renounce and disclaim her, and never desire to see or hear of her more. Your affectionate tho' sorrowful kinswoman.*'

Slowly Jenny laid the letter down, positioning it exactly as it had lain before. She drew herself tall and as straight-backed as her aunt before saying, quietly, 'My father was a good man and I loved him. I will mourn him in my heart. My mother does not want me – there is no place for me now, in Glendessary or here.

111

If I caused my father's death, however inadvertently, I owe him penance as well as grief. I will obey my chief.' With the dignity of desolation she walked slowly from the room.

In the silence she left behind her, the old woman sat on, unmoving, while a single tear furrowed the powder of her mask and fell unnoticed on to the motionless hands.

Part 2
France

1

Miss was placed in a nunnery of which a Scotch Lady of the House of
Seaforth was Abbess; by the Favour of the Lady Abbess Miss had more
liberty than is common, which she generally improved to serve such
of the Sisterhood as she had contracted an intimacy with.

The convent was quiet with fading sunlight. From a high
distance came the plainsong of Vespers; from the cloisters close
at hand, the sweet evening trill of a bird. There was no other
sound. Jenny felt the now-familiar panic swell inside her.
Trapped eyes slid over narrow, sun-warmed wall and cooler
shadow, over stone-flagged square of floor, square stool, square
table sufficient only for wooden feeding-bowl and prayer. Her
breviary lay open at the prescribed page, her restless hands
threaded the prescribed rosary, her knees stiffened on the
prescribed wooden prayer-stool, while through the window slit
the evening sun lanced free and golden, its shaft dancing with
a thousand motes of taunting dust. Jenny was nearing the end
of her novitiate and knew the prison gates inexorably closing.
   She had been delivered to the convent tormented in body and
in mind, for the long sea-journey and the overland travelling in
France had accomplished what none of her aunt's doses had
managed. Jenny had not been in the convent twenty-four hours
before she miscarried. The nuns were kindly women and when
the girl loosed her anguish in days of uncontrollable weeping,
they nursed her with a tenderness and solicitude which, coming
as it did on the heels of her family's rejection and the loss of her
baby, touched an answering chord in her heart. She turned to
them as a storm-tossed ship to a quiet haven and for a time found
peace in the ordered regime, the prayers, the undemanding
quietude of contemplation. Willingly she submitted to instruction. Cut off from all other influences, on the convent diet of
little food and much thought, she grew light-headed with
canticles and dogma.
   In the long winter darknesses of candlelight and soft-falling
snow, she had neither strength nor will to resist such indoctrina-
tion but with spring had come an unexpected rebirth, a
resurgence of spirit small as a hare-bell shoot, but thrusting. She
had made atonement, paid her mourning due, and she had heard

no 'call' except the call of home. Surely her expiation was complete and she was now free?

But where could she go? Her family had turned against her. What little money her father had left her was gone into the convent's coffers. She had no means of her own, no friends – there was no place for her anywhere but here. Yet her resistance grew.

'You must learn acceptance,' the Abbess told her, 'and submission.'

The Abbess was a tall, well-favoured woman, regal in her absolute authority. She had accepted Jenny Cameron both for her entrance money and as a favour to Lochiel, for whom she had a warm regard. The girl was not the first well-born young lady to have misbehaved and been disposed of thus: past faults must be atoned for, naturally, but the moulding of the spirit to accept necessity was the most important. Looking at the girl before her, the Abbess had inwardly sighed. This would be a tough block to fashion. But she had been so herself, once. 'Blot out all past life from your mind,' she had advised at the outset. 'Contemplate only the present and what *must be* the future. Sister Cecilia will instruct and guide you.'

So, white-clad and silent, Jenny was told what to do and when, with every minute of the day allotted to some task, while inside her head the sound of the closing convent gate beat with the relentless pulse of doom. Orders were now her life. From Matins in the small hours of dawn to Compline and the *Nunc Dimittis*, she had no regimen but the breviary, no territory but the pathways of the convent and the vault of her cell.

As the strains of the *Magnificat* floated mellifluous from the coolness of the chapel, Jenny tipped an ear to the distant plainsong. There would be candles on the high altar and more before the figure of Our Lady. She had been taught to look on that figure and raise her thoughts to heaven, but candlelight on stone reminded her only of the great hall at home.

'*Hail Mary, full of grace, the Lord is with thee,*' she gabbled and slammed the beads hard together. '*Blessed art thou among women and blessed is the fruit of thy womb . . .*' Perhaps it was as well the child had died, destined as it had been for an orphanage and inevitable servitude. '*I confess to Almighty God and to you, Father, that I have been disobedient . . . unclean . . . defiled my body and my spirit by licentious living . . . that by my actions I caused my father's death.*' She had done penance enough for a dozen murders, she thought with a flash of her old spirit, and still she must search her soul and confess. '*I have sinned in thought, word and deed . . .*' But was it a sin to show affection? To seek comfort when the heart wept? Was it a sin to

116

think with such constant longing of Glendessary? They had told her it was.

'I have never forced any girl to the life of the cloister against her will,' the Abbess had said. 'You must open your heart to God and await His call.'

'God calls to all,' explained Sister Cecilia when Jenny at last confessed she heard nothing. 'But if you fill your heart with homesick wailings, is it any wonder His voice is drowned?'

Sister Cecilia was in charge of the novices: an old woman with a gentle, kindly face. From the first she had felt for the girl a loving compassion. For Miss Jenny was not like the others: truth shone from those splendid eyes which were never veiled or sly as many in the convent were. Left to herself, she would one day hear and understand God's guidance. Her spirit was strong and therefore rebellious: to attempt to subdue it would be fatal, for like a trapped bird it would beat itself against the walls of its prison until it died – or soared, bloodstained but singing, to freedom. Only patience and time could hope to achieve Jenny's conversion, but Sister Cecilia had an endless supply of both.

She was from Ireland, with a host of nieces and nephews in the old country and one of them serving with the Royal Irish Brigade in King Louis' army here in France, fighting against the English and the Dutch in the interminable wrangle over the Spanish succession. 'If he ever comes to visit me, *ma petite*,' she had told Jenny, 'you shall meet him. For if anyone can satisfy your craving for news of the outside world, then Finn O'Neil can do it. He fought against Marlborough himself – and lost, poor boy – this year at Oudenarde.'

'Does he visit you often, Sister?'

'He is a soldier,' and she smiled away disappointment in gentle excuse. 'He will come when he can.'

Sunlight warmed the cloister, grass thrust thick and green, nesting birds busied themselves and sang. All around her the sleeping earth awoke to renewed life, yet the round of the allotted hours remained unchanged. Summer blazed and waned, and with the slow-growing horror of the condemned, Jenny too late understood her plight. When her novitiate was complete, she would take the inevitable vows and be incarcerated for life. The money was paid, the bargain sealed.

That was why, as she knelt in her cell on a sunlit autumn evening to the sound of distant Vespers, panic churned through her mind while her beleaguered spirit scurried to and fro, fruitlessly seeking escape.

'*You will speak a foreign tongue in a foreign land*,' Uncle Ewen had said. That part at least of his prophecy had come true. '*Before you ride in glory to your King.*' She had thought that to mean military glory, that the king was Scotland's true King James. Perhaps after all it had meant only this – a convent in France and the King of Heaven?

So many words had proved not what they seemed. There had been too many broken promises, discarded vows. '*A Cameron never breaks his word*,' her father had told her, yet her aunt had broken hers with as little heed as for a broken biscuit, and Hugh had snapped his like Communion bread ... '*May I be stabbed with this same weapon*,' he had vowed that windy April day above Glendessary, '*if I break my oath*.' He had made the *creach* and had fulfilled the letter – but he and she both knew he had broken the spirit of his vow. And her spirit with it. As memory blotted all else from her mind but Hugh, Jenny surrendered finally to despair.

The strains of Compline roused her in the moonlit darkness of her cell. '*Lord now lettest thou thy servant depart in peace according to thy word* ...' Hesitantly at first, then with deliberate strength, Jenny joined in the familiar words until the final, diminishing '*Amen*'. Then she made the sign of the cross and prepared herself for sleep. Tomorrow she would tell Sister Cecilia she wished to rise with the rest of them for Matins, Lauds, Prime, Terce, Sext ... *ad infinitum*. There was no other way. Sister Cecilia would believe she had heard God's voice at last and offer prayers of thanksgiving. Jenny no longer had the strength to correct her. With a bleak and empty heart, she closed her eyes for sleep.

Autumn burned inexorably on, and the breezes which licked the cloisters with cat's tongues of warmth brought a scent of vigorous life which Jenny found unbearable, in spite of the blanketing fervour of her prayers. These she entered into with a consuming energy which baffled her superiors and left her hollow-eyed and febrile: but though she pursued sanctity with the galloping frenzy of the chase, imploring Sister Cecilia for yet more penances or meditations, the lowing of a distant cow, even a cockerel's boasting was enough to shatter any tented seclusion her prayers might have contructed and send her heart speeding beyond the convent walls.

'I *will* do it,' she vowed, combating desperation. 'What other course can I take?'

A morning in early spring brought the answer.

2

Her confessor happened one Day to bring along with him an Officer belonging to the Irish Brigade, a Gentleman of a good Family in Ireland, who had an agreeable Address, a good Share of Sense, and wanted nothing of that Assurance, or any other Qualification, necessary to recommend him to the Fair Sex. The young Colonel was much charmed with the Conversation of Miss Jenny, and she with his . . .

It was early March and in the wintry silence of Ste Marie de la Roche, Finn O'Neil was restless. It was four months now since the French Royal Irish Regiment, in company with the armies of both sides, had withdrawn to winter quarters, and he was impatient for action.

It was always the same: the armies were so cumbersome. They took so long to dismantle and pack their ovens, load their baggage into wagons, collect their flour sacks and fodder, rope up their pack-horses and harness their mounts, that winter was upon them before they could follow up any advantage they might have won. After Malplaquet, O'Neil's own cavalry had worried and snapped at the enemy while the French army gathered itself together beyond the Rhonelle in order to protect Maubeuge, but like Marshal Boufflers he would have preferred to attack the besiegers of Mons and relieve the town. King Louis, however, forbade it. Maubeuge was vital and must be preserved at all costs; therefore Mons capitulated, O'Neil was denied his battle, and since the end of October both armies had been in winter quarters – and his were this stinking, rat-ridden post-house of an *auberge* where no door nor window fitted its frame, the ceiling sagged, and the place was so riddled with draughts even the fire coughed its life out in putrid smoke. As for French cooking . . . he would sooner live like a Highlander on honest kale: at least you knew what went into that. When would it be spring?

The Duke of Marlborough, they said, was back in England, but found more troubles at home than in Flanders by all accounts, with the Queen turning against him and appointing his enemies to commands in his own army. But Queen Anne was old and fat, and there was one in St Germain – and fighting in the ranks of the *Maison du Roi*, in season – who was ready and waiting to step in and rule the old country as it should be ruled, and would have been had not that Orange Protestant usurper come to stir up trouble back in '89. O'Neil had been a child of four then or he would have fought, as his father had, at the Battle of the Boyne. But he had made up for that: one day very soon the Stuart king would be restored and the old religion flourish. Meanwhile, he fought every campaign with the fervour and involvement of the natural soldier and the exiled patriot.

Colonel Finn O'Neil was not a big man, but tight-muscled and compact, his clear blue eyes still mischievous with youthful spirits in spite of the sabre scar which scored his face from brow to chin. That he had won at Ramillies, at the height of the cavalry battle, from an unknown hand. But with 25,000 horsemen locked in charge and counter-charge, it was a wonder anyone rode out again unscathed. The Colonel flexed his knee to test the healing of his latest wound – a musket ball through the thigh just above the knee. Damn those boots of his for not reaching higher – and that skiving Daniel for turning the cuff too low – but the knees of a cavalryman were notoriously vulnerable and he had been lucky. The ball had missed the bone. Not like Marshal Villars whose knee had been shattered, they said, almost beyond the surgeon's powers to heal. But for that, thought Finn O'Neil for the hundredth time, we might have held the field . . .

Again he flexed his knee, sprang testing to his feet to crumple instantly, lopsided, to the dirty floor. 'By the Blessed Mary,' he gasped, 'and all the saints in heaven!'

'Do you be resting, sir, a while longer. Impatience never healed a wound yet.'

'Who is impatient?' roared Finn as his colour returned. 'Is it not ten weeks past that I was winged? And you'll not go fetching the surgeon, Daniel, or I'll stuff his leeches down his own throat – and yours! And I'll not be bled again, understand? I've shed enough in battle without spilling more into that poxy surgeon's bowl.'

'Aye, sir.' His monkey-faced, bog-wiry servant was unperturbed by this outburst. He had been Colonel O'Neil's man since he was a sprig of an ensign seven years ago; given to Finn by Finn's father to serve son, as Daniel's own father served old O'Neil. Daniel had accompanied young Finn from Ireland with his splendid, beloved, white cavalry charger, Oberon, worth all of twelve pounds, his gleaming cuirass unmarked then by dent or scratch, and his creaking, squeaking thigh-boots of leather thick enough to block a musket ball at point-blank range. On his white charger with its scarlet saddle cloth and tail ribbons, himself in black velvet and gleaming steel, and the pair of them rivalling the Sun King himself for gold braid, Finn O'Neil had been a master for any man to be proud of, though he was a hot-tempered, foul-mouthed, bog-devil when the drink was in him – or the pain.

'Will you be taking a sup o' broth for your strength, sir?'

'Broth is it? *Broth*! And me weak with loss of blood and tediosity? Order me a roasted *poularde* – none of their French *ragoûts*, remember – with fresh bread and a bumper of Burgundy wine. And send it up by the innkeeper's *daughter*, do you hear, while you seek forage for my horse. For if Oberon be not as fit as when I was picked off him by that sniping son-of-a-bitch with his traitor's musket, I'll nail your ears to the stable door and have your guts for a bridle!'

'God, how I hate winter quarters!' he finished, as Daniel disappeared through the ramshackle wooden door. He heard his steps loud on the uneven stair, voices from below, the clang of cooking pots and a girl's high laugh. That would be Marianne, the daughter of the house and the only ray of hope in this black purgatory of a winter.

He glared morosely through the clouded glass of the window. Its shutters were folded back to let in what winter light there was from a snow-clouded sky and with it came the odour of rotting straw from the cobbled yard below and the sour smell of the midden. But O'Neil preferred a room over the stable yard: that way he could keep a close eye on Daniel and on Oberon. Fodder was always a problem in the winter months; though he paid willingly for the best oats and straw, it was wise to check that he received what he paid for. With St Germain not fifteen kilometres away, he must send Daniel further afield to buy the best, for James Stuart's Court in exile had long milked any local reserves dry as a witch's tit, but he didn't grudge the laddie that. O'Neil frowned deeper as he looked to the north across huddled roofs of stableyard and village. He could just see the outline of the Château of St Germain-en-Laye on its eminence above the Seine, with Paris out of sight somewhere to the east. A magnificent palace once, second only to Versailles, but crammed too full of exiled, penniless Jacobites to maintain the gilded splendour at its original lavish level. The French King Louis was generous to his exiled kinsman, but that exile had continued too long. First James Francis Edward's father, with Queen Mary Beatrice and his infant son, ousted from his own Kingdom by that Dutchman William; then that same son, James, the Chevalier de St George, now come of age and still denied his throne.

They could pass their Acts of Settlement giving the throne to

121

the House of Hanover; their Acts of Attainder, threatening James and all Jacobites with death; they could form their Grand Alliance and line up all the European powers against France in the endless wars of the Spanish succession, but no man-made law, no military victory, could alter the fact that James Stuart was Britain's King by right. If Queen Anne did not herself name James as her successor – and there were many who vowed she would have done so long ago were it not for his religion – there were thousands now in France prepared to do it for her; and in Ireland too, and England, while the Scottish Highlands would rise to a man in James's favour when the call came.

O'Neil's face lightened at the thought. Spies passed regularly between St Germain and Scotland; letters sped by willing messenger to London and to Edinburgh ... that attempt two years ago had been bungled by ill-planning, in bad weather: next time would be more successful. They said the Duke of Marlborough himself had a foot in the Jacobite camp.

God, if only spring would come, the armies could move again, chase Marlborough and the Dutchmen back where they belonged beyond the Flemish border, clear France for Louis, and move on to London ...

Damn the winter, damn the pot-holed roads and overflowing waterways, damn rotting straw, sour wine and all flea-ridden, worm-eaten, dung-stinking inns where a man could get neither warmth nor food nor service!

'*Marianne*!' he roared. '*Dépêche-toi*!' Marianne was the only female villager not toothless with age or locked prudently out of sight: Marianne was a peach, a nectarine ripe for the picking, a soft-bloomed, plump-fleshed delight ... But it was the *aubergiste* himself who brought the wooden platter of chicken and set it unceremoniously on the trestle table with a pewter flagon of wine.

'Where is Marianne?' demanded O'Neil. 'I pay for *service*!'

'That does not include my daughter!' growled the *aubergiste*, slamming the door so violently that cobwebs cascaded from the rafters in a cloud of ancient dust.

'*Merde*!' growled O'Neil as he dusted the downfall from his jacket. There was scum on the wine, too, but it made little difference: it was piss anyway. But he drank it and polished off the chicken to the clean bones. If only he could ride again ... He flexed his knee several times, stood up with care, and walked the room slowly, testing and bending at every third step, his teeth clenched firm against the stabbing pain. 'One, two, *bend* – aagh. One, two, *bend*..'

He did not hear the door open, but the sudden gush of air set the small fire sputtering and he whirled on an oath to see an old man in peasant's leathers, a folded paper in his hand.

'*Un message, monsieur.*' He hovered, awaiting recompense, his trepidation strengthened by obstinacy, for the paper sported the seal of St Germain. But as he read the note, O'Neil's face lost its angry lines.

'*Merci, mon vieux.*' He tossed the old man a coin. 'Tell your master my wound is of no account. I will be delighted to join the hunting party. *Daniel*!' He leant half out of the window and bellowed across the courtyard. 'Saddle Oberon! We go to Fontainebleau for the hunt.'

And when the sport was over, he thought on a sudden whim, he would ride on to the convent of Sacré Coeur and pay old Aunt Cecilia a visit. Perhaps if he did that, he argued with tortuous logic, the campaign season would come upon him all the sooner?

Sister Cecilia was in the herb garden with Jenny when the bell at the great gate rang out to announce a visitor. She had been instructing the girl in the basics of herbal medicine, for though it was early March there were plants in green leaf – agrimony, camomile, lemon balm and dill. The old woman had thought much about Miss Jenny and her increasing restlessness. There was something Jenny needed that the contemplative life could not offer, and until that need was satisfied, she would not find peace of mind. Sister Cecilia watched her shrewdly, noting the troubled eyes, the restless hands. But all Jenny said in answer to her question was, 'No, Sister, I am not troubled, merely unprepared,' and resumed her endless penances.

Sister Cecilia thought these excessive. She used her discretion to have Miss Jenny's confessor changed. The old priest of sour rectitude was replaced by a livelier, younger man. It made no difference, apart from a rumour, carefully kept from the Abbess's ears, of sudden laughter from the confessional and as sudden a request from the priest himself to return his charge to his senior. Jenny was as restless as before and, with dismay, Sister Cecilia noted a return of the trapped look in those honest eyes. The kindly nun decided it was intellectual stimulus the young girl needed, an outside and outdoor interest to divert her energy from the endless track of spiritual self-argument which prevented her acceptance of God's will. She herself was overseer of the convent's small dispensary and saw in the pounding and mixing of medicines and elixirs an answer to her charge's disquietude.

'Why do you persevere with me?' asked Jenny, her eyes

123

downcast. 'I am not worthy. There are far better novices than I to claim your time.'

'But none more deserving. Remember the parable of the prodigal son? Of the search for the one sheep strayed from the fold? Your heart is still darkened with resistance and doubt, but we pray constantly for your enlightenment, which *will* come.'

Never, thought Jenny, with rising panic, and soon she must take her final vows. But a Cameron's word was sacred: if she were not to perjure herself, there was only one alternative. Increasingly she avoided Sister Cecilia's eyes lest she give herself away, while her mind worried at plans and possibilities. But she enjoyed her lessons in the herb garden, finding diversion, as Sister Cecilia had hoped, in the strange qualities of plants.

'Agrimony is most beneficial, dear, for treating looseness of the bowels. Gather the whole plant, remember, to make an infusion or tisane. Now here is hyssop, ideal for distracting butterflies from the vegetable garden. Our Benedictine brothers use the herb for other purposes – a delightful liqueur with undoubted medicinal qualities – but here we put our plants to simpler use. Hyssop flowers in an infusion are beneficial for weak chests.'

'And what of digitalis?' asked Jenny remembering the High-land foxgloves gathered by the lads at home to send to the apothecaries of Inverness. There was no sign of foxgloves in this symmetry of herb beds, neat behind miniature battlements of clipped yew or lavender. Beyond the herb garden to the south was the apple orchard, branches already threading a green haze of promise, to the east the Abbess' private rose-arbour and peach-garden, to the west the vegetable patch. Around the whole was a sunwarmed wall where plum tree, pear and apricot spread budding arms, joining their barrier to unscalable stone to keep her safe inside – and at her back the serene, unconquerable bastion of the convent. How could she have imagined the thrusting purple vigour of a foxglove in this lilied piety?

A novice had appeared in the convent archway and was moving towards them with unseemly haste.

'Sister Cecilia,' she said, breathless both with excitement and the need to suppress it, 'there is a visitor to see you. An officer of the Royal Irish Regiment who says he is your nephew. He is waiting in the audience room, Sister. Shall I accompany you?' she added eagerly, knowing the old nun approved of chaperons at all such meetings.

'No, my dear. You may return to your duties. Miss Jenny shall accompany me that I may continue her lesson with as little loss as possible – and revive her with a breath of outside air,' she finished with an almost impish smile behind the crestfallen novice's retreating back. Jenny felt a quickening of interest which set her heart beating exhilaratingly fast. An officer of the Irish Regiment! He would have news of the outside world, of the last campaign, perhaps even of St Germain, and, indirectly, of Sir Ewen and home. Impetuously, Jenny put an arm round her instructress and kissed her cheek. 'Thank you, Sister Cecilia. You are too good to me.' Her voice faltered and she turned her face aside to mask her excitement, but Sister Cecilia was already hurrying along the path towards the convent and her visitor.

'My favourite, most winsome aunt!' The officer seized the old nun by the waist and swung her, laughing, into the air. 'The best aunt in the world – is she not so?' he asked, turning mischievous blue eyes on Jenny who stood in the doorway, looking on with pleasure at a scene of such open affection. The stone walls were as bare, the sunlight as hostile, the shadows as cold as before, yet the plain grey audience room with its candled niche and statue, its wooden *prie-dieu* and simple, narrow window, was suddenly warm as the great hall at home on a banquet day and as full of life, for the Irish officer radiated vigour. He was dark as Uncle Ewen, muscular as Hugh, with an impudent good humour which reached straight to her heart and found its pair. Here was no smooth-tongued cleric, but a man of open truth and splendid deeds: one had only to note that scar which he wore like a battle-prize. Jenny felt her heart absurdly light: she could have sung aloud for the joy of approaching spring and this young man's visit – which reaffirmed, as nothing else could, the existence of life outside Sacré Coeur.

'Well, Aunt,' he was saying, 'I see you dared to bring company. Are you not frightened that I will corrupt the maiden with my soldier's manners and my soldier's talk?'

'Away with your nonsense, Finn. I knew him as a baby, Jenny, and look at him now, the overgrown rascal that he is – and as mischievous as ever, no doubt. Well, don't stand there dithering, Finn O'Neil. Have you no news for us, no tales of victories? You have not let Marlborough's men get close enough to hurt you again, have you?' she asked with sudden concern. 'Were you not limping, just now, when we came in?'

'It is nothing, Aunt. An old wound but lately healed, that is all. But please introduce me to your companion, lest I add discourtesy to ignorance.'

'This is Miss Jenny Cameron of Glendessary in Scotland, come to join us a year past last Michaelmas.'

'*Voluntarily*?' Finn O'Neil lifted an expressive eyebrow. 'I see you, Miss Jenny, on horseback, in the hills, with the wind's fingers in your hair, the wind's kiss upon your cheek and . . .'

'And nothing, Finn O'Neil. Take no heed, Jenny. Finn loves the music of his own voice too well to note what words he speaks.'

'Nonsense, Aunt. I never speak unless with something to say. Am I not right, Miss Jenny? You are an accomplished horse-woman, are you not?'

'I was once. But I rode only Highland garrons.'

'You must see Oberon,' said O'Neil, boasting. 'He is the finest stallion in the Irish Regiment, white as milk, hair as fine as silver thread and with a rump as full and creamy-smooth as any virgin's . .'

'*Finn!*' cried his old aunt, shocked. 'I will not have you mention such . . . such unmentionables before a novice.'

But Miss Jenny was laughing as she had not heard her laugh in all her time in the convent – the uncomplicated laugh of her childhood, clear and sweet, so that Sister Cecilia, in spite of her shock, felt her own lips widen.

'A stallion with a maiden's rump! What sort of unnatural beast is that? Give me an honest garron any day. My uncle Ewen does not scorn them, and for sureness of foot in the rock-tumbled gullies of the mountains you could not find a better.'

'Your Uncle Ewen? Not Ewen Dubh, Lochiel himself?'

'Aye. Why not?'

'Then you will be a Jacobite as I am, Miss Jenny. Tell me,' he added, mischievous, 'are you a Compounder?'

'That I am not, nor ever shall be! Besides, there can be no compounding now. If Queen Anne name an heir, it must be James, already King of Scotland.' The Compounders had suggested, back in King William's time, before James VII's death, that William should name James Francis Edward as his heir, thus bypassing his unacceptable father: a suggestion regarded as treason by James himself and all true Jacobites. 'James is the only rightful heir and truth is truth. It cannot be "compounded" to suit expedience.'

'Well spoken. Yet these campaigns have lasted too many years, cost too many lives. The peace negotiations in Utrecht are difficult enough as it is. On your argument they would be impossible. Would you admit *no* compromise?'

'None. If the wars are long, the fault lies in the strategy,' retorted Jenny. 'There is a battle, a conceded victory, and then nothing while your infantry busy themselves with baggage trains and billets. Why do you not pursue your started quarry to the kill?'

Colonel O'Neil regarded her with amusement behind which was surprised respect. 'Curious,' he remarked to Sister Cecilia. 'You did not tell me that your convent studied military strategy.

Have your novices planned the ending of the wars for us? If so, pray tell me at once that I may send a message to Boufflers and Villars to end the matter before summer.'

'Jenny likes to be informed,' said his aunt, smiling. 'She is intelligent, and we do hear a shred or two of news, now and then. You wrote to me yourself about Malplaquet.'

But Jenny could not keep silence. 'Yes, I have planned it,' she said, her dark eyes challenging Finn to contradict. 'You cannot move so many men so often without impossible delay. I would limit my striking force to a number who could carry provender sufficient for a week if necessary, so they could move swiftly to catch the enemy unawares, not trundle at snail's pace in a morass of baggage trains while enemy horsemen ring them easily with spies, reporting numbers of men and ordnance. I would give each man a cheese of mare's milk as the Tartars do, or bid him forage. I would carry hand-mills for flour . . .'

'And the ovens?' asked Finn, his face expressionless. 'Or are your striking force to eat their fresh ground flour in handfuls, raw?'

'I had not thought of ovens,' said Jenny, crestfallen. 'Can you not requisition in the village where you strike camp?'

'Poor villagers. Already their mares are to be milked dry for cheeses, their barns and fowl pens robbed by your foraging soldiers, and now they are to bake bread for 60,000 men. But I forgot. You are fighting your war with a mere brigade, all strong and brave and wise. I see it all. The field of 40,000 slain, felled by little hand-mills and mare's-milk cheeses and the terror of 130 fierce moustaches!'

'Fool,' gasped Sister Cecilia, helpless with laughter, while Jenny flushed with mortification.

'Then *tell me*! How can I know if I am told nothing and have never seen . . .'

Finn's laughter stopped on an instant and the blue of his eyes deepened to seriousness. 'I apologize, Miss Cameron. I love to tease; Aunt Cecilia will tell you it was always so, but I forgot myself. If you will allow me, I will be delighted to tell you all you want to know. First, the ovens: an army needs bread. Even a small army of, say, 30,000 would need 450 hundredweight of bread a day. As you know, it is the practice to march three days, and rest and re-supply on the fourth, so . . . to feed your 30,000 men for each four-day stint would take at least thirty ovens and more than 300 hundredweight of flour. No village, as you see, could provide that. So we transport our own ovens, building and dismantling at each camp. So many baggage-loads of bricks, so many builders, so much fuel to fire and heat the ovens . . . the task, you see, is monumental. And the horses, too, must be fed.

'Every Grand Forage takes men who could be fighting bolder battles. You cannot hope to move a cavalry regiment, for instance, before the spring grass is lush and plentiful enough to counteract the winter's deprivations. Then there is ammunition ... ordnance ... quagmires ... floods...'

Finn talked fluently, without condescension, addressing himself direct to the girl with the dark, intelligent eyes and the eager face. He made no compromise for femininity or ignorance, speaking to her as he would have spoken to a fellow-officer, his speech moderated only by his aunt's presence and the hushed sanctity of his surroundings. Jenny fixed her eyes on his and drank each word deep into her thirsty soul until the two of them were tight bound together in their private, martial world.

Sister Cecilia watched with benign approval. This was what Jenny needed ... a life-line to reality which would steady her and give her strength.

'What would you do, Finn,' she interrupted as last, 'without a war to fight? You would be dull as Oberon in his winter stable, for where else are you able to flaunt your splendid caparisons?'

'In the forests of Fontainebleau,' retorted Finn, 'where we were at dawn this morning.'

'What did you hunt?' demanded Jenny eagerly. 'Are there deer in the forest, as there are at home?' Her eyes grew dreamy at the memory of Sir Ewen and her father, with hounds, horses and her father's gillies. The scent of crushed heather was in her nostrils, with the reek of horses and men's sweat. 'I dearly love to hunt ... At home,' she went on excitedly, 'they will be hunting the arctic hare. Its flesh is sweeter, though it be so small. They say an infallible lure is honey and caraway comfits, though Hugh and I used only snares and subtilty...'

Finn O'Neil was fascinated. Even clad as she was in the shapeless gown and headdress of the novice, the girl was striking: dark colouring, clear eyes, strong face and tall, arresting figure. She could have been a Highland queen – or colonel of a regiment. Yet she spoke with such innocence. Finn could not take his eyes from her face.

'Tell us of the hunting, Finn,' his aunt was saying. 'We are cut off here from all news. Is St Germain very grand still?'

'St Germain is seething as ever with penniless, quarrelsome Scotsmen so that the Queen needs all her time and art to make ends meet. James himself is not content to stop there, except when winter demands it: he fights his campaigns with us. A more valiant soldier you would not find anywhere, nor a better huntsman. He rode with us in Fontainebleau and made merry sport.'

Jenny was enthralled, her whole face alive as it had not been for many months. Though his own remained fixed on his aunt, Finn O'Neil knew Jenny's were on him: his back straightened, he held his head an inch higher, even his moustaches preened themselves for her admiration as his story gathered colour and intensity.

Sister Cecilia, looking from one animated young face to the other, felt no apprehension. Only gladness that her favourite nephew and her favourite novice should find so much in common and be so obviously happy in each other's company.

After that first visit, Finn O'Neil came often. There was good hunting in the vicinity, he had found tolerable lodgings in the village and his knee continued to heal, but these things would not have been sufficient to keep him longer in a place so far from Paris had it not been for his Aunt's young novice, Jenny Cameron. The party from St Germain had long returned, yet still he lingered . . .

Jenny Cameron intrigued him. After that first encounter when her eyes had seemed to drink his very presence, they had met often, though always in the company of his aunt. On the few occasions when he found his aunt alone, he had been oddly restless and had returned early to his lodgings to shout for Daniel and wine.

When she was there, they talked; he found her at first serious, then, as she learnt more of his campaigns, argumentative, even pert.

'You mean it was the *French* King who would not let James land in Scotland, but posted him about the seas like a decoy to draw off the English troops from his precious France?' Jenny was astonished, then outraged. 'And no one lifted a finger to help His Majesty?'

'How would you have had us help him?' asked Finn with a twinkle. 'Would you have us mutiny, take the ship and all the Frenchmen with it, and sail it alone through the blockading English fleet? Or should we have urged His Majesty overboard to swim ashore? We did the prudent thing – came swiftly home again to await a better time.'

'When a man talks of prudence, he means only to save his skin.'

'Would you have had us lose our lives, and His Majesty's too, in the German sea?' teased Finn, secure in the knowledge of his own bravery.

'Did Marlborough win at Malplaquet by prudence?'

'No. But we escaped by prudence, to fight another day.'

Jenny was silenced, but she did not mind. It was such a blessed relief to hear an open, honest argument she could follow and, if she chose and had the necessary knowledge, refute, instead of the featherbed frustration of the convent's casuistry.

'What would have been your strategy, Miss Jenny?' teased Finn with a wink at his aunt. 'I await your answer.'

'*Falbh is ithdo chachd*!' retorted Jenny, unashamed. After an astonished moment first her aunt, then Finn, then Jenny herself dissolved in helpless laughter.

The Abbess heard the merriment from her study and frowned. Sister Cecilia was entirely reliable. As mother of the novices, she had never failed to deliver them suitably prepared. But it was not wise to take unnecessary risks. That Cameron girl had better take her final vows at the earliest opportunity – in May.

In early spring Marlborough, Captain-General of the English army, left England once again for Flanders. The winter had not gone well. His victory at Malplaquet the previous September was judged by many as too bloody. The Tories called him 'Butcher', while his wife Sarah, supplanted in the Queen's affections by Abigail Masham, had forfeited royal favour. The Queen's displeasure showed in her treatment of Marlborough himself. Slighted, mortified by the calculated insult of appointing Mrs Masham's brother to the Oxford Regiment, an appointment customarily in the Captain-General's gift, Marlborough saw clearly that he too had lost Queen Anne's favour. The rift was eventually patched up, for Marlborough was vital to the Grand Alliance and could not be allowed, as he threatened, to resign command.

But these intrigues at the English court gave the Jacobites new hope. Mrs Masham had a cousin – Robert Harley, a Tory and a Jacobite. Anne herself was at heart Tory and known to be against the Hanoverian succession. She was gross and forty. She would not live long. With the right people about her, she might still name James as her successor. Meanwhile her disgruntled Captain-General took himself off to Holland to the interminable peace negotiations which had occupied the winter recess for most of the past seven years.

But as March drew towards its close there came an easing of winter weather. Every tree, every bursting bud, proclaimed the onslaught of spring; days grew soft with promise, evenings lengthened. Finn O'Neil felt the stirring and was troubled. For the first time in his life the arrival of spring did not bring unadulterated joy. With the opening of the highways, gun-carriages could roll again, columns of horse move forward freely and at night men sleep in their cloaks beside their horses without danger of frostbite: the summons would come at any moment. But when it did he must leave the village in which he had found such unexpected pleasure.

Since joining the regiment O'Neil had been heartfree: he found a girl (for he was undoubtedly attractive) whenever he felt the need, and for the rest was content to be his own man. But Jenny Cameron intrigued and fascinated him. He saw her face when he closed his eyes in sleep, heard her voice in the silence, breathed her breath. Her mind spoke to his as directly as twin to twin. She was open and honest as the naïvest child, yet with the shapely allure of a seductress: and she was forbidden. The combination was irresistible. He knew as clearly as if she had spoken it that she had no wish for the life of a convent, sensed as clearly as if his aunt had told him that Sister Cecilia knew it too; yet from the barred and twice-locked gate to the high, enclosing walls and constant supervision, Sacré Coeur was a fortress equipped for any siege. He was a soldier, on leave and in love, she an unwilling novice soon to take her final vow. On either count he saw a challenge thrown at his feet.

In the herb garden, scents gathered sweet over thrusting leaf and thickening stem. Singing from the morning chapel flitted light as birdsong through the shadowed cloisters as dawn light spread sunny hands over sequestered passageway and walk. Jenny felt her heart beat fast and high in her throat. In May she was to make her vows: already with the other postulants she was rehearsing for the ceremony. She had little time. She knew what she must do.

'I come to take my leave, Aunt Cecilia,' Colonel O'Neil kissed his aunt on both cheeks. 'And of you, Miss Jenny.' He bowed low over her hand. 'Word has come that Marlborough is preparing to open the campaign. His armies are already assembling and I must join my regiment for the march to the French frontier. My man is packing now.'

'May God watch over you and bless you,' said his aunt, her eyes moist. She moved to the niche where the painted statue of Our Lady raised a hand in permanent blessing, the infant in her arm echoing the benediction in miniature, and knelt on the wooden *prie-dieu* at its foot. 'I will light a candle for you, Finn, and pray for your safe-keeping.' She bent her head, eyes closed, over her rosary.

It must be now, thought Jenny with agitation. There would

131

not come another chance. She moved closer to where he stood, head bent, eyes closed in deference to his aunt's prayer. His left hand rested on the hilt of his sword, his right hung loose at his side. She slipped her own hand into his, put her lips to his ear and whispered, '*Take me with you.*'

His eyes jerked open, his head turned towards her and he looked into her imploring eyes with an expression of astonishment. 'Please,' she mouthed, one eye on Sister Cecilia, still on her knees at the little altar. 'You are my only hope. Take me to St Germain. I have kinsmen there who will help me. Can't you see it is *death* for me here?'

Her face was a mere three inches from his own, her eyes huge with pleading, her breath warm on his cheek, her hand tight held in his. He felt laughter bubble rich, full-throated, inside him and his blue eyes danced. Then Sister Cecilia stirred, one hand on the prayer-rail to aid her. Without a word, Finn stepped forward to place a helping hand at her elbow and lift her to her feet.

Mortification and dismay dispersed as Jenny became aware of the folded paper in her hand. That he had slipped it to her in secrecy could mean only one thing – and the laughter she had seen in his eyes had been because not only were their minds in tune, but their hearts too...

'Go with God, my son,' Sister Cecilia was saying. 'And may we meet very soon.'

'*Amen,*' said Finn and Jenny together.

'Sister Cecilia,' Jenny's voice was troubled, her eyes veiled. 'I wish to meditate alone tonight. Forgive me, and may God's will be done.'

'You are beset by doubts, *ma petite*. It is usual when the day of dedication draws close. Do not let it prey upon your mind. Open your heart to Him and God will guide you.'

'Thank you, Sister, for your understanding – and for all you have done for me.' Jenny felt her eyes blur with unshed tears. But it was *not* treachery. They forced such methods upon her by their own intransigence: she had told them of her doubts and they would not listen. They would never voluntarily set her free. Deep in her heart, Jenny's conscience warred with reason, but, whatever the outcome, she knew how she must act. 'Pray for me, Sister,' she finished, unusually humble, 'and forgive me. I shall not attend Vespers, but use the time to examine my conscience, if I may.'

'As you will, *ma petite*.' The old nun was to remember every word of that conversation in the days that followed, but even in the light of the Abbess's fury she could not find it in her heart to condemn. 'It is God's will,' she said and though she sorrowed for the girl, she was secretly content.

3

He proposed to free her from the Cloister, to which she consented. For
this Purpose he procured a false Key for a Garden Door, through which
Miss passed, where he and his Servant with Horses were waiting to
receive her.

It was cold in the herb garden, the shadows black with frost, the
bands of hyssop, lemon balm and camomile a uniform grey in
the colourless night. The sky was clouded, the moon fortunately
obscured. From the chapel came the plainsong of Vespers: if he
was waiting as he promised, there would be time.

She pulled the dark velvet close around her to obscure the
lighter gleam of her novice's gown. She had no clothes of her
own. They had vanished long ago, taken, she supposed, for the
poor. The cloak she had found by chance in the apartments set
aside for ladies seeking brief retreat from the cares of the
fashionable world and paying generously for the privilege. She
had taken it without hesitation, deeming it equal in value to the
clothes she had lost. When she reached St Germain she would
buy replacements for the too-identifiable robes of the convent.
Till then the camouflage cloak would suffice.

She had reached the end of the path now and paused in the
deeper shadow of a bay tree, listening ... The evening air was
chill on her cheek, the ground underfoot cold ... From the
dovecot behind her came the sleepy murmur of roosting birds,
while somewhere far away beyond the village a dog barked.
Then, from beyond the boundary wall, she heard the shaking of
flared nostrils, the gentle thud of hoof on turf..

She sped through the archway into the Abbess's own garden,
past the rose-arbour and the fountain to the small gate in the
wall. This gate was kept always locked, to be opened only by
the Abbess's permission for essential gardening, but when Jenny
tapped it lightly, twice, it opened on the instant. Three horses
were grouped close, one man holding their reins, another
holding open the door. Not a word was spoken. She slipped
through the crack and he closed it, turned the key in the lock,
tossed the key into the meadow at his back, took her waist in
his hands and swung her into the saddle of the nearest horse. He
mounted the second, his servant the third. Then they were

moving silently across the convent meadow to skirt the village in a wide detour, hooves muffled by the new-sprung grass. The only sound was the creak of leather, the rustle of moving cloth, the occasional chink of harness. Even the horses' breath was silent.

Once, Jenny looked back to where the convent rose black against the night sky, the long flat line of the boundary wall solid as a defence-work, with behind it the battlemented line of dovecot and cloisters, audience rooms, offices and gatehouse, and, high above the rest, the chapel and its bell-tower. Here and there yellow light prickled; she heard the distant choir, ethereal in the gathering darkness. They were singing, appropriately enough, the *Nunc Dimittis*.

Then they were on the highway below the village, with the countryside opening out on either side in flat, dark-sleeping meadows, skeletal vineyards and bony patches of winter trees. Finn O'Neil reined in his horse. 'Now, Miss Jenny Cameron, let us see how well you can ride.'

He touched spurred heel to flank and leapt forward into the darkness. Jenny tucked herself more firmly into the unfamiliar saddle, dug in her heels and followed. Wind buffeted her cheeks, stung her eyes to tears, numbed the tips of her ears; her hair broke loose from its pins and streamed behind her with her billowing cloak. She gave herself completely to the speed and the wind and the flashing landscape of the night countryside. They met no one, saw no one, heard only the steady beat of their horses' hooves, the straining of their own lungs. A river glinted to the right of them, ahead a wood rose black on the horizon, slipped aside and back as they drew close. There were bridges, a village or two, once a mire where the river had overflowed its banks, then they were at the top of a long incline at the foot of which lay a village, larger than the few they had traversed. On the skyline beyond was the outline of a castle.

'St Germain,' said Finn, and Jenny allowed herself the first long breath of freedom. In St Germain were Jacobites, exiles like herself, friends...

'The Colonel's *sister*?' The *aubergiste* raised an eyebrow as he looked Jenny over in one comprehensive glance. 'Then you will not mind sharing your room, for there is none other to be had, with the village full of soldiers, and no peace till they've gone.'

'Which will be soon enough,' replied Finn cheerfully, 'and you with nothing to do but count your profits. My old room will suffice for my sister. I will sleep below, or in a chair. It is only

135

for one night, for tomorrow we go to St Germain. But I will have no *table d'hôte* eating, remember. Send up a good supper to Mam'selle's room, for we have ridden hard and long; and none of your watered wine. I'll have a flagon of the best. See to it, Daniel.'

The Colonel took Jenny's arm and led her up the creaking, ill-made stairs to the bedchamber where Marianne was attempting to blow life into the paltry heap of sticks and birch-bark in the grate.

'Bring a lighted faggot from below,' ordered Finn, 'And more candles!' he called after her as she clattered downstairs. How plain and dull she had become, he reflected briefly. He had thought her beguiling a month back. 'I apologize, Miss Jenny, for the accommodation, but at this time of night and with the horses exhausted, we have no choice. I will sleep in a chair.'

'It is not only the horses that are exhausted,' said Jenny, laughing. 'I would welcome a ditch on the open hillside, or Oberon's stall. Anywhere, now that I am *free*! Oh Finn, I thank you for it with all my heart!' and she flung her arms round his neck and kissed him. Had not Marianne returned at that moment with a smoking shovel of embers to add to the fire, Finn might have forgotten himself . . . but the innkeeper's daughter was scurrying about the room, setting the trestle table in place, plumping up the heap of feather-beds, twitching the curtains to rights, disappearing down the stair in a clatter of sabots to emerge again almost immediately with a copper bed-warmer which she thrust into the pile of quilts and slid expertly up and down.

'Enough,' said Finn. 'Cannot you see my sister is exhausted? Fetch food. I have such a hunger on me I could eat an ox.'

'My petticoats are sodden,' said Jenny when the maid had gone. She kilted them high and spread them in front of the struggling fire. 'What will they think of me at St Germain?'

'Did you bring no other garments?' Finn looked at her in surprise. It had not occurred to him to worry about practicalities such as dress.

'I have none. Don't look so dismayed,' she said. 'I will have a gown made as soon as I can find a sempstress and cloth.'

'At least you brought money?' The sight of Miss Jenny in her obviously convent garments, lifting her dirty hem to knee-height to expose stockingless, shoeless feet and firm bare legs, was a charming one – but she could not go to St Germain like that. He would be branded convent-robber before he'd taken two steps past the threshold. As it was, they would have to be wary: the Abbess was sure to have sent out search-parties. Thank God Jenny had had the foresight to bring that cloak.

136

'Money?' Jenny's face lost its animation. 'The Abbess keeps all money. I have not even a brooch or ring. I am sorry, Finn, I did not think ...' She had never been required to consider money – not at Glendessary, at her aunt's, not even on the journey to France, and certainly not in Sacré Coeur. 'But all will be well tomorrow, Finn,' she went on as he did not speak, but bit his lip in sudden, apparently sobering thought. 'I am sure to find a kinsman at St Germain who will help me, and my brother will make recompense when I am home again.' Alan, she was sure, would always help her.

'With the prize money from my last campaign I have money enough for both of us.' Finn's unease had been due not to the absence of Miss Jenny's resources, for he was rich and needed none, but to the responsibility it laid on him as her abductor. He had thought of her as independent, free as he was to come or go as he chose ...

But the *aubergiste* and Daniel together had appeared at the door with an ashet of chickens, a beef *ragoût*, white bread and a flagon of wine.

'Come, let us eat and forget our problems till tomorrow. See to Oberon and the rest, Daniel, and take this,' he flipped a coin across the room and Daniel caught it expertly in one hand. 'Buy yourself a bellyful of good food and better wine – for it will be marching rations tomorrow.'

'Will you really march tomorrow?' asked Jenny later, when they had eaten everything provided and Finn had called for more wine. The fire burned steadily now, casting a warm glow over the dusty wooden floor and rough furnishings. The candles lit each grimy window pane with reflected starlight and even the dirty yellow bed-hangings softened to gold, so that the bleak, cold room had shrunk to a fire-wrapped and intimate cocoon.

'We go to Paris,' he said slowly, 'to report for duty. After that it will be Maubeuge, no doubt to take up where we left off in October.' He looked at her with steady eyes. 'And you, Jenny,' he said quietly, 'what will you do?'

'Go home, when I can. But why do you look at me so?'

'Because you are beautiful and I think I love you.'

'*Think*?' Jenny's voice was light, but her heart had leapt in her breast at the banked fire in his voice.

'I would not swear to something unknown,' he said, with quiet seriousness, 'and what I feel for you I have not felt before for any woman.'

Jenny studied Finn's face, so close to hers across the table, searching for some truth on which to anchor her trust. The candlelight touched his face with shadow, and his eyes were very blue. She could not look away. 'What is it you feel for me?' she asked, when he did not speak.

'So many things ... wonder, awe, admiration, desire ... I know I am at ease with you ... and yet not at ease, for the longing for you is a torment, a pain...'

'Is *that* why you rescued me?' said Jenny, teasing, though her cheeks were pink and her breathing fast. 'And I thought it altruistic gallantry. St George rescuing the maiden from the dragon of the convent – or one Jacobite rescuing another to fight again for the cause.'

'That too.' He leant across the table till his face was a handsbreadth from her own. 'But most of all I wanted you free, for me...'

'As your wife?' asked Jenny, surprised.

'I know not. And that is the honest truth.' He had thought only of snatching her from the jaws of the church before they closed on her for ever; he had refused to think beyond the moment of escape lest he tempt Fate too far. 'I had not thought to marry anyone...'

'Nor I,' said Jenny, suddenly sober. She remembered that vow to Hugh so long ago and her own renewal of it when he had betrayed her. But she had been younger then, untaught, and Hugh was married to another.

'Why are you sad, my little one?' Finn reached out a hand and lifted her face.

'I was thinking of betrayal and the wounds it causes.'

'If you are concerned for Aunt Cecilia, there is no need. I know she wants you to act according to your conscience and your conscience would not let you make a vow you knew you could not keep. She will understand, Jenny, and forgive.'

'Do you think so?' Determinedly, Jenny pushed back the memory of Hugh. He was a shadow now, no more, a wraith from a childhood dream. Her broken trust with Sister Cecilia was of more import. 'I was fond of her, Finn. I did not want to hurt her, but I could see no other way.'

'Nor I. Come, Jenny, smile for there is no going back. When you spoke to me in the little chapel, I knew God was on our side.'

'Surely Finn O'Neil 'tis blasphemy you are speaking! Would God himself send a soldier to carry off His nun-elect?'

'Why not, if she had strayed into cold and alien places?'

'It *was* cold, Finn.' Jenny's eyes widened with remembered anguish. 'Cold death.'

'I know.' He reached across the narrow table and laid a hand, warm and conforting, over hers. Then he took her hand, turned it palm upwards and raised it to his lips.

'More wine, mavournin?'

The wine was velvet-smooth on the tongue: it seemed to soften her whole body with its warmth, to set her senses quivering, expectant, like a flower opening to the sun. He held the goblet to her lips and his face was very close. Her hands closed over his and touched the cup to his lips, too. Then he took the vessel from her hand and set it aside.

'Come to the fire, Jenny, and forget the cold. It is past now, for ever ... and your garments are still damp.' He drew her to her feet. 'And if you will not do as I say,' he continued, imprisoning her close against him as she feigned resistance, so that his lips were against her ear, 'then I will take the petticoats off you myself.'

But the fire had died to smouldering embers, the room sunk deep in shadows before Finn O'Neil spread petticoats and shift over a chair back at the hearth. His fingers lingered over the cotton, caressing in memory of its owner's warmth, while his eyes still held the wonder of her loving. There was no sound from the room below, nor from the village; only the rattle of a shutter in the night wind and, somewhere, a sighing draught ... while from the high and shadowed altar of their bed came the slow rhythm of her breathing, warm and low as a cat's contented purring.

For the first time in his twenty-five years of swash-buckling life, Finn O'Neil knew humility. She had come to him joyfully, in friendship and shared warmth, had welcomed him as naturally as the sea receives the river, or the river the stream, and now, he knew, their lives were as inseparably bound. He had known many women in his time, but none who had given so freely or made him feel so close to primeval truth. Already he was cold without her ... He stirred the ashes to small flame, touched a candle to the sudden flickering tongue and held it high. She lay in slumber deep as a child's, curled on her side, cheek on the pillow, lips parted and dark hair tumbled over bare shoulders. One arm was stretched over the place where he had lain and he could see the curve of her breast against the rough cambric of the bed-coverings. Gently he peeled back the coverlet and stood looking down at the curves and valleys of her body, the graceful lines, the planes of pure delight. He felt wonder, awe, and above all, responsibility. He had not planned it, he hardly knew what he had planned beyond her rescue from the convent, but now the plan had been made for him.

He snuffed the candle between finger and thumb, set it aside and lay down beside her, drawing the bed-curtains closed. His

139

eyes stared unseeing into the enclosing darkness and his face was solemn as he thought of his past, gone for ever, cut out of his life by those tawdry bed-curtains – his freedom, his wayward, carefree living, his heart-whole irresponsibility. But the bed-curtains were cloth of gold now and there was no help: tomorrow he would find a priest.

Jenny woke to full sunlight and an empty bed.

'I brought your washing water, Mam'selle,' said a voice from beyond the bed-curtain, and Jenny wrenched it back to see Marianne busy at the fire, a steaming jug on the washstand and no sign of Finn.

'Monsieur said to tell you he will be back this evening, Mam'selle. He said to send you *café* and any viands you required, and to find you a sempstress and cloth.'

'I am ravenous, Marianne. Fetch me anything you have while I wash and dress. Then we will talk of gowns.'

Finn O'Neil was a rascal, she thought happily as she splashed the rapidly-cooling water over breast and thigh and armpit. Leaving her asleep . . . But she had not slept so long and deeply since her childhood. She stopped in amazement, remembering, then snorted with repressed delight. Matins, Lauds, Prime, Terce . . . how many Orders of the Day had she missed since last night's Vespers?

Was it only last night? She paused in wonder at the thought, for that one night with Finn had obliterated her time in the nunnery as cleanly as a wave smooths sand. Sacré Coeur was already a dream, a holy, silent dream of purity and cold; but a dream still, over and gone. She stretched her arms wide, stood a-tiptoe and felt herself grow tall and full with freedom.

Through the grimy window she could see the distant edifice of St Germain, high on the skyline to the north. Today Finn had said, they would go there. But he was right. She could not go dressed as she was. She would not have minded for herself, but it might be wiser to go as a less obvious refugee.

She stepped quickly into shift and rough-spun petticoat, then the heavy cotton convent gown, and shook out her hair. She had forgotten to bring even a comb!

But Marianne had returned with bread and goatsmilk cheese and a dish of steaming coffee. Jenny ate indiscriminately and with gusto till the board was cleared.

'The sempstress is *en bas*, Mam'selle' said Marianne hesitantly.

'Send her up. What is there to wait for?'

'Your hair, Mam'selle. Shall I make your *coiffure*?'

140

'If you must,' laughed Jenny – another month and they would have shorn her bald in Sacré Coeur. 'But I must tell Monsieur when he returns to buy a comb and pins.'

'I have them here,' said the girl shyly and produced a tortoiseshell comb and a handful of hairpins from a pocket at her waist.

'You should wear green, Mam'selle, or crimson,' Marianne said as she worked. 'Monsieur said to fetch bolts of cloth of various colours, for you to choose, but I think...'

'Whatever you say, Marianne,' interrupted Jenny. 'Colour is of no consequence to me so long as it is bright and warm.'

'Then I will fetch the sempstress.'

Jenny spent an impatient hour being measured and looped about with material of differing kinds before Marianne and her assistant were satisfied. But while they snipped and pinned, folded and stitched in unswerving concentration, Jenny ranged the room from window to trestle table to door to window, impatient to be outside and riding.

'How far is it to St Germain?' she asked once.

'Not far. Fifteen kilometres perhaps,' said Marianne.

'Not far enough,' grumbled the sempstress. She was old, her face a mesh of lines and her back crooked, but her misshapen fingers were nimble as a child's and her eyes clear-sighted and shrewd.

'Why do you say that?' demanded Jenny. 'Do they harm you?'

'The Queen is grace itself,' mumbled the old woman, placating, 'and La Consolatrice is an angel.' La Consolatrice was the nickname given to James's sister, Louise Marie. 'But there are too many hangers-on with too little money and too much time on their hands. Trouble ... only trouble ...' and to prevent further indiscretion, for it was plain the young Mam'selle was angry, she filled her toothless mouth with pins.

'La Consolatrice,' said Marianne quickly, 'is almost eighteen years of age now. It is said that she and the Duc de Berry are in love, but the King her grandfather will not allow the match.'

'Why not?' asked Jenny, interested in spite of her annoyance.

'They say that James Stuart, like his father, will never be a king in his own land – only in ours, Mam'selle. Perhaps it is not true, but...'

'It is *not*,' said Jenny with a dignity worthy of James himself. 'It is a lie put about by his enemies. But he has friends, too. Atholl, Panmure, the Duke of Berwick, my own uncle Ewen – and your King Louis is his friend, Even the great Duke of

Marlborough, they say, would jump swiftly to his side if the time and tide were right. Oh yes,' went on Jenny as neither woman made reply, 'the day will come. I know it. Queen Anne will die very soon, and when she does King James is waiting. So you see, Marianne, you are wrong. La Consolatrice, as you call her, is a most fortunate woman, well fitted to be the Duc de Berry's bride.'

'She looks adorable in her hunting-habit,' said the old sempstress, on safer ground. 'It is scarlet, they tell me, laced with gold. She turns all heads at *la chasse* and her eyes are huge and black as forest pools . . . like yours, Mam'selle,' she finished, sitting back on her heels and studying Jenny with new interest. 'You too would look well in scarlet, in the Bois de Boulogne.'

'If I am to hunt,' said Jenny, 'I will wear green. But if you do not move your fingers faster, I will wear nothing but these con . . .' – she stopped herself on the brink of indiscretion – 'confounded homespun garments till I *die*.'

'*Tout de suite*, Mam'selle,' said Marianne, her eyes anxious; Monsieur had promised her a *cadeau* if the work was done by sundown. She would make the sempstress stitch all day to complete the first gown in time. 'We will leave you now,' she said, 'and bring the gown to you by evening.'

'Then I will ride abroad. Call Daniel to saddle my horse.'

'Daniel is gone, Mam'selle, with his master, and you are to stay in your room,' she lowered her voice, 'lest you are seen by enemies. Monsieur has ordered it. He has ordered you a partridge, too, Mam'selle,' she added quickly 'and a *soufflé au Calvados*. You are also to have whatever wine you wish.'

'So be it,' sighed Jenny, subsiding on to the bed as the two women left with their arms full of green and apricot-coloured cloth. Finn was right to be cautious on her behalf – the Abbess would surely have search-parties scouring the country by now – and at least the convent had taught her patience.

It was late afternoon before the women came to her room, and still Finn O'Neil had not returned. They fitted and tucked the bodice, flounced the skirt and declared the garment finished.

'I will fetch a glass,' said Marianne and returned a few minutes later with the promised article. 'Wait till I light the candles, Mam'selle, so that you may see.'

'Magnificent,' said a voice from the doorway. Finn O'Neil was flushed with riding, hair wind-blown, boots mud-spattered. He tossed his tricorne hat on to a chair, strode across the room to the fire and spread cold hands to the warming flame. 'Now leave us, Marianne. You will be well rewarded.' When they had gone, their sabots loud as horses' hooves on the wooden stairs, he took Jenny's waist in his two hands and swung her high on a whoop of laughter. 'Tonight, mavournin, is our wedding night.' He kissed her, lingering, then held her away from him, his blue eyes teasing. 'Last night was merely a rehearsal.'

'Wedding?' Jenny was puzzled. 'You mean the dress?'

'That too. But where do you think I have been today?'

'To St Germain, of course.'

'Later.' He brushed aside her protests, took both her hands in his. 'I told you, Jenny, that I did not mean to marry. Like you, I hold my given word as sacred: I was not prepared to make a vow I knew I could not keep. But you and I are one: we can make the vows required of us without fear. There is a priest downstairs and . . .'

'No!' Jenny snatched her hands away from his on a cry of involuntary horror. 'I will see no priest!'

'But Jenny, he is not from the convent,' said Finn, misunderstanding. 'He will not betray you or seek to reclaim you in any way. He is happy to marry us by the simplest ceremony, tonight.' He did not add that it had taken him the better part of the day and a goodly amount of *louis d'or* to secure the priest's attendance.

'No. I will live with you, Finn. I will be handfast, if you want it. I will love you . . . I *do* love you . . . but I will go before no priest.'

In spite of all his arguments, cajolings, bullyings, pleadings, she remained adamant until Finn retired, angry and defeated, to a bumper of consolatory brandy at the *auberge* fire.

Jenny herself did not know what drove her. She knew only that deep at the very root of her being she had already made that solemn vow, and it had not been to Finn. Though she loved Finn as she had loved no one else, it was a vow she could not make twice.

'I have given you all the pledge you need, Finn,' she pleaded when he returned, drawn inexorably back to her in spite of his still-smouldering anger. 'Do not try to make me marry.' She put her arms about his neck and kissed him on the lips, the eyes, the lips again. Finn held back, rigid with hurt and mortification and with a fear he could not explain. He wanted her bound to him lest he lose her: before he had wanted only to be free.

'I am already your wife, Finn,' she was saying. 'Your handfast, loving wife. Why can you not believe me and be content, as I am?'

But Finn O'Neil had never yielded ground to any woman, or any man, come to that. 'Because', he said through clenched teeth, 'I want you *mine*.'

Disconcertingly, Jenny laughed. 'Oh Finn, you look so fierce with your splendid moustaches. If only you had a little hand-mill and a goatsmilk cheese, I swear you would terrify me!'

'Why you...' Finn seized her roughly by the shoulders with some idea of shaking her into submission. Instead he found himself the suppliant – bemused, surely bewitched, he thought with private wonder, entreating her forgiveness and her welcoming, drowning love.

'What did they tell you at St Germain?' asked Jenny, stripping the last of the beef from the rib with firm white teeth and licking the juices from her fingers, one by one. She tossed the bone expertly through the open window and reached for another. From the *auberge* beneath came the usual roisterous clamour of French and English voices mixed, for King Louis had many foreign mercenaries in his armies. From the stable-yard the noise of hooves on cobbles, and ostler's shouts, rose clear to the casement which Jenny had flung open to air the overheated room. Not that the air was clean, with its undertones of horse-dung and midden, but it was at least cool.

'St Germain?' Finn's voice was for a moment puzzled, then his face cleared. 'I did not go.'

'Not go?' Jenny was appalled. 'Why not? When you promised?'

'Because my dove, my love, my singing bird, you are now my *wife*. Handfast or priest-fast, what is the difference, as you said yourself.'

'But what of James?' faltered Jenny. Her plans had never stretched beyond that castle on the skyline. At St Germain all would have been settled, somehow. Her Uncle Ewen or her Uncle John would have accepted her, welcomed her home into the Cameron clan and she would have done as they did, following their King...

'King James will claim his throne one day, mavournin. When he does, his armies will go with him. Until then, we fight for the cause of his kinsman Louis, in whose land we live. I did not go to St Germain', he said more kindly at the sight of her crestfallen face, 'because it was not necessary. King James has gone already to the northern front with the rest of the regiment. There is only Queen Beatrice at the Château, with her daughter, Princess Louise Marie.'

'La Consolatrice,' said Jenny, remembering.

'They call her so. Her mother needs all the consolation a daughter can offer, with her husband dead and her son at the battle-front. But these wars will soon be over. Even now they are arguing in Utrecht over peace terms.'

'Then why fight?' asked Jenny, surprised.

'Why indeed. Except that terms are not yet settled and every battle fought and won may be to our advantage. It seems Marlborough has decided against the attack from the coast – a blessed decision for us. Had he followed up that plan, he would have cut in behind the line of our best and strongest fortification, though had he done so, we could have seized the opportunity to leap forward into Brabant.'

'How?' demanded Jenny. 'Where is Brabant in relation to your lines?'

Finn swept aside the ashets, all argument forgotten, and scratched a line in the table-top with the point of a knife.

'This,' he said, 'is the French frontier. These,' and he scored a series of crosses, 'are our fortresses: Maubeuge, Condé, Douai. Here to the north is Brussels, here Ghent. This line is the river Scheldt, this the river Lye. Marlborough could have chosen either, for both lead into regions as yet untapped by foraging armies, theirs or ours, and both have waterways. But the Dutch insist on keeping the allied army between us and their precious territory, so Marlborough will come this way, along the Scheldt, and move southward to threaten here, at Douai.'

'Can you stop them?' breathed Jenny, enthralled.

'Marlborough has 110 battalions, 161 squadrons, Eugene of Hanover another 45 battalions and 100 or so squadrons – together, as you see, they have massive forces. But we have more. Villars can muster a full 200 battalions at least and more than 300 squadrons, though Marlborough's army is better equipped and better supplied.' Finn frowned down at his own sketch map. 'We will have four armies in the field. The Duke of Berwick asked to be allowed to forestall the attack, but the King will not agree. If only Villars were sufficiently recovered ... but Montesquiou is to take charge of preparations in his place.'

'What will they be?'

'Ypres is to be reinforced and La Bassée, but the grass is not grown thick enough for forage: he can feed only 40 battalions there as yet. Tomorrow I will look for better lodgings for you, Jenny. In Paris, perhaps, where you will have friends.'

'But I need no lodgings. I will be with you.'

'It is not possible. We march for ...'

'Three days and rest the fourth,' interrupted Jenny. 'I can do that too.'

'We sleep in our cloaks, at our horses' sides.'

'At home, I have slept in the heather often enough, and on colder nights.'

'But it is a *man*'s war, Jenny. You cannot come.'

'I come,' she said, quietly now, 'or I am no longer your wife.'

145

For a long moment they glared into each other's eyes, the blue eyes angry with determination, the brown ones adamantine, but it was the blue which finally softened in capitulation.

'Jenny, Jenny . . .' he sighed. 'To what a pass have you brought me that I, Colonel Finn O'Neil, should give in to a sprig of a girl in a flame of a gown with hair as black as the raven's wing. But the great Finn MacCoul himself was known for his gentleness to women.'

'Aye, and for his leadership of warriors,' retorted Jenny, remembering fireside tales of childhood. 'If he could combine the two, then why not you? Besides,' she added, dark eyes dancing, 'I will keep you warm at night.'

That was the beginning of a strange new life. Though Finn, as he had promised, took her with him, she found that even he could not conquer the protocol which required her to ride with the other camp-followers behind the baggage train, while he headed his cavalry unit at the forefront of the column. He made her hire a maid, a cousin of the sempstress, though Jenny swore she needed none. But Colette was useful in her way and unobtrusive, and soon learnt when to leave her mistress alone: when the white rump of the Colonel's charger disappeared into the early morning mist, it was time enough to busy herself with the bivouac fire and the filling of the day's canteens.

For Finn came to her whenever he could, and Jenny, who had talked once of sleeping, plaid-wrapped, with Hugh above a summer shieling, found a campaign blanket in a French field with Finn a warmer re-enactment of that dream. For in childhood, unknowing, she had dreamt only of the separate closeness of friendship under the freedom of a summer sky; not of the sweeter fusion of two in one. Even on rest days when they halted for two nights instead of one, she stayed with the column, rather than in a village, watching the never-ending activity of an army on the move as they made their slow way northward towards the frontier.

The convent at least had trained her for rhythm, for long stretches of mindless endurance. Her childhood had trained her, as her father's educational methods were designed to do, for hardship and privation, for the sharing of what little there was without complaint, for survival without the palliatives of civilized living, . . . and Finn gave her all the purpose she needed. Had her inclination turned to self-analysis, Jenny would have perceived that she was deeply happy: her future no longer troubled her, her past was obliterated, and she was content.

146

Jenny Cameron slipped easily into the rhythm of the campaign: rise before dawn, douse fires, saddle horses, pack blanket roll and cooking-pot, clothes bundle, wine jar and bread, lend a hand where needed, with strayed horses or overturned cart, and finally take one's place with the other women at the back of the column while far ahead the kettledrum rolled for the march, the trumpets and hautboys sounded and the standards unfurled.

The splendour of it never failed to stir her. As the dawn mist cleared, leaving lingering pennons ethereal white in the forest trees and a pink-washed gauze over poppied meadows, the sun would roll like a dusty coin over the horizon and scatter cloud and shadow in a gush of scarlet and turquoise-green, while against the wakening sky the jagged outline of the column sharpened. The overall greyness split, sun-brightened, into splashes of white and buff, green, scarlet and blue from the regiments' coats, the gold of epaulets and braiding, the silver gleam of sword. She knew the order well: first the fusiliers, with engineers and pioneers to repair the road where necessary for the gun-carriages and wagons; then four guns with their horses, crews and ammunition, then the treasure and baggage of the royal household, the belongings of the Commander-in-Chief and the Quartermaster-General, the wagons of the Provost-Marshal and other dignitaries, then the pontoons for bridges, carried upside down on wagons. After that came more gun-carriages, dragged by their specially chosen horses; their gun crews and supporting infantry; the kit of the *Maison du Roi* and the advance guard cavalry (including Finn's); the great mass of the regimental baggage with the Paymaster's and Quartermaster's; the wagons and carts of the *vivandières*; the provisioners and sutlers; and the miscellaneous cartloads of powder, rope, fuses, tools, bombs, and the rest of the column's indispensable hardware. Last of all, behind the rumbling, mud-splashing wooden wheels of the last cart in the column, came a motley assortment of women and children – and Jenny.

They marched all day, stopping only to rest the horses, to free a mud-embedded wagon, or to wait for the pioneers at the head of the column to make the road cartworthy or to erect a bridge.

Then they were at the front. The forces were dispersed, the camp set up with its magazines and grain stores, in regimental tents, its officers' quarters and cavalry lines. And Jenny consented to go into lodgings.

'Marlborough's and Prince Eugene's men are assembling at Tournai,' explained Finn. 'They plan an assault at Douai, but spring is late and forage sparse. Only half their troops are assembled as yet, so it will be a long process. I will stay in camp and find you lodgings in Lens.'

But when the enemy moved earlier and far more swiftly than expected, broke the lines and caught the French unprepared and foraging, it was on Lens that they advanced: Jenny and Colette fled with the rest of them, leaving undefended walls and abandoned stores. All the French could do was count their losses, while the enemy prepared to besiege Douai exactly as Marlborough had planned.

'He is a military genius,' said Finn with admiration. 'To move so fast and soon! He had dry forage brought by water while we thought he must wait for the grass to grow, and now we must fall back as far as Cambrai with all our forward magazines lost to the enemy. If only Villars would come! Montesquiou does nothing but procrastinate and wait for reinforcements.'

'What will Marlborough do now?' asked Jenny, her eyes on Finn's face, the chicken wing forgotten in her fingers: Daniel had been on a forage of his own to a nearby hen-house.

'Lay siege to Douai of course, but it is well prepared, thanks to the winter's refurbishings, and we will pick off their water convoys and attack their baggage trains. We had best find lodgings for you behind our lines, for it will be a lengthy siege.'

This time Finn was right. When Villars arrived at last to take command, and Berwick joined him, there was talk of a battle to relieve the town. Both armies went through elaborate and threatening maneouvres till they faced each other, menacing, 15,000 strong on either side, within cannon-shot of each other on the plain below Vimy ridge. But discretion prevailed, and it was the end of June before Douai finally fell, to be followed by Béthune, Saint Venant and, in filthy November weather, Aire.

'And not a battle in the whole campaign!' complained Finn as they repaired to winter quarters.

'At least you are not wounded,' comforted Jenny, 'and your old injury is healed far better than poor Marshal Villars'. He wears an iron contraption to keep his knee in place on horseback and his wound, they say, still suppurates.'

This was to be the pattern of the next two years – winter quarters of loving and laughter, of hunting, riding, and, when Finn had military matters of provisioning or strategy to attend to, more domestic pursuits for Jenny. In the spring the opening of the campaign season, the march north to the frontier, and the slow maneouvring dance of battle-line and siege . . .

She grew accustomed to the cannon-fire, the musket-shot and kettledrums, the trampled cornfields and suddenly wheeling birds, the wounded, the sweating medical teams, the screaming horses, the blood-spattered uniforms, muddied rivers and bodies broken in the summer meadows. She gave help and comfort where she could, and strangely did not fear for Finn or for herself. They spent what time they could together and, when apart, knew companionship in waiting.

Sometimes when the bivouac fires burnt bright in the evening and the camp was settling for sleep, he would talk to her of home.

'We will go to Ireland one day, acushla,' he told her, 'and ride together through the emerald beauty of my father's land. I see you,' he continued, dreaming, 'in a sea-green riding habit with scarlet lapels, trimmed with gold. There will be gold, too, on your velvet cap and a huge scarlet feather ... I will buy you a fine bay gelding and deck him with caparisons of the same sea-green, also fringed with gold. All who look on you will say you are a sea-princess, lovelier than Deirdre, daughter of Fedlimid, bard of Conchaber, and I will ride at your side and be proud.'

As she listened, she remembered Lochiel in Aunt Cameron's house when he had talked of her riding to meet her king. One day she knew it would come true, when she and Finn rode out to meet King James at Edinburgh Castle. One day, when this campaign was over and the treaty made.

She thought little, now, of home; rarely of her family. Her sisters she supposed would be married, or dead. Her mother too. Her brothers at the University, if the smallpox and the fever had spared them. As for her brother Alan, he was Cameron of Glendessary in her father's place and the others would go their own way. They would think as little of her as she of them.

In the jubilation of Finn's company and the excitement of the long campaign she forgot even the cause of her exiled King, James Stuart. For if he was content to spend his waiting time with the armies of King Louis, then so was she. At least she was near her King's headquarters.

She saw him once, by chance, as he rode beside a river. The two armies were camped on opposite sides, but within shouting distance. They were resting or Jenny would not have been, as she was, on horseback on a nearby hillside. She saw another rider, motionless as she was, at a distance along the river bank and would not have known who he was had not someone called out and the horseman moved forward so that she saw the blue ribbon of the Garter. Even then she might not have recognized her sovereign had she not seen that several of the opposing army, Englishmen and Scots, were doffing their hats and bowing on the far side of the river. Jenny watched in awe as James moved slowly along the bank acknowledging their homage. He was more handsome than she had imagined, taller, straighter, his young face perfect in its dark-eyed solemnity: she could not have wished for a more regal king. After that she watched always for the blue Garter, but the élite of the cavalry corps did not cross paths often with the tail-end of the baggage train. She had no fears for him as she had none for Finn, or for herself, and was wholly unprepared for Bouchain.

'Damn! Damn! Damn!' roared Finn O'Neil, hurling his sword in a crash of steel against the wall. 'Curse those devils on horseback! Curse the villain Marlborough! Curse every blind-eyed, snoring, pea-brained, bog-rotten look-out in the French army and curse Oberon for a spavined, broken-winded *nag*!'

Jenny raised an eyebrow in surprise. She was used to hearing curses heaped on the armies, French and English, indiscriminately, but the insults to Oberon were new. 'What set-back has befallen your cavalry this time?' she asked, lightly enough but with a wariness behind the smile: she had faced Finn many times in anger, for they were both too impetuous to escape it, but this time there was a new element to his wrath. 'Is Oberon failing? He has fought a hard campaign.'

'We are all *failing*, you dagger-tongued houri! *I* fail!' and he booted the table-leg so hard that the trestle snapped and platters, bread and the wild strawberries Jenny had scoured the countryside to find cascaded to the floor. 'Villars *fails*! Montesquiou *fails*!' He seized a chair by one leg and hurled it against the tester. At the crash of wood on wood the door eased open on a careful crack. 'Can I fetch ..?' began Daniel and retired with notable speed as the water-pot cracked a door panel in a roar of obscenity.

Jenny stood, hands on hips, and watched, knowing his fury would burn out. 'When you have finished breaking what miserable furniture they give us, shall I fetch you more? Or shall we move downstairs and start on the landlord's parlour?'

'Oh Jenny, Jenny!' He clasped her painfully tight against his chest and pressed his cheek against hers. She felt moisture on her face and knew him to be weeping. Tears of remorse. 'They have breached our lines – what Villars himself called the Ne Plus Ultra – and I spurred my darling Oberon till the blood ran ... I am ashamed.' She soothed him with childhood endearments long forgotten: they brought back memories of firelight on gilded leather bindings, her father's gentle voice and reassuring arms. 'Tell me,' she said when he was quiet again, and moved to set the room to rights.

'Leave that,' he said wearily, subsiding into the one whole chair remaining and pulling her on to his knee. 'It was a masterly trick – I cannot deny it – a stroke of genius on that villain's part. And we fell for it. We expected a battle – they had lined up their armies in battle formation – 100,000 men at least, their spontoons and halberds massed thick as hedgehog spines ... We too were in position, ready to fly at the villains' throats the moment they attacked. I rode with Villars up and down the line. We could not have been more prepared. It would have been a struggle fit for the gods, mavournin, and we would have triumphed. Marlborough himself rode along the battle-front to reconnoitre. I *saw* him, Jenny, with his cavalry, and was so busy counting horses and assessing strength, that I saw nothing beyond the villain's party – as was his obvious design. *I fell for it*, Jenny!'

'It was natural,' soothed Jenny. 'When an opportunity presents to assess the enemy, anyone would take it.'

'But Marlborough's exploitation of it was a strategy we should have seen. He lured us deliberately. While all our eyes were on his party, the artillery at his back began to slip away. Even at sunset when we surveyed their ranks – as we thought for the last time before the battle – we saw nothing out of place. There was even a group of cavalry riding *west* as if to reconnoitre an escape should the battle go against them. We did not hear their drums or the thud of hooves and marching feet. It was only when the moon came up that we saw ...'

'What?' prompted Jenny as his face darkened again in remembered rage.

'The whole army had upped camp and gone! To the *east*. And Villars had withdrawn men from there to aid us in the battle. We moved, too, as soon as the scouts came back to tell us where Marlborough was heading for, but they had too much start on us. I spurred poor Oberon wickedly ... They breached our lines, Jenny, and without a battle! Now they will lay siege to Bouchain.'

'But Bouchain is a fine fortress, you told me so yourself. With our army close at hand to block their baggage trains and prevent them bringing up more cannon, surely Bouchain will endure?'

'It is too late. That devil marches as swiftly by night as by day. Already he has cannon enough for ten sieges and a system of redoubts and ditches dug in the darkness. He is walling himself in on all sides, Jenny. It will be a long, long siege. But', he went on more cheerfully, 'Albergotti's men have already constructed a fine entrenched camp for us west of Bouchain. My brigade will serve there.'

'But are there not marshes? A bog of rushes and willow? How

151

can you move horses if they be knee-deep in mud? And a cannon would sink with no trace but a bubble!'

'The camp is on the high ground and the marsh is both a protection and a blessing. There is a cow-path through it to the walls of Bouchain – a single track, meandering, yet our men have improved and protected it by an ingenious system of parapets. They bound long faggots from tree to tree to make a two-mile path which takes us right to the walls of the town! It's a life-line, Jenny, which links army and besieged together, and together we'll beat that villain yet.'

He pushed her to her feet with a slap on the behind and roared, with his old good humour, 'Daniel! Where is my *wine*? I sent the devil for it an hour ago.' He added, with a wink at Jenny, 'We'll beat them yet, my darlin'.'

'Take care, Finn.' For the first time in their life together Jenny felt anxiety. 'It does not sound good ground for cavalry.'

'All ground is the same, Jenny, for Oberon.'

But later, when the meal had long been eaten, the wine drunk and the fire had died, Finn lay with her head in the crook of his naked arm and stared at the shadowed canopy above him. 'You are right, mavournin. The marsh is treacherous. Were a horse to shy or step aside, it would be lost. I will leave Oberon here with you, and take another mount until Bouchain is freed. Besides, I ill-treated him and he has earned his rest. You will care for him?'

'I will ride him every day,' she murmured in contentment. 'I will be the envy of every colonel's lady in the garrison and every cavalryman in the King's army. And I'll not spur him, neither, for I have none.'

'I dispute that, madam,' he growled with a low laugh of pleasure as her hands moved over him, 'for you drive me hard enough . . .'

It was August of 1711, Jenny's second campaign, when the two armies converged on the fortress town of Bouchain. The corn stood thick in the fields, sun-burnished, heavy with heat. Dust rose in clouds from rutted tracks as wagons rumbled to their allotted places: the smoke of bivouac fires rose straight as a plumb line to the evening sky. It would be a long siege, Finn had said. He had taken lodgings for her in Cambrai, but she rode forward every evening now as far as she dared, for she knew well enough what Finn's reaction would be were she to trespass rashly on to dangerous ground. If Oberon or she were to be wounded, she wondered ruefully which he would mind the most, but felt no jealousy.

'Care for him well and wait for me,' Finn had said as he kissed her in farewell, and she did both with patience. Even when Daniel came to her, breathless, ten days later with the news that the cow-path had been taken and the Colonel was now trapped inside the garrison with the defending force, she did not worry. Bouchain was strong, Finn had said, the French army close at hand. Even without the cow-path they would survive.

But with the cow-path taken, Bouchain was alone. The enemy siege-trains arrived unimpeded, and their ordnance was set in place. Jenny heard the bombardment from Cambrai as Marlborough battered Bouchain and, at his back, Villars did the same to the English entrenchments. But Marlborough's army was too well-fortified: though the besieged could see the supporting French army clearly across the martial masses of their English attackers, they could not reach them and the life-line of vital supplies was cut.

Jenny saw the white flag from her look-out post on an evening in mid-September. They said in Cambrai that the Governor had offered to surrender the fortress if he were allowed, as was customary, to march out with the honours of war. Jenny felt sorrow and anger for their defeat, but no anxiety. It was always Marlborough's custom to accord such terms.

'They say he means to teach us a lesson,' reported Daniel, separated from his master by the walls of Bouchain. 'I'll bring you word as soon as we hear his terms.'

But when word came it brought disaster. 'Unconditional surrender: the entire garrison taken prisoner.'

Finn a prisoner? It was inconceivable. Jenny woke repeatedly in the throes of the same nightmare – she and Finn, either or both she knew not, in the cell in the convent, with no light but a barred square high out of reach. She clawed for that square, over a wall that slipped from her hands until she woke in a cold panic of despair, and for the first time since she left Sacré Coeur she prayed . . .

'Please God, keep him safe and bring him back to me.'

That was a bleak winter of waiting in Cambrai. The town was dismal with winter rain, then sleet, then driving snow. Food was scarce, fodder almost non-existent. Rats prowled the cobbled streets, scavenging. Both armies had dispersed in October, though Marlborough had garrisoned and fortified Bouchain, and all who remained in Cambrai were the sick, the wounded and such camp personnel as had been detailed to lay in supplies and restock the magazines against the resumption of hostilities in the spring.

'He'll come back, Miss,' Daniel assured her. 'There will be negotiations ... exchanges of officers ... there always are.'

But he did not come, and they said the Dutch fed their prisoners atrociously.

Cambrai was full of suffering. The children in the narrow, cobbled streets were hollow-eyed and ragged; cats with hip-bones sharp as pikestaffs loped through gutter and midden. But the women still spun linen, if they had the flax: Jenny would see them occasionally through open doorway or lamp-lit window as she walked each day to the Porte de Paris. This was the part of the town which had been taken over by the winter staff – intendants whose job it was to build up supplies for the coming campaign, strike bargains with local contractors, wine-growers, and millers. But Jenny's business was not with them. While the money Finn had given her lasted, for she would not touch the store in his campaign trunk, she was able to find food without their help; she was known to pay ready money, unlike the Government intendants who paid with promises which might or might not be honoured.

This great gate, the Porte de Paris, was part of the town's defences and it was in a room below the keep that Dr McKinnon had his surgery, such as it was.

McKinnon was a small, wiry man, red-haired under his wig, with big, freckled hands. He had studied medicine at Edinburgh University with Archibald Cameron, grandson of Lochiel. Jenny remembered Archibald well – she had had a snowball fight with him and his brother Donald one winter afternoon in Achnacarry. In these dark winter days of waiting she was lonely for male company, and McKinnon gave her news.

For his part, the doctor welcomed her as a reviving breath of youth and health in the festering misery of the wounded in his charge. They talked of Edinburgh, of Achnacarry, and of James Stuart who would one day be king.

'I'll be glad to leave this foreign desert,' said McKinnon with feeling. 'I drank better claret at home, and the flatlands oppress me.'

He told her that Marlborough was back in England, in disgrace, that the Tories were in the ascendant, that Queen Anne would die at any minute, 'so swollen wi' the dropsy she should ha' died long since, and if she hasna' the sense to name James heir for hersel' then James's men will do it for her. Come spring, lass, and we'll settle the business here. It's a short step then to London, and to Edinburgh.'

But Jenny could not share his optimism. Once the thought of sweeping home on a wave of triumph in King James's wake would have been enough to keep her buoyant; now she could think only of Finn.

'What do they do to prisoners?'

The doctor looked up sharply from his accounts; the laudanum was running short in spite of meticulous husbanding; someone was surely selling it off to a local apothecary – to sell back again at double the price to him. 'Who?'

'Marlborough's men and the Dutch.'

'That depends,' he said carefully. 'The common soldiers might have their weapons taken, their breeches' belts cut, and be sent home with their hands in their pockets: or put to pioneering for their captors . . . The officers, well that's another matter. If they have money they'll live well enough, under house guard or word of honour, until they are ransomed or exchanged. The Colonel will come home,' he added and patted her shoulder in awkward reassurance. 'Only give him time.'

But time hung heavy on her hands. Jenny took to visiting those of the wounded who were well enough, to talk to them of home or the campaign; even, on McKinnon's suggestion, to write occasional letters for them. She was grateful now for her aunt's instruction, for with French, Italian and her native Gaelic as well as English she moved equally freely among French and *étrangers*. Moreover she wrote a swift and legible hand in any language required of her. In return, they told her of their summer campaign, of the attack on Bouchain and its defence, of conditions in the camps, and she found, through their confidences, a new closeness with Finn. And with them. By the turn of the year she was accepted everywhere as one of the company.

Only once did a soldier misunderstand the nature of her friendliness, and waylaid her in her lodging. But when he put a hand on her hip and another on her breast, she threw him in a surge of fury half across the room, and when he took a step towards her, she shot at him.

The flint was damp, the shot misfired, but he did not wait for her to reload. She was not molested again. The Colonel's 'Miss' was as fierce as her man, went the rumour, and even the *canaille* gave her wary berth.

She rode Oberon every day, with Daniel at her side and both of them armed, but forage was an increasing problem. Though Jenny dipped deep into the Colonel's pouch and sent Daniel further and further afield, she began to pray for spring for Oberon now, as well as for Finn. She wrote letters or provision lists for the favour of a measure of oats or fresh hay, and somehow they managed, though Oberon grew lean as the winter dragged reluctantly towards spring, and there was a vicious, hungry look in many a man's eye.

Jenny took to sleeping with Finn's flintlock pistol under her pillow lest a marauder thwart even Daniel's vigilance and make off with what little of value they had left.

She had been asleep perhaps two hours when she was jerked sharply awake. She raised herself on one elbow, straining into the silence while her hand slid under the pillow and found the pistol butt. A gust of wind stirred the curtain; a board creaked; she snapped the flint at the ready, aiming at whoever it was beyond the bed-curtains ... She heard the scrape of tinder, a candle flickered, a hand looped back the curtains and he looked down at her kneeling, naked, on the bed, the pistol held tight in both hands and her hair tumbling to her waist.

'Do not shoot me, mavournin, not now when I am home ...' but she was already in his arms, weeping and laughing, saying his name over and over, while he crushed her naked breasts against the serge of his coat and kissed her with the hunger of the starved.

The pistol fell forgotten to the floor, the candle burnt out unnoticed, but it was late into the night before they slept, and late into morning before they woke and Jenny saw how thin he was and haggard.

'I need air, my darlin',' he said, brushing aside her solicitude. 'and you. Is Oberon well?'

'As well as I am,' said Jenny, laughing, and took him straight to the stable where Daniel earned a cuff for a misplaced hair in the animal's mane and another for an imagined sore. But they were blows without malice and Daniel grinned. 'The world is set right again, Miss,' he said, 'and the master's hand as sure as ever.'

But it was not and Finn knew it. Jenny knew it too and was concerned for him. His voice had lost its volume and he coughed too often. His old thigh injury, he confessed, had plagued him on the march from Bouchain and he was pale behind the weathered tan of his skin. But by the end of the first week he was regaining his strength; by the end of the second he announced that he was going out early, alone, in search of forage.

Finn O'Neil slipped back his tricorne hat till it hung by a thong under his chin and let the frosted wind comb freely through his hair. It was good to feel Oberon under his thighs again, to feel the ripple of muscle, the power waiting to loose itself at his command. It was a clear morning, the ground hard underfoot. The sun was a huge disc low on the eastern horizon as he rode out through the gates into the open country and saw the fields and woods, the ravines and the glinting ribbon of the river Scheldt, with somewhere in the northern distance the battlemented fortress of Bouchain. That surgeon fellow, McKinnon, had told him of a farm in the area of Arleux which might have oats at a price, but first he would enjoy his freedom and Oberon's company.

There was mist in the valley; the meadows sparkled with dew-frost and on the hedgerow a cobweb hung thick with pearls. Somewhere a cock crew, hoarse-voiced, in skinny-necked impatience, and Finn laughed.

'He too wants his oats, my beauty,' and he touched his heels to his horse's flanks and quickened pace. 'We will be in sight of the village soon and you shall have your fill. But the day is fine and clear; we will go the long way round.'

It was the sight of Bouchain which undid him. He had not meant to ride so far north, but that fortress with the wrong flags flying was a taunt he could not ignore. He had fought for that town, defended it, seen it battered into ignominious submission. He had marched out of it, disarmed, disgraced, a prisoner-of-war of his own countrymen, and it left a bitter taste. But in the spring, he vowed, they'd win it back.

'Shall we take a closer look, Oberon?' He turned the horse's head northwards and spurred him to a gallop across the open country, forage forgotten. The cow-path should have alerted him, but he was exhilarated by speed and the thought of victory, and when he came to a stream in a patch of willow-trees and rushes he set Oberon at the jump without a thought.

It was late into the night when Jenny heard them on the stairs, but she was not a-bed. She had kept the fire blazing and the candles lit, a flagon of wine ready on the table with bread and a smoked ham Colette had bargained half the morning for. Jenny had rewarded her with ribbons from her own dress, for when Finn came he would be hungry.

He must have ridden farther than he intended, she thought, but she did not worry – she knew from childhood that dusk was a good hour for hunting. But the voice which set her starting to her feet was not that of a successful huntsman.

'Blast you, man, don't touch me!'

'But master, you . . .'

'Get back where you belong, you bog-rotten son-of-a-bitch!'

The door crashed open on a roar of fury and she saw him fall against the lintel, ashen-faced, mud-soaked, his stock ripped away and his sword strapped to his leg by dirty rags which to Jenny's horrified gaze revealed themselves to be his own dismembered shirt.

'Finn!' Jenny's eyes flew to Daniel's face and he answered her unspoken question in a nervous half-whisper. 'Oberon took a jump awkwardly. The master fell and . . .'

'Get out, poltroon! See to my horse as I told you!' But Daniel held his ground. Speaking more firmly now that Miss Jenny was in charge, he said, 'His leg is broken, Miss. He strapped it himself, but he'll need to take off the boot and . . .'

'Get out before I kick you down the stairs!' O'Neil moved incautiously to carry out his threat and had not Jenny caught him, would have fallen. The oaths, this time, were faint and scarce distinguishable from a groan.

'Fetch Dr McKinnon,' ordered Jenny. 'Never mind if he is abed. Tell him I need him. And hurry!'

'I'll see no leech and Daniel knows it. They're fit for nothing but to bleed a man to death. I mean to live a good while longer. Get me to my chair, woman – and *Daniel*! See to Oberon or I'll skin you alive.' But Daniel had already gone.

'Colette, tell the stable lad to see to the Colonel's horse, and then fetch brandy.' The startled maid who had scurried out of her cupboard in the attic to the door of their chamber at the disturbance of her master's return, sped as hastily out again. They heard her sabots loud on the cobbles of the yard.

'Finn, Finn,' soothed Jenny when she had helped him to the chair as best she could. 'McKinnon is a good man. He is a relative of Lochiel's,' she added, stretching consanguinity, 'and no common leech.'

'Was it not a clever idea, mavournin,' he said, his eyes closed on his pain, 'to stiffen the joint with my sword? You said yourself that Marshal Villars had a steel support till he was healed, and he kept the saddle well enough.'

'How far did you ride?' asked Jenny quietly, praying in her head for the surgeon to hurry.

'Five miles? Three? I know not . . . that damned cow-path . . .'

'But the cow-path is at Bouchain! You took a fall, broke a leg, strapped it yourself and rode *eight miles* home?' She was horrified and at the same time humbled by his courage.

'My leg is not broken,' he said, but they both knew he lied.

McKinnon cut the boot from his leg, splitting the leather from

158

cuff to foot and Finn did not protest. His stocking, too, had to be cut away; even his breeches; when he swooned they carried him to the bed, for he had refused to go there sooner, and he recovered consciousness to find the surgeon binding the wooden splints in place.

'Damn you, man, I made a better job of it myself with a sword and a shirt-tail! And no doubt you'll want a fee for your hamfisted pains.'

'Aye,' said the doctor, unperturbed, 'and think yourself lucky I dinna' charge for the abuse I get, or you'd be bankrupt. See you lie still now, for a month or so and then . . .'

'A *month*? I'll not lie still a day, do you hear?'

The doctor sighed. 'As you will. But if you're that set on crippling yoursel' for life, why send for me from my bed?'

'I did not send, you drivelling, poxy, lick-spittle quack . . .'

But the doctor ignored him. 'Thank you, Miss Jenny, I will take a glass of brandy.' He moved away from the bed and drew her with him to the fire. 'It is not easy work to set a bone at the best of times.' He mopped his brow with a kerchief and she saw with surprise that it was damp with sweat. 'Not easy to know one is inflicting pain. It is a bad break. It will set in time, but you must see he does not move.'

That, as Jenny found in the days that followed, was no easy task. He swore continually, shouted at her if she touched him. 'Take no heed, Miss,' said Daniel in awkward comfort after a particularly violent outburst in which Finn had struck her in the face and the rings on his fingers had raised a livid bruise. 'He has been the same all his life: pain makes some men humble, some silent, others whimpering weak, but with Finn O'Neil 'tis always violence and foul words. He does not mean it, and when you are gone from him, he frets.'

Jenny steeled herself against the pain of it and endured, though her pride was sorely tried: had it not been that she loved him, she would have left him alone, but if she moved from the room for an instant, he accused her of desertion, treachery, even whoring, 'in that poxy surgeon's bed, God rot the pair of you'. The next time she left him to barter for clean linen for his bed, she returned to find Finn at the window, standing defiantly on both bare feet. He mistook the shock of her expression.

'I know I am a figure of derision to you, arsebare in my shirt-tails, but I'll not lie idle another minute. Fetch my clothes, woman, and do not dare to hide them from me again.'

'Go to your bed, Finn,' she managed, appalled. 'You will dislodge the bone. The doctor said to . . .'

'Blast the doctor,' roared Finn, 'I'll be obeyed in my own house, you filthy bitch.' Jenny's control snapped. She loosed on him every long-forgotten oath of her Gaelic childhood, every fouler one from the Edinburgh taverns, even the latest French obscenities she had culled, unknowing, from the surgeon's wounded, and she finished, 'Be a *man*, as you used to be. I have known a wounded dog behave more nobly than you.'

She went to him then, put a supporting arm around his waist and he laid his head on her breast. She felt his tears on her skin and knew her own eyes moist. God keep him safe, she prayed, with sudden silent terror, as he whispered, 'I am sorry, mavournin. 'Tis only you I love or ever shall. Forgive me. I am not sufficiently acquainted with pain.'

Jenny knew what he meant. She too took health for granted. Hunger, cold, aching limbs, were natural hazards, easily overcome, but illness was a hostile stranger and she was lost as he was how to tackle it.

But both, instinctively and with equal horror, recognized the final betrayal.

'*Colette*!' The terror in her mistress's voice brought the girl clattering breathless to the door. 'Fetch Daniel. Send him *at once* for Dr McKinnon. He is to come . . . without . . . delay,' she finished on a low and shuddering moan of pure despair. Then she crossed to the casement and opened it in the vain hope that air might blow away that unmistakable odour of decay.

Jenny could never smell brandy again without the memory of that terrible night: Finn's screaming, his wild, contorted aspect as he gulped from the bottle she held to his lips, the crushing grip of his hand on hers, the surgeon's sweat-drenched, ashen face as the saw rasped on and on . . . and the sudden silence as Finn swooned to merciful oblivion in the smoke of searing flesh.

McKinnon snatched the brandy bottle to his own lips with trembling hands and emptied it. 'I have done all I can for him,' he said, with compassion. 'He is in God's hands now. Rest while you can, Miss Jenny. He will need you when he wakes.'

But when he regained consciousness after too many silent hours, it was to call for a priest.

'I wish to be confessed, Jenny.' His voice was scarce above a whisper, and at first she could not believe it. 'Daniel must ask at St Gery's. And stay with me, Jenny.'

When the priest had gone, Finn lay at peace, and his quietness terrified Jenny as nothing had till then.

'I have £300 in my trunk, mavournin. It is yours, with everything I possess. Be good to Daniel, and to Oberon.'

'There is no need, Finn, to concern yourself.' She smoothed back the hair from his brow, and fought to keep her voice from trembling. 'You will be well again in no time. There is a smith in Cambrai, the surgeon says, who will make you an iron boot so skillfully that even Oberon will not know the difference. As soon as you are well enough, we will send for him to take measurements. You and Oberon will drive Marlborough out of France and end the war, and we will go together, to Scotland. When we ride to Edinburgh Castle, James himself will welcome us as old comrades from the Flanders campaign...'

'Old comrades. Much more than that, Jenny. You have been my sweetness and my fire, my brief taste of paradise. But I stole you, mavournin,' and his eyes were full of sadness. 'You were my *creach* and I must pay the penalty.'

'I was no Highland heifer,' she managed through her tears, 'to be lassooed in a gully at nightfall. I came to you willingly, my darling.'

'I stole you nonetheless ... from God ... but you were so beautiful.' He looked at her then, his blue eyes suddenly clear and far-seeing. 'I wanted you, for mine.'

'I *am* yours, Finn, your handfast, loving wife, for ever ... Finn? *Finn*!'

As she felt the hand in hers go limp, saw those clear eyes glaze, she loosed her torment in a cry of such wild, primeval anguish that women in the streets of Cambrai crossed themselves in dread. As the bell tolled slowly from the belfry of St Gery to mark the Colonel's passing, Jenny Cameron's voice still keened across the rooftops in eerie, alien grief.

Jenny heard the birdsong as from a far distance and lay contented, listening to the trills and pipings, the scufflings of leaf and feather, the sudden sharp call of a blackbird's alarm: a cat was prowling too close to the steading. She heard the lowing of a cow in the distance and a bell – a little bell, surely not the church bell at Kilmalie? She was too drowsy to pursue the thought. She heard cartwheels on cobbles and horses' hooves. Strange: the road to Glendessary was too rutted for wheels. It was Edinburgh after all and her aunt's house. No matter. The sunlight behind her closed eyelids was yellow and the skin of her face warm. It must be summer. In summer everyone left Edinburgh for the country and she would go home, to Hugh. That was her aunt's maid, packing... and in the street below her window, someone singing. Idly she listened to the words. '*A si mon moine voulait danser, A si mon moine voulait danser, Un chaperon je lui donnerais ...*' With the slow, raw pain of returning memory, Jenny opened her eyes on the yellow camlet curtains of the bed she had shared with Finn, and in which first he, then his baby son, had died.

She lay a long time remembering, but it was as of a different life, lived by someone other than herself. Her discovery, in the wild anguish of Finn's loss, that she carried his child ... her refusal to obey Dr McKinnon and go home, 'for my baby must pay his respects to his father's grave'. . . . Colette's and Daniel's loyalty ... the birth of her little son ... then only fever and confusion. She could scarcely remember her baby – so small and new, so soon gone from her. Finn had gone, too ... She saw Finn as he had been on that first day in the visitors' room at Sacré Coeur: the convent walls had not shut out his bursting vigour, nor his laughter. She remembered him with gratitude and an overwhelming love in which there was no bitterness of loss. He had stolen her from God's service, and had paid the price. She in her turn had paid, with Finn whom she loved and with Finn's son. The convent had no further claim on her. The account was settled, the slate wiped clean. She was free now to go home to Lochiel, who had banished her, and ask forgiveness.

But suppose she did, and he refused? It might be best to wait a little, till she was stronger; till King James himself was safely home. There would be such universal celebration then that Lochiel would not be able to refuse her – had he not said himself that she would ride in glory to her King?

When Colette arrived with a bowl of *bouillon* and the news that Dr McKinnon was here to see her, Jenny gave her the first weak smile of many months.

'I have lit a candle to the Holy Mother,' beamed Colette, 'in thanks for your recovery. You have been ill for too long.'

'That girl looked after you well,' McKinnon told her a week later, as she sat at the table in a bedgown and cap, with a blanket over her knees and a dish of consommé in her hands. 'What do you intend to do with her when you go?'

'Do with her?' Jenny looked at the serious-faced young doctor in his powdered wig and sober clothes, too old by far for his years. 'I had not thought . . .'

'Then it is time you did. She has earned your consideration, Jenny, as has Daniel. Without them you would have been delivered to the poorhouse or the Sisters of Mercy.'

Jenny was sobered by his stern tone and a little ashamed. 'I took it for granted,' she said slowly, 'that where I go, they will go too.'

'To Scotland? Colette can speak no language but her own and Daniel was Finn's man, not yours. How will they fare in Glendessary?'

Jenny felt tears of weakness blur her eyes. 'I cannot think . . .

but I will, Calum, I promise you. When I am strong again and ready to go home.'

'And when will that be, Jenny?'

'Soon . . .'

But spring turned to summer and she made no move. For since the Treaty of Utrecht, ending the war, had been signed in April, things had changed. In exchange for the recognition of his grandson as Philip V of Spain, the French King had been obliged to recognize the Hanoverian succession: he could therefore no longer openly acknowledge James Stuart as the rightful King of England. James, to save Louis the embarrassment of ejecting him, had left for Bar-le-Duc in Lorraine. There was no point, therefore, in Jenny's returning yet to St Germain: and none at all in pursuing James to Bar-le-Duc. She would wait, as the world did, for James Stuart to make a move, and while she waited she would stay in Cambrai.

With the cessation of hostilities the garrison had been reduced to a mere holding force and the armies had dispersed, but the surgeon stayed on as garrison doctor, and, to Jenny anyway, purveyor of news.

Queen Anne was failing fast, and when she died there were many who would not welcome the chosen Hanoverian King George.

'James Stuart's preparations are made,' reported McKinnon. 'It cannot now be long. If not this summer, then the spring.'

'Will you go with him?'

'Perhaps. But I am a doctor, not a soldier. If I go it will be to mend the bodies men have broken, and I can do that here.'

Jenny looked around her at the high French bed with its wooden steps, the wooden walls and ill-fitting, rough-hewn windows, felt the hot French air, heavy with garlic and *pot-pourri*, and cried in sudden agitation, 'Do you never long to go *home*?'

'To the hills and the clean air? Aye, but a man needs more than the freedom of the mountains. He needs the freedom to worship his God in peace.'

Jenny had forgotten he was a Catholic, as James was. She herself felt no such deprivation, being free from dogma and content to worship God by whatever means were at hand – family prayers in Glendessary, candles and incense in a French church, or a song from the heart on an open hillside. But, remembering her suffering in the prison of Sacré Coeur, she could feel something of McKinnon's need to know himself free to pray as he chose.

'James will restore your church,' she said. 'All men will be free.'

McKinnon did not answer: if James had not been a Catholic, he would long ago have been declared Queen Anne's legitimate heir. But he refused steadfastly to abjure the Roman church: while McKinnon's admiration was increased because of this, his faith in James's future reign diminished. But he would not destroy Jenny's animation. It was too young a seedling and had taken too long to emerge from its winter darkness. He said only, 'When James is King of England, I will join him. Until then, I will treat my patients here, in France. And you, Miss Jenny, have spent too many months indoors. I order you a course of exercise, both on foot and on horseback.'

So as summer burned contentedly towards autumn, Jenny went abroad again by stages, at first on foot and then, when she was strong enough, on Oberon. Often McKinnon rode with her and it was soon reported throughout the garrison that McKinnon had taken up with Colonel O'Neil's woman. It was true, though not in the way they meant. Both were lonely: they enjoyed each other's company and never flagged for want of conversation. They talked of James, of Scotland, of the war newly over, of medical history and practice, of the Highlands and their childhood, of James and Scotland once again.

But it was not till the following summer that the long-awaited news arrived. Queen Anne of England was dead.

'Take Oberon,' said Jenny, her eyes large with pleading. 'I would like you to have him as a token of our friendship. I have little else to give.'

It was true, for in spite of Colette's miracles of husbanding, Finn's gold had alarmingly diminished.

'I need no token,' said McKinnon, 'and you must guard what wealth you have. When you reach Scotland the horse will be an adornment to the King's court, and should circumstances go against you he will fetch a good price.'

'How should they go against me? With James gathering forces for his triumphal return and the whole of Scotland, and most of England too, agog to welcome him? But you were aye a long-faced pessimist, Calum.' She looked at him in sudden silence, her eyes brimming with affection. 'Thank you for all you have done for me – and farewell.' She laid her hands on his shoulders and kissed him. 'May we meet again, in Scotland.'

But in St Germain, which they found aboil with rumour and expectation, Calum's pessimism was confirmed. Queen Anne was dead, but already George of Hanover had taken over. His Whig ministry angered the Tories, increased Jacobite fervour to boiling-point, yet still James had not gathered his forces to go

164

'home'. He had already lost the force of a *coup d'état* and if he waited any longer, winter would make invasion impossible.

The delay had other, more immediate effects: Jenny's purse was emptying fast and Colette determined to speak out.

'Madame, Daniel and I wish to marry. We have served you well,' she hurried on before she could be interrupted, 'and faithfully, but we do not wish to go to your Scotland. My home is Ste Marie de la Roche and Daniel's home is with me.'

Jenny stared at Colette in astonishment, seeing the small, pink-cheeked and pale-haired girl as if for the first time.

'But what will you do?' At home, no servant ever left. 'What will I do?'

'You will go home,' said Colette, 'and so will I.'

The girl's unconscious eloquence moved Jenny's heart to remorse. 'Of course, Colette, and I am sorry. I know what it is to be homesick. You shall be married at once . . . Now, leave me, while I think how best it can be done. And tell Daniel to ask again for news.'

Jenny locked the door of her room, took the key from its ribbon at her neck and opened Finn's trunk. Dear Finn. He had left her all he had – his rings, his clothes, his prize money from the wars, his horse. She would give his fine linen shirt to Daniel, her own yellow damask gown to Colette . . . and they must also have gold. But the leather pouch was disconcertingly light. Her lodgings here were too costly: if Daniel brought no better news from St Germain, they would take the next coach south for Colette's Ste Marie de la Roche and the post-horse inn where she had first stayed with Finn.

It was strange to be back in Ste Marie de la Roche, to see the same cantankerous *aubergiste* and his daughter, Marianne; more than strange to be shown to the same bedchamber and to sleep in the same bed, alone. But Jenny was accustomed now to loneliness and saw this retracing of the steps as a necessary path. Here she had taken up a new life with Finn: that life done, she would start out from the same place on a fresh path home.

Logically, she thought in the grey, small hours, she should return to Sacré Coeur: but once there she would not be allowed again to escape, certainly not to retrace her girlhood journey home to Edinburgh. Sacré Coeur had been a cul-de-sac, and one she would be wise on her return journey to avoid.

Meanwhile the grey winter dragged on through mist and rain, through casement-clattering blizzard and chimney-howling gale, and the price of oats grew steadily higher in spite of Jenny's spirited argument and Daniel's haggling on her behalf. He was well placed now, on his father-in-law's tenant strip of land, to find out unexpected sources of supply, but the winter was too long and spring too late in coming. When it came in a sparkle of April sun on dew, green buds bursting on chestnut branch and green life spreading through winter fields, it brought swallow and song-thrush and a host of busy, nesting birds, but it brought no news from Bar-le-Duc of James's march. And though the forage they needed would soon be plentiful, the damage was done.

'Daniel, I want you to sell Oberon for me.' Jenny's voice was firm but veiled with sadness, and the man who had come in answer to her summons felt his heart twist with compassion and shame. His master Finn O'Neil had bade him care for her, yet she had freed him willingly to marry his Colette. She had given them more than he had hoped for, had sent them to their cottage with her blessing. Yet his conscience troubled him. The girl could not be much past twenty and already she was widowed, homeless, perhaps destitute. Why else should she require him to sell the horse he knew she had planned to take to Scotland with her, to ride to greet her King? 'If there is anything that I can do, Miss ... ' he began, uncertain how to circumvent her pride. 'Colette and I have a room with a fire and a good feather-bed. We will gladly...'

'Thank you,' interrupted Jenny, and her head lifted imperceptibly. 'I will remember your kindness should I ever have the need. But I sent for you to find a buyer for Oberon. He is a campaign horse. He needs a soldier or a battle. We are on the post-route here and many gentlemen pass through *en route* for Paris or the south. But the buyer must be a soldier, understand, of proven valour.'

Daniel understood. He looked at Miss Jenny with admiration, remembering the days spent in the royal hunting forests, the old, soft-leaved, dark-crowding trees, and Miss Jenny, splendid in hunting-green, on Oberon's back. He remembered her trotting brisk and pink-cheeked through the chequered plane-trees, their trunks pale-blotched as an artist's palette, their leaves crisped golden at the edges with the approach of autumn. He saw her in the snow, dark-haired on a white horse, in a solitary landscape, and his heart stirred with long-forgotten poetry. But all he said was, 'Are you sure, Miss?'

'I am sure.' Control slipped and her eyes were suddenly pleading. 'But you must find the right man, Daniel, a good man, like the Colonel, brave and kind.'

'I'd find one for Miss Jenny, too,' reported Daniel later to

Colette, 'if it were in my power. She's a lonely lass and needs a man.'

'She will find her man at home, Daniel, in Scotland,' said Colette. 'I know it.'

'If she ever gets there. It looks as if that King of hers will never shift, and she will not go without him.'

'He will shift, *chéri*. A Quaker lady told Queen Beatrice herself on the King's own birthday. "Thy son will return to England," she said. The Holy Spirit told her.'

'Then let the Holy Spirit tell her son to hurry up!' retorted Daniel, and laughed at his wife's scandalized expression. But the waiting was not a subject for laughter: Daniel determined to find the best possible price for Miss Jenny's horse lest she, like many others, be ruined in her dilatory monarch's cause.

'There is a visitor below to speak with you, Madame.' Marianne stood in the open doorway on a morning in early May. 'He says that Daniel told him to call here to see Madame about a horse. Daniel himself is working in the fields and cannot come, but he sent word by Monsieur that all is as you wished.'

Jenny looked at Marianne in alarm. 'What is this monsieur like, Marianne? Is he a noble gentleman? A fine soldier like Colonel O'Neil?' For Marianne remembered the Colonel, and who would not, thought Jenny wistfully. 'Tell me honestly, Marianne. Is he a man of stature? Is he the Colonel's equal?'

'*Mais oui*, Madame. They say he is a hero. He was carried from the field of Malplaquet unconscious after leading a charge with a bayonet blade in his leg. He was wounded at Béthune, and Marshal Villars himself commended him. I think he is a fine gentleman, Madame, and will look well on Madame's Oberon. He is a nobleman,' she finished as Miss Jenny turned her back and made no answer, 'and rich.'

Daniel had done as she asked. The buyer was ideal. Yet how could she part with Oberon so abruptly? 'Tell him ...' she began.

'He is on his way south, Madame,' interrupted Marianne, anticipating objection. 'He stays only a few hours in Sainte Marie. You will not find a better, and he will pay ready gold.'

Jenny thought of her empty purse, Finn's much depleted trunk, the cost of stabling and forage, the money owed ... 'Tell him I will come.'

Later, as she stood alone in her room, mourning the loss of her last link with Finn, her fingers traced the crosses he had made on the table-top on that night so long ago, when Finn O'Neil, Colonel in the Irish Regiment, had explained the Flanders campaign to a runaway novice ... Mauberge, Condé, Douai. There was no cross for Béthune or Cambrai ....

She stood a long time, motionless, remembering. Then with regathered courage turned her eyes towards the future and St Germain. Surely the news must come soon?

'There are to be three Risings, to happen simultaneously.' Jenny's eyes were brilliant as Daniel spoke. 'In the south-west of England, in Northumberland, and in Scotland. The port of Bristol will be captured, Plymouth too. Your King will land on the south coast and sweep from there to London.'

'And Berwick?' Jenny knew how much her King relied upon his half-brother's support.

'He is a Frenchman now, a subject of King Louis. He may not support King Louis' enemies or leave his country without permission.'

'And since when has James been Louis' enemy?'

'Since Utrecht,' said Daniel, and shrugged. Jenny was silenced. That treaty might have ended the Flanders wars which had been a drain on men and land for too many years, but it had also ended French support for the Stuarts. Could they really win without it? For the first time Jenny felt a tremor of doubt.

Beyond the village, fields newly green were bright as velvet between hedgerows misted with may blossom and ragged robin. Orchards were a froth of milk and raspberry sherbet, and the air which rose warm from the valley was scented with blossom: apple, plum and peach. That small, contented landscape was not her country: why should it concern itself with James Stuart? Jenny felt suddenly isolated, an observer in a foreign land, for she wanted nothing now but to speak her own language again, among her own kind. She stayed only for her King.

But James kept more than Jenny Cameron waiting while he tried to enlist Berwick's support, only to decide too late to undertake the venture without him: for by then the seas were treacherous.

And not only the seas. Somehow the plotters in England had been betrayed and many of the leaders arrested. When Mar raised James's royal standard on a gusty day in early September, 1715, the Highlands rose to back him to a man; but south of the Tay it was a different story – for Argyll's Goverment forces blocked their passage and in November the battle of Sherrifmuir confirmed the stalemate.

'Why does James not *move*?' cried Jenny, exasperated beyond endurance by the news. There would be Cameron men in Mar's army, Cameron men on the battlefield of Sherrifmuir, Cameron men dying, wounded, maimed . . . her own brother, perhaps, her uncle, Hugh . . . Why was she not with them where she belonged?

Anxiety was with her daily now, as her resources dwindled, and with them her hope. For the first time in her life she felt the fear of starvation, of homelessness, of the shame of destitution. If the Rising succeeded, all would be well. If not . . .

She would take work: teach English, write letters or accounts, 'model' young ladies as her aunt in Edinburgh had done. At the thought, Jenny smiled in rueful self-mockery. For who would employ her? A *soi-disant* widow, a foreigner without wealth or influence? If she had land or livestock she could have managed somehow, but she had nothing.

'If James Stuart fails,' she told herself with sober clarity, 'then I am truly destitute.'

In the freedom of her Highland childhood the possibility of destitution had never threatened. But here she must pay Marianne's cupidinous father whose demands increased as the soldiers disappeared; or go to Daniel and Colette who had work enough to do to feed themselves. Means forbade the one course, honour the other. 'What am I to do?' she asked over and over, with mounting panic, and knew herself trapped.

'You must go back to St Germain, Madame,' urged Marianne, 'and ask help from Queen Beatrice. As a faithful supporter of her son's cause, it would be no dishonour.'

James had sailed at last for the kingdom he had never seen and, as Jenny waited superstitiously for confirmation of his victory before rushing home in triumph, had turned tail again and fled. In his deserted kingdom, his loyal leaders were arrested, attainted, condemned . . . It was a shame too deep to bear. Jenny could not meet Marianne's eyes as she answered, 'No.' She would not join that pitiful jumble of parasites, some genuine enough, some paupers, who swarmed the once-grand corridors of St Germain.

'But you must, Madame,' insisted Marianne. 'Papa will allow you to stay no longer. He says he has room for three in your *chambre* and there will be many fugitives . . .'

'I will not beg at St Germain,' said Jenny quietly. For there was one last refuge. With a shudder of cold dread she remembered Sacré Coeur . . . But if I cannot go home, she thought with desolation, there is no help . . . 'Fetch me paper, Marianne, and a quill. I wish to write a letter.'

'*Sister Cecilia*,' she would begin, '*I humbly beg forgiveness for my past misdoings . . .*'

From the yard below her window came the noise of the *diligence* from Paris, the usual clatter of wheels and whinnying of horses, the usual shouts for ostler and servant, the usual grumbling complaint as travelling trunks were manhandled from the roof of the vehicle, and ladies handed carefully to the muddy ground. The air was suddenly thick with the scent of damp wool, sweating horses, tobacco-smoke and dust. But Jenny heard nothing, for the scent of rain-drenched woollen cloth reminded her with stabbing intensity of the hillside above Glendessary, of herself and Hugh lying in the frost-stiffened heather under a blissful, empty sky, and in the far valley a solitary stirk. She would not see Glendessary again.

When Marianne burst into the room, she held out her hand for the paper without turning her head, lest the girl see her face.

'Madame! Madame! There are the gentlemen *Écossais au dessous* and oh Madame!' She clasped her hands together in tearful delight. '*Le bon Dieu* has answered all my prayers for you! One of the *Écossais* is a Monsieur Cameron!'

Part 3
Scotland

1

Accordingly she set out and upon her arrival, her brother received her
with abundance of Tenderness. She then managed the Affairs of her
Brother's House, and behaved with great Prudence and Decency,
insomuch that she had in a small Time gained the Affections of all the
Gentry in the Neighbourhood; she had naturally a flow of Wit, and a
solid Judgement, without that Mixture of Malice, or that satirical turn
which Wits generally have . . .

Hugh Cameron stood on the wharf at Leith and stared in dread
across the glittering waters at the packet-boat from France, its
sails billowing in the fresh sea wind, the spray a white cascade
at its bow.

It must be ten years since he had seen her, but that scene
under her aunt's window in Edinburgh High Street was
preserved in every detail, clear-cut, bright-coloured, complete
as the miniature which hung beside the fireplace in Glendessary. His *creach* . . . his vows . . . their laughter together . . . their
embrace. What would she say to him?

But it was long ago. She would have changed: forgotten him.
Whereas he could not forget. He knew now that the fault was
not his, but although he had been tricked he should not have
allowed it, should have held firm somehow, gone to Edinburgh
to fetch her, run away with her . . . anything except the
humiliation of what he had done. He had failed her, betrayed
her, broken his vow. How could her meet her eyes, which were
always clear as a mountain pool with truth, and say, 'Welcome
home, Miss Jenny,' as Alan, Laird of Glendessary, had bid him
do?

The vessel was close in, now, to the shore. He heard the rush
of lowering canvas, the clatter of boom and winch, the shouts
of men. A rope snaked through the air and slapped, spray-wet,
on to the quay-side. Someone twisted it expertly round a bollard
and the boat creaked closer till it thudded against coiled rope
and settled to a dipping halt. Oh God, what could he say to her?
What would she do?

Jenny saw him long before they berthed, standing head and

shoulders above the rest of them. She would have known him anywhere: that huge, well-ordered strength, that corn-gold hair. As the vessel drew in towards the shore she saw that he was kilted in full Highland splendour of plaid and broadsword, brass shoulder-boss, jewelled dirk . . . She had forgotten how imposing a Highlander could look. Hugh had been just seventeen when she last saw him, with a boy's slimness and unschooled strength. At twenty-six he was bearded, square-built, powerful, and, from the set of his head, proud as she was. He should not see the hurt he had caused her all those years ago and which the sight of him brought rushing back, though not with the agony it had caused her once. She felt only sadness now, as of a distant but remembered pain . . . a mere *tristesse* beside her grief for Finn. And Hugh's betrayal was a peccadillo set against James Stuart's ignominious flight from his own kingdom, his own and loyal subjects.

I am glad to see Hugh, she reflected, her eyes on his face as the sail cascaded to the deck behind her in a rush of ropes and shouting. But too many things have come between us.

She looked away from him, then, to the hills which filled the horizon: to the north misted, heath-wrapped, some snow-whitened; to the west, purpled with distance and a dying sun. Seagulls wheeled and cried, swooping low over the water in the boat's wake; sunset tinted the waves with pink and watered gold. Behind her, the firth stretched limitless, already darkening towards the horizon where it met the German sea; ahead of her, a calm blade parted the hills with tinted silver on which small boats bobbed, harmless, trailing lobster-pots or lines. Jenny felt her heart fill with an emotion which blocked her throat and stung her eyes with tears. When she stepped from the gangplank to where Hugh Cameron waited, she looked up at him with brimming eyes and said only, 'It is good to be home.'

'How is Alan?' she asked as they rode slowly along the estuary in the evening light, the gillies following with her small luggage – Finn's campaign trunk and one valise. They were to stay the night at Cramond and begin the journey north the following day.

'Well enough. Sir Ewen plans for him to marry.'

Jenny remembered her Aunt Cameron's warnings that she would be a tolerated poor relation in her brother's household; Uncle Ewen's that Glendessary would never be hers; and her own far-off dream of ranging free in the hills with Hugh. Aunt Cameron, like her mother, was dead, John Cameron had told her; his father, Sir Ewen, was old and ailing. John himself was

174

attainted and could never return to Scotland – his son Donald would be chief in his stead when old Sir Ewen died. As for Hugh ... She studied his profile, searching for the faith and eagerness which had been there in childhood, but saw only a stranger, awkward in her company.

'How is Sir Ewen?' she asked when they had ridden a while and still he had not spoken.

'Weak – and sorely disappointed by the failure of the Rising.'

'As are we all. Did you ... did many Cameron men go?'

'I was at Sherrifmuir where my father fell.' He did not elaborate and she did not ask. John Cameron, Younger of Lochiel, had told her of Alexander's death and of other Camerons killed in the abortive Rising of '15.

'And Alan is alone at Glendessary?'

'Aye. Your brother Ewen is at Leiden at the University; your brother John in Aberdeen. We rarely see them. And since your mother's death, your sisters have not returned.' Catherine and Meg, Uncle John had told her, were both married and had moved south, the one to Perthshire, the other to Dumfries.

'How is your wife?' she persevered, when they had journeyed on a while in silence.

'Well.' Hugh could not look at her.

'You have children?'

'Four.' That too was a betrayal. With shame, Hugh recalled the futile vow of his wedding night. It had been broken soon enough. He remembered his frenzied journey to Edinburgh when he realized how he had been duped and Jenny betrayed, his murderous, primitive retribution, and the anger which had been with him still, unassuaged, as he crashed home to the turf-roofed shieling and Bess. She had been feeding their baby son at the breast and her shift was disarranged ... he had killed a man and lost a woman, and the grief in him cried out for solace. After that, there had been no going back; and with Miss Jenny gone, what did it matter?

'Are you happy?' she was asking.

He turned his head, then looked away as he saw in her eyes a sadness which echoed his own. He thought of Bess who loved him, of his children Ewen, Donald, Isobel and little Jean.

'I have been ... content.'

'And I.' They looked at each other briefly as the past unrolled for each of them and furled again, still separate. 'She has loved a man,' thought Hugh with a jealousy which almost choked him. 'I am forgotten...'

'He has a wife and children, and is content.' It made her lonely...

175

As they left Edinburgh behind them and moved northward, Jenny felt the years slough away. The hills were unchanged as she had known they would be, and though the taverns were as dirty, the food as bad, with rancid butter and ill-cooked game, what did it matter when she was going home?

They travelled now in single file, sometimes Hugh in front of the column, sometimes Jenny, the small, sure-footed garrons, linked by tail and rope together, following, the baggage in creels across their backs. They saw deer and ptarmigan, plover and skylark, half-naked Highland children wild as foxes, smelt the sweet smoke of peat fires on a frosted evening; and with every step that drew them closer to Arkaig, Jenny felt mounting joy and apprehension. Ahead of them rose the distant fastnesses of Argyll and Glen Spean, Glenfinnan, Glendessary . . . There was snow on Ben Nevis and more in the gullie as they approached Loch Linnhe. At a flooded ford Hugh carried her across the green-frothed, icy water, though she would gladly have ridden her swimming horse to avoid the contact of his body. But he held himself aloof, strong arms stiff with rectitude, face carefully blank. He might have been carrying her mother – or a bale of valuable cloth. Jenny would have laughed had she not felt close to tears.

'Hugh,' she said as the path narrowed through a steep ravine and the gillies fell behind, 'my reputation, I hope, is not entirely bad. I know you have a wife whom you love. I do not, in spite of any tales you might have heard, range over the countryside seeking men to seduce. I will not compromise you, so you need not behave like a terrified virgin in a villain's evil grip.'

He had forgotten how outspoken and shrewd her wit could be, but she mistook his expression. 'I see I have offended you. I am sorry. I merely wanted you to know that the past is forgotten between us, except for the pleasure we took in each other's company. I hope we may do so still?'

When he did not answer, but kept his grey eyes on the path ahead, she added, as if to herself, 'I have known happiness.'

He looked at her then, and as swiftly away, while the jealousy lacerated his heart. If it had been in his power to undo the wrong he had done her, he would have done so gladly. As it was, he must see her every day, knowing her unattainable, knowing she thought him happy. It was a punishment apt enough for his crime.

'Be cheerful, Hugh,' she was saying, 'or are you on the look-out for raiders? You certainly look fierce enough to terrify an army of cattle thieves,' but her words only turned the knife of memory deeper. 'Tell me about Glendessary,' she persisted, determined they should be friends. 'Are the Macdonalds as big

176

a set of thieves as ever? Who is tacksman in Fassefern, and are the salmon good this year?'

Haltingly, he told her, until her enthusiasm and his own knowledge wore down the awkwardness between them and they rode side by side as wary but remembered friends. The barrier, however, remained.

Then they were in the woods below Loch Lochy, a tiny path narrow as a ship's plank, ridged with tree roots, cushioned with oak leaves and a dozen kinds of moss. At her right was the river, narrow and powerful between high banks, its waters churning in thunderous green-tinted arabesques. Autumn leaves burned on the trees and again under her feet in a fire of tangled bracken stems. Somewhere close at hand she heard the roar of a cataract and knew it to be Cia-aig. Her heart beat fast with sudden fear. They were almost at Achnacarry where she must appear, a suppliant, before her chief.

Fear, however, vanished when she saw the old, familiar face, the thick grey beard and thicker hair, the black, jet-sparkling eyes.

'Uncle Ewen!' She ran to him as she had done in childhood, throwing her arms around his neck and kissing him over and over. 'It is good to be home.'

The old man's eyes were moist as he held her at arm's length and looked her over. 'You have worn well, lass.'

'And you, Uncle.' It was true. Although approaching ninety, Lochiel held himself erect as ever, eyes undimmed. She had felt the frailty of ageing bone under his rough-spun coat but it did not show, and when he laughed, as he did now, his voice had almost its old volume.

'I thought I'd seen the last of you, lass, long ago.'

There was a hint of pain below the teasing and Jenny dropped her eyes. 'I am sorry, Uncle, for my past misdoings. I am come before my chief to ask forgiveness.'

'Which you have, Jenny, and freely. You were aye the jewel o' the clan.' He took her hand and pulled her to the fire. 'Fetch brandy, woman!' he ordered as his wife appeared, hands fluttering, in the doorway.

'Not for me, Uncle,' said Jenny. 'Wine if you have it, but not brandy.'

'You have picked up fancy ways in foreign parts, have ye?' He looked at her shrewdly, then his face grew serious. 'Aye, lass, there's a deal o' pain in the world, which no amount o' brandy can cure. You shall have your wine. Well don't stand there, woman: fetch it! I knew you would come,' he continued, taking

177

her hand and looking into her eyes with a gaze she remembered from long ago. 'I see things, lass. They tell me I am wandering, but it is not so. I saw you, Jenny, long ago riding to our King, and it *will be*.'

'But James has failed, Uncle.' She spoke with gentleness for his age. 'Those who supported him have lost their lands, their freedom, their country. Had you not had the foresight long ago to make over your inheritance to Donald, you would have lost yours – or Uncle John would have lost it for you.'

'Aye, lass. But I *had* the foresight. And I tell you, Jenny, that there will come a time, though I may not live to see it. Where is your haunchman?' he asked, with apparent dislocation.

'Hugh Cameron? With the horses below. He is waiting to take me home, for I may not stay long if we are to reach Glendessary by nightfall.'

'I see him, too, Jenny, at your side. You are made to be together. We did you wrong.'

Jenny was silent, disturbed by the old man's words. He was old. She had let appearances deceive her into thinking his mind still strong as his body. But he shook his head as if to clear it and said, 'Pour the wine, lass, and tell me of France. What plans have John and our King's party for a return? I hope they will tell young Jamie to bring more men with him next time, and money.'

Jenny heard the door open behind her, then footsteps on the wooden floor. 'Hugh! take a glass with me, boy, for your journey. And guard the lassie well.'

The old chief stood with his back to the hearth, the firelight flickering over oil paintings, tapestries, and polished floor, and raised his glass to the young pair before him: Jenny with her dark eyes and darker hair, her proud bearing and splendid figure, and the lad Hugh, head and shoulders taller, with hair and beard as thick as Sir Ewen's own and the colour of ripened corn. 'Bless you both. May you prosper,' he said quietly, 'and walk together in peace.'

Neither of them spoke as they rode out of Achnacarry for the last stretch of the journey. Lochiel had blessed them as if in marriage: both knew that could never be.

Wind whipped the surface of Loch Arkaig into a thousand wings of foam as they threaded the shore path homeward, Glendessary a dark block against the evening sky. Then as they drew closer they heard the piping, lights glowed high in the windows, more bobbed like a string of glowworms towards them along the shore, while the piping swelled to an exultant glory which echoed jubilant from crag and gully and brought the tears to Jenny's eyes. Her brother Alan was welcoming her home.

Alan welcomed her, as she had known he would, with uncritical affection. He was a gentle, diffident, scholarly man, more fitted to the library than the office, and soon began to hand over estate matters to Jenny and to Hugh. She made out the accounts, received the rents, disposed of the tacksmen's various pastures, ordered stores, kept the cellars and the meal-kists stocked.

Hugh saw to the cattle, buying stirk or branded bull, selling the same, or directing drovers for their annual journey south to Kelso, Edinburgh or Stirling. They made a good team, though unyoked and taking care never to be alone together, never to touch hands. The barrier between them remained unbroken, each conscious of it with a quivering, raw-nerved awareness which made them unnatural in each other's company. It was a barrier founded on deep-rooted misconceptions: Jenny believed he had married for love and loved Bess still; Hugh believed she had rejected him years ago, and knew from her face that she had loved another man completely, that she mourned whoever it was even now as she rode beside him in her beloved Glendessary. The past ten years were a bottomless ravine with Jenny on one side, Hugh on the other, across which they called occasionally for necessary information: and each of them was lonely.

A year after Jenny's return, her brother Alan married: Isobel MacLean, a cousin of Lochiel's wife. Lochiel himself had arranged it, and Jenny liked her well enough. She was a pale girl, unobtrusive, content to leave the ordering of the household to her husband's sister whom she regarded with a mixture of reverence and fear. She and Alan were well suited, both undemanding and unassertive. Jenny tolerated them and they her: as their lives took diverging paths there was little friction between them. A daughter was born, then another, and both parents were absorbed in their growing family. Alan abandoned all pretence of management, leaving everything entirely in Jenny's hands. She assumed the responsibility willingly. Inevitably it meant that she and Hugh must spend more time together, but she treated him now as a colonel might treat a trusted officer: any urge to confidence was checked by protocol.

Besides, she had young Ewen. Ewen was Hugh's eldest son, a boy of eight when she returned to Glendessary and soon her chosen companion, as she was his. Under the pretext of teaching him French, which Jenny spoke now like a second tongue, and English, for like his father Ewen spoke the Gaelic, she spent long hours in his company, and though his mother disapproved with a brooding jealousy, she could not logically complain. There was no tutor yet at Glendessary, the school at Kilmalie too distant to attempt except in summer – and in summer there were better things to do.

Jenny was a good teacher, if unorthodox. Remembering the years of frustrated boredom in her own childhood schoolroom, she sat the boy on horseback and took him with her to the hills where they spoke only French – until the lure of moorcock or speeding hare diverted them. Eventually Ewen's brother Donald joined them, but it was Ewen Jenny loved, for he was his father in miniature, with the same grey, far-seeing eyes and golden hair, the same strong limbs.

Hugh watched them together with a mingled sadness and pride: Ewen should have been her son.

In the winter of 1719 that other Ewen, seventeenth chief of the Camerons, died at Achnacarry. His son John became chief in his stead, but as John was forfeited and exiled, living alternately in Paris or with James in Rome, his son Donald assumed leadership in his place, and slowly the pattern of life in Lochaber began to change. Donald had new ideas about estate management, his clansmen's education and welfare. He planted trees. As for the age-old custom of cattle-lifting, he dubbed it theft and forbade its practice, extending his interdict to cover all who harboured thieves or received the goods they stole. The *creach* was to be a thing of the past.

Perhaps it is as well, thought Jenny, staring out of her window as she often did when the house was sleeping, the candles doused. A *creach* can cause too much pain. Low at the loch's edge was the dark bulk of the home farm. A light burnt faint in one of the windows. Hugh must be working late. She stood there a long time, watching moonlight on water, the movement of silent cloud, a flurry of wind on the loch's surface, till that distant light was extinguished – and she went to bed.

So the years fell into a pattern and passed, uneventfully, but in a kind of peace . . .

A son was born to Alan and Isobel, and the heir to Glendessary was welcomed with as much rejoicing as the new heir to the Scottish throne in Rome, little Charles Edward, Prince of Wales, born to the exiled James and his wife Clementina.

With the coming of the news came a new hope. Jacobite loyalties were strained almost to breaking point by the failure of yet another attempt by the unfortunate James. His grandiose plans of a two-pronged invasion, backed by Spain and aided by an Irish diversion, had been reduced by the weather and a string of misfortunes to a tiny band of Jacobites holed up in the castle of Eilean Donan in Loch Alsh, to be driven out and trounced by overwhelming Government troops.

Government troops were now increasingly in evidence, even in the hitherto impenetrable fastnesses of Lochaber, for General Wade had begun his road-building designed to open up the Highlands and destroy their centuries-old seclusion. But with a new Stuart heir, disheartened Jacobites realized that all hope had not, after all, died with the failure of the '19. As she looked down at the sleeping face of her nephew, John, Jenny felt a long-dormant excitement stir again to life. Sir Ewen had not lived to see the restoration of his King; she might not live to see it either; but here in the cradle lay someone who might – and in another cradle in Rome lay the infant who might one day be that King.

'We need money,' she announced to Alan as they sat together in the drawing-room one evening in early autumn. Isobel, tired out with nursing, had retired early to bed.

'Why?' asked Alan without emerging from his book: a treatise on the new husbandry which cousin Donald at Achnacarry had lent him. It held some interesting ideas.

'To buy arms.'

This time Alan did look up, with a shock of surprise. 'You would be better employed buying trees,' he said, 'as Lochiel has done. He plans a splendid avenue one day, he tells me, in the Dark Mile.'

'Then it will be a fitting road by which to welcome our King! Listen, Alan. There is talk in London of forbidding Highlanders to carry arms: it is to be their way of ensuring there will be no Rising. Can you not see, when those roads which are already started in Inverness reach south into Lochaber, we will be vulnerable to every law they choose to make? We cannot stop the roads, but we can lay in a supply of arms against the day we are called to use them. I was checking only yesterday and find we have nothing but a few fowling-pieces, a pistol or two, and a rusted matchlock musket. A matchlock! They threw those out of Marlborough's army ten years ago!'

'We need no arms, Jenny. If laws are made, we must obey them. We must learn, as others do, to live peaceably with our neighbours.'

'Of course, Alan, but it is not domestic law I talk of! This law forbidding Highlanders to carry arms is not to prevent us shooting each other – it is to prevent us rising to support our King. Oh, I know James Stuart is become a sombre, retiring man more concerned now with his soul's salvation than his throne –

understandably so, with the deaths of so many men on his conscience – but he has a son as you have, a fine, promising boy well fitted to be Scotland's King. One day Prince Charles will come to claim that throne. I know it as surely as Uncle Ewen knew it. And when he comes, we must be ready, Alan.'

'I will buy no arms, Jenny, for there will be no Rising. The Hanoverian succession is now assured, accepted by Parliament and the people. We have stability. One day, we will also have prosperity.'

Jenny bit her lip in frustration, then in thought. When she spoke again, it was on a different tack. 'Alan, if you will not buy arms for our King, then at least do so for your own protection. Have you thought what riff-raff may come into our country once that road is built? Broken men, thieves, marauders who could rape and kill and burn to their heart's content if we had not the means to stop them? Think of Isobel, of your daughters, and of wee Johnny. You said yourself that prosperity is not yet in sight. Until it is, we are vulnerable – and we have a solitary matchlock between us.'

'Do you really think the road might bring us trouble?' Alan looked suddenly unsure, vulnerable as in childhood, seeking her reassurance.

'I do. In the past our isolation has protected us. That gone, we are at the mercy of every thief in Scotland.' As still he hesitated, she went on, 'Where is the harm? I mean only to buy guns enough for Glendessary, not to arm a regiment.'

'Then you must have money.' Jenny was right. He must protect his little family. 'The drovers will go south in a few weeks. There will be money enough then.'

'And that gone, how would we pay for the winter oatmeal and salt? For the wine and the servants' ale? Remember, we must lay in stores for five months at the least.'

'I could ask Lochiel,' faltered Alan, 'but I know he is straitened, as are most.' The abortive Rising had left many a family poor that had once been wealthy.

'There is cousin Campbell,' said Jenny slowly. 'I remember our father talking of him – a prosperous merchant in Edinburgh. You must go to him and ask. Go with the drovers at the end of the month, and take Hugh with you.'

Reluctantly, Alan agreed, and Jenny drew up a careful document which listed all the provisions he must make against exorbitant interest or the pledging of irretrievable land. But as the day of departure approached, Isobel took to her bed with a fever brought on, Jenny was sure, by nervous apprehension of her husband's absence. She begged Alan not to go.

'You must go in my stead, Jenny. Hugh will guard you on the

journey and cousin Campbell will not refuse *you*. Please, Jenny, for all our sakes?'

Jenny viewed the prospect of revisiting Edinburgh, and in Hugh's company, with dread, but unaccountably Hugh refused to go. Jenny took it as one more indication that he shunned her company and offered to take Ewen instead. He was sixteen now, tall as his father and eager to make his first journey out of Glendessary. The decision taken, Jenny looked forward to the visit with a mixture of excitement and apprehension, as the cattle collected, firm-fleshed and restless.

'Be alert for ambush, Ewen, as you go through Macdonald country,' warned Hugh at the leave-taking. 'Summer-fattened beasts on the move are a favourite target.'

'I will, father. No Macdonald will get past these.' Ewen was proudly armed with broadsword and dirk, and a pistol at his belt.

'You'd best carry a pistol too, Miss Jenny,' said Hugh and handed her a weapon, flinching as he always did at the rare touch of her hand. She was used to it now, but lost as to how to handle a relationship as opaque and dangerous as Hugh's was with her. That it was dangerous, they both knew: Hugh's flinching from all touch confirmed it and Jenny dared make no move towards closer reconciliation lest she loose an uncontrollable torrent – of what, she did not know. It made an uneasiness between them which she had learnt to tolerate as she might a persistent pebble in a shoe. But she faced him calmly enough. 'Thank you, Hugh. Take care of Glendessary for me till my return.'

'Good weather ...' Jenny touched heels to her mountain garron and the column moved round the lochside and away to join the drove-road south.

It was like campaigning days returned, except that there were no cannon, no armed soldiers, no trundling, ungainly carts – and no Finn. Instead, Hugh Cameron's son led the column of lowing, meandering cattle, with its outriders and professional drovers; or, fearing raids on any stragglers, brought up the rear. Jenny took turns with Ewen at the head of the column or at the rear, and was as happy as she had learnt to be in her years at Glendessary.

Then, as on that day so many years ago when she had first ridden south with her father, the outline of Edinburgh Castle rose on the skyline, the shimmering vastness of the Firth of Forth lay at her feet.

Their business was soon done, the money borrowed, hidden

183

away in a pouch at her waist, the pledges signed. By the third day arrangements had been made with a discreet agent to have the goods they required ready for collection by sundown. When she joined Ewen where he waited for her at the entrance to Campbell's Close, they were earlier than she had anticipated.

'I have an urge to visit the haunts of my wicked childhood,' she said. 'Let us walk a little in the High Street until the drovers' work is done and the stores I ordered safely packed away. You can buy ribbons for your mother while I buy comfits for my nieces. And sugar-plums for Johnny, who likes them inordinately well – I caught him with his fingers in the jar only last week. See, there is my aunt's old house,' she hurried on, 'with Sir Patrick's up above. I wonder what became of him? He had a daughter, Charlotte, a pretty girl.' She talked now deliberately to keep memory at bay, but later, their errands done, it was memory that made her cry out in astonishment as a sedan chair brushed past them, its liveried bearers red-faced and panting, its velvet curtains swaying like a galleon's canvas in full sail. '*Wattie!*'

A hand looped back the curtains to reveal a small, alert face sandwiched between a monumental powdered wig and a pile of ruffles unsuccessfully secured with a jewel the size of a pigeon's egg.

'It canna' be Miss Jenny?'

'It can and is!' cried Jenny, laughing, as the chair was set down and the one-time caddie stepped carefully out on to the cassies.

'Baillie Tom Watt, Madam, at your service,' and he bowed. Then he saw Ewen and his swaggering confidence evaporated on the instant with an expression close to fear.

'Whatever is the matter, Wattie? You remember Hugh Cameron who came once to my aunt's house with a young bull? This is his son.'

'His *son*?' Wattie laughed nervously and drew down the front of his embroidered waistcoat. 'My regards to your father, young man.'

'Though your father would not recognize Wattie now, Ewen,' smiled Jenny, noting the fine stockings, the buckled shoes, the braided cuffs and lapels of his coat, 'for he never dressed then in yellow satin with enough rings to furnish a goldsmith's shop. You have done well for a barefoot caddie with cheek enough for three. But take a drink with us, Wattie, and talk of old times.'

'I will be honoured, Miss Jenny, if you will take wine and sustenance in my own house,' and he stepped back to indicate the doorway behind them.

'Surely you do not live here?' The 'Land' he indicated was among the most prosperous in Edinburgh.

'Aye – and on the best floor.'

'Then we will be delighted, will we not, Ewen? If only to see how well the caddie who slept on my aunt's seventh step has done for himself. It *was* the seventh, wasn't it?' she asked later as they sat in Wattie's parlour, having duly admired the table, the panelling, and the oil portrait of Wattie himself done, he assured them, by the best Edinburgh artist of the day.

But in spite of Jenny's open admiration of all he had achieved – two goldsmith's shops and half a dozen apprentices, as well as a seat on the Town Council – Wattie did not seem at ease. His eyes kept moving to Ewen and quickly away again. To bridge the awkwardness when conversation flagged, Jenny said, 'Do you remember Andrew? I wonder what became of him.'

Again the glance at Ewen as the Baillie said, through dry lips, 'No one knows. He just . . . disappeared.'

Ewen stood up, took a step towards him, and in spite of his wealth, his position and his damning knowledge, Wattie cringed. But Ewen said only, 'You will excuse me, I have business to attend to. I will call back for you, Miss Jenny, in an hour.'

'He is too big, that haunchman of yours,' said Wattie with a nervous laugh. 'As his father was. I would not like to meet either of them alone on a dark night after curfew.' He remembered that scene by the nor' loch and shuddered. Then with returning confidence, he added, 'Hugh loved *you* once, and wasn't the Neb mad to see it!'

'Once . . . But *Baillie* Watt!' Jenny hurried on, savouring the absurdity. 'Who would have thought it.'

'I told you so, Miss Jenny, years ago, when you sneaked on to the stair to gossip.'

'And not always only for that, I fear!' With Hugh's son gone they fell to gleeful reminiscence, like a pair of children, till there were sounds from the stairs and a manservant announced that Miss Jenny's man was come to fetch her awa'.

'Good-bye Wattie. I am glad you prospered.' She bent to kiss him on the cheek and he blushed with pleasure.

'Awa' wi' ye, Miss Jenny,' he said, reverting to his childhood speech, 'afore ye get me into mischief. I'm a Baillie now, ye ken.'

'And a rich one. 'Tis you who need the caddie now.' In the pleasure of Wattie's rise to wealth, Jenny forgot her sadness at the memory of days past, of mistakes too dearly made. Her mission was safely accomplished, their cattle sold, muskets and pistols rolled in canvas concealed under salt, flour and other stores which had been ordered for the house and stowed in creels across the baggage-horses' backs.

It was a quiet but contented cavalcade which made its slow way north towards Glendessary, and they were above Loch Linnhe before she realized it. This was the last stop before home: as the night was dry with autumn frost, they elected to stay on the hillside rather than at the one bug-ridden, overcrowded tavern in the valley.

When the gillies had dispersed, their meal of whisky and oatmeal finished, to lie wrapped in their plaids among the horses, Ewen made up her fire, fetched fresh heather for her bed and spread a plaid to soften it. Then he too disappeared, leaving the tiny shieling to her alone.

And suddenly contentment vanished in a wave of loneliness too strong to bear. Ewen was a good lad – he looked after her well – but it should have been his father . . . As she looked round the empty, turf-walled, turf-roofed shieling with its central fire and blanketed heather bed, the memory of Finn pierced her heart with the sharpness of a sword. Finn would not have let an hour of misunderstanding pass between them. He would have sworn, smashed furniture, spent his rage in a roaring fury in which coldness had no place – and finally would have loved her, drawing her close and shutting out all loneliness. . .

Jenny could bear the constriction of her empty hut no longer, pushed through the narrow entrance and ran, barefooted, up the hillside till she was high on the ridge and breathless. Then she leant back against the rock and felt its coldness spread through plaid and bodice into her very bones. The line of the hills was black against the frost-clear sky: stars clustered thick and bright as candle-flame.

She did not move as Ewen came to stand beside her.

'What is it, Aunt Jenny?' Ewen asked anxiously, seeing the glint of tears on her face. 'I looked for you everywhere and I was worried. Are you sad?'

'A little . . . it is nothing.'

'Father says that, too, when Mother finds him looking, as you were, into silence.'

'Does he do that often, Ewen?'

'Oh yes. He reads till we are all abed, then puts out the lamp and stands at the window, gazing across the loch towards Glendessary. Sometimes, I think, for hours.'

Jenny sighed. Ewen was her friend, warm and guileless, but his father was cold as the frost at her back, aloof and inaccessible as the far mountains. 'Come, Ewen, it is time for sleep. We must be on our way early tomorrow lest the ford be flooded and we be forced to take the long way round.'

'If it is flooded, I shall carry you,' boasted Ewen.

And he did, holding her effortlessly in his arms, her own twined round his neck and both of them laughing.

Bess saw them from a window and her heart beat fast with fear: that woman had tried to take away her husband, now she wanted to take her son.

Hugh also saw them, and was wrung with jealousy, but he set his face in its familiar mask and strode out to meet the returning cavalcade.

It was the winter after Jenny's journey to Edinburgh. At first there was no particular anxiety: though the little girls each had measles, the disease took its natural course through rash and fever to recovery. But little John was barely two and without the resistance of his sturdier sisters. The fever took hold of him and burned him to a delirium which was torment for his parents to watch. There was no time to fetch a doctor, for the road to Achnacarry was blocked with snow, the glens impassable.

Jenny dipped into the long-stored knowledge which Sister Cecilia had imparted and did her best, though Glendessary's medicine chest lacked many of the convent's ingredients, while Alan and Isobel grew more distraught with every hour that passed. One or other of them sat constantly at the cot-side, sponging the infant's forehead and his hands. 'Help us, Jenny,' begged Alan as Johnny's delirium burned to frenzy. 'I cannot bear it if he should die.'

'Hush, Alan,' she soothed, as she had done in childhood. 'He will not die. The convent's remedies will work very soon . . .'

And she was right. But though the child recovered, Isobel did not. She grew spiritless and wan, took to weeping for no reason, woke on a scream in the night; and when her two daughters took the whooping-cough and died within a week of each other, Isobel went distraught.

'Her mind is gone,' said Alan sadly. 'I doubt she will recover. And John does not thrive as he ought to do.'

This was true. Whether the illness had affected his brain or whether the brain itself had always had a weakness, no one knew, but whereas Hugh's children were strong and vigorous, Alan's Johnny remained ailing. He suffered fits and could not speak without a stammer. By the time he was five he had only just learned to walk alone. But by that time Isobel was dead. Alan shut himself away in his study, and the care of young John fell largely to his aunt.

Jenny assumed it gladly. With surprising tenderness she taught the lad to ride and took him with her everywhere, with

Hugh's sons Ewen and young Donald; and as well as a knowledge of French, she instilled in Hugh's sons a loyalty to the Stuart cause. Even young Johnny listened, wide-eyed and wondering, as she talked of the Union of the Parliaments; of the rioting there had been in the Edinburgh streets when the Scottish Parliament sat for the last time; of the build-up to that first Rising of 1708 – she told them of Marlborough's campaigns; of James Stuart, the Chevalier de St George; of how she had seen him riding by a river in France with the Order of the Garter across his breast. She told them of the Rising of '15 and how the French and the weather had betrayed James Stuart yet again – for she could bear to blame her King only in secrecy, in her own heart – and of how their dead chief Ewen Dubh, seventeenth Lochiel, had foretold their King's coming.

'Be it James himself or his son, Prince Charles, on his behalf, our King will come. We must only be patient, and prepared.'

Over the years Jenny had learnt patience, and as she had done long ago, in that homesick loneliness of Edinburgh, she sank all other longings in loyalty to her exiled King and in the hope of his return. And while she waited, secure in the knowledge of Sir Ewen's prophecy, she found contentment in the daily running of Glendessary estate and the changing seasons.

But for Bess contentment was impossible. Hugh spent long hours on the estate or at the big house with Miss Jenny, and she saw little of him. When he came home he hardly spoke – and never came to bed before she slept. She felt him slipping away where she could not follow, until she knew there was only one course left for her to take.

All will be well when I get the potion. Last time it worked for me and it will again. He will take the cup, unknowing . . . drink it . . . and then we will have such loving . . . *She* will not get him . . . And I'll find a girl for Ewen. Ewen needs a young lass, not a woman old enough to be his mother. And she is, for all her black hair and her flashing eyes. Witch's eyes. Taking where she fancies . . . other women's husbands, other women's sons. But she will not get my Hugh . . .

The woman stopped to regain breath. The path was steeper than she remembered, the way much longer, but once she had travelled there and back again between Hugh's sleeping and his waking. When she returned she had given him the precious potion and he had given her Ewen . . .

She had the money, safe in her tight-closed hand. She would buy love with it as she had done that night so long ago . . . tears blurred her eyes and she stumbled faster as rain lashed down on a sudden squall and blotted out the hills. There had been cat's paws on the loch that morning and a whining in the chimney. She should not have come. But how could she bear it? It was that woman's fault. But Bess would beat her yet. The stocky figure pulled the plaid tighter, dipped her head into the snatching wind, closed her eyes against the arrows of rain and battled on towards Macdonald country where she would buy her happiness. She did not see the gully until it opened under her feet.

It was evening of the following day before they found Bess, and only after every cottar in the valley had joined Hugh, on horseback or on foot, to comb the hill slopes and the gullies, the tumbling burns and copses, of Glendessary estate.

Jenny saw them from the upper drawing-room, in a thin procession, slow-moving, picking their way home down the hillside in the dying light. It was raining still, a thin haze which blurred the near hills and set the cataracts racing in every cleft and gully, while in the distance, snow-capped mountains lowered, brooding under a clouded sky. At the head of the procession walked Hugh, his sons on either side, and in his arms a burden, reverently borne.

They laid her in the great hall in Glendessary, set hot stones at her sides and feet, and kept the fire blazing to melt the ice which had entered her bones as she lay among the rocks of the ravine. They gave her brandy, hot gruel, and Miss Jenny's special mixture, but no ministration on earth could heal her broken back.

She lingered for a week and Hugh hardly left her side, tending her with the gentleness and solicitude of remorse. For on that first evening when he carried her home he had found her right hand clasped tight and could not prise the fingers free. Only when she opened her eyes and recognized him did the grip relax, and he saw the coin in her hand.

'What is that, Bess? Did you find it?'

'It is mine . . . It was to have bought me your love.' She closed her eyes in returning pain and did not see the shock in his face.

'I am sorry, Bess,' he whispered. 'I have failed you.'

'No. It was my fault. I should not have sought to buy what cannot be bought.'

He smoothed her hair from her face then, and kissed her closed eyes. 'Forgive me.' Jenny, arriving unnoticed in the doorway, turned and went away...

They buried Bess Cameron in the graveyard at Kilmalie, beside her mother. At the graveside Hugh stood sombre-faced but erect, his sons at his shoulders and his daughters clinging close. It was a tight-knit group; Ewen his father's image, Donald smaller, dark-haired like the girls; Isobel and Jean at once protective of their widowed father and seeking his comfort in their loss.

'I am sorry,' said Jenny quietly when the short ceremony was over. 'You will miss her sorely. I know what it is to lose a dear companion whom one loves.' But Hugh at least had Ewen and the others. Watching their solicitude for their father, Jenny knew there was no place for an outsider in that little group, not even for their Laird . . .

And Jenny was their Laird in all but name. Alan took no interest, gave no orders, made no decisions. Since his wife had died he had withdrawn increasingly into a world of books from which it was now impossible to call him back. Even Johnny could not arouse him to interest: poor Johnny, backward still, his limbs too thin and unco-ordinated, his head too large, and his wits free-flying as dandelion seed in an autumn breeze.

But he was an affectionate child and well-loved. There was no malice in him, no awareness of his difference: as long as he could be with his Aunt Jenny, he was both tractable and content. Only when she left him to ride out to one of the remoter farms, or on a journey she thought too arduous for his strength, would he become uncertain-tempered and restless.

'You will care for him, Jenny, when I am gone?' said Alan on one of the rare evenings he spent with her. 'You know he will be Laird in my stead, if he lives.'

'Would it not be better to ask one of our brothers?' One was still in the University at Leiden, the other now in Paris. 'After all, they will inherit in their turn.'

'John will obey no one but you, Jenny. You are best fitted to care for him – and for Glendessary. I know you love them both. Please?'

'Of course, Alan.' Jenny slipped an arm round her brother's shoulders in reassurance and kissed his forehead. 'If you are sure.'

'You were always better suited than I to take command,' said her brother with sudden wry amusement. 'Even in childhood. Remember how you tormented poor Mr Graham? And ran away to the hills whenever the urge moved you? I was always terrified and overjoyed when you allowed me to come with you.'

'Terrified?' echoed Jenny. 'Of me? Or of those bogles I used to threaten you with?'

'Of neither. I was terrified that I would fall behind and lose you.' His face grew sad as he finished, 'Now it is I who must go first into the unknown.'

Jenny said nothing. His pallor, his thin chest, and the cough which too frequently ended in blood, confirmed his words. She drew him closer and said only, 'I will care for John for you, all my life. And for Glendessary.' To the last crumb of earth, the smallest pebble, the weakest new-born lark-chick, the most ailing child. It was what she had dreamed of in that far-off childhood which Alan had recalled, though she had not dreamed to bear the weight alone.

'I have drawn up a deed of guardianship,' said Alan. 'My signature is already made and witnessed. I would like you to sign it too, Jenny, then I can be at peace.'

Before the year was out John Cameron, six years old and utterly dependent, became the new Laird of Glendessary, though everyone on the estate, including himself, continued to refer to him as Johnny.

On the Continent his little counterpart, Charles Edward Stuart, had a new governor, James Murray, Earl of Dunbar and a Protestant. While Queen Clementina saw the appointment as a conspiracy against her own Catholicism, others recognized an astute political move. The little Prince was healthy, intelligent, well-favoured, with a charming manner and a high-spirited, volatile temperament: he promised well for the future, and was being most properly schooled for his royal destiny...

But in London Robert Walpole as Chief Minister had gone a long way to establishing a stable political system, linking Crown and Commons. The country had settled into peace and the promise of prosperity, while in Scotland the building of roads continued, with the establishment of forts to garrison the out-posts. Gradually the boundaries of the Jacobite Highland strongholds were being driven back...

'General Wade's men are blasting at Loch Lochy for the next stretch of road,' said Hugh Cameron one morning in the spring following Alan's death. 'The cattle must be moved further west lest the noise alarm them.'

'Take drovers and see to it,' said Jenny. 'We do not want them to stray into Macdonald land, for we are forbidden now to fetch them back. In all duty to Lochiel I could not ask you to do it.'

Hugh looked at her sharply: her expression was unnaturally demure, only her eyes betrayed her, being alive with a mischief which brought the past flooding back.

'Do you remember, Hugh, how you lay on the hillside in the snow and planned to steal Macdonald's cattle?'

Now is the time, he thought. *Now*. He clenched his hands tight and searched for words. 'Miss Jenny, I ...' The 'Miss' had been a habit assumed on her return to keep that dangerous distance between them: now it slipped automatically from his tongue as he sought despairingly for words to leap that self-made abyss – and destroyed his courage. He had made a vow and failed her. She was his Laird now. She had Glendessary as she had always wanted. Why should she need him? Yet he must speak, if only to set things right between them.

Jenny saw his confusion and misread its cause. It had all been too long ago ... twenty years or more ... they were both changed. In her eyes he was as fine a man as she had always thought him, though his face was weathered now, his blonde hair greyer and his beard as speckled at a thrush's egg. But he had been more withdrawn than ever since Bess's death. He mourned her still. He had lost the taste for levity – or love. She dropped her eyes to the papers on the desk in front of her and said quietly, 'I am sorry, Hugh. I should not have made a lightness of such a matter. Of course I would not ask you to do what is forbidden.'

With the acceptance of defeat, Hugh knew the moment lost. It was too late. For her, for him, for all of them, it was too late. Now only a monumental catalyst could bring them together.

It was too late, too, apparently for Scotland. When the unpopular Hanoverian George died in 1727, another equally unpopular succeeded him. Though James had two sons now to ensure the Stuart dynasty, his efforts to collect support enough to put him back upon his rightful throne were fruitless. Not George's German preferences, not his ghastly mistresses, his family quarrels, his cupidinous ministers, not even the financial crash of the South Sea Bubble which implicated King George himself, could swing the balance in favour of the Catholic James, and too many countries now were allied to England to risk giving support to his cause.

But Prince Charles Edward Stuart was now a handsome, high-spirited lad of thirteen who could, according to popular report, do anything he set his hand to with outstanding brilliance and lure the birds from the trees with his devastating charm.

'It may be too late for James,' said Jenny, ever hopeful, 'but surely not for his son?' 'We are at peace now, Jenny,' replied her cousin, Donald Cameron of Lochiel, on one of his rare visits to Glendessary. 'Here in the Highlands we have the chance to consolidate, develop, become civilized. It is better far to accept, to live in peace one with another, to let old wrongs lie in the ground where they belong. Besides, James never lived in Scotland and nor has Charles, his son. We are nothing to them but a dream, Jenny, as they are to us. We want no wars, though

192

I doubt the young Prince Charles would agree. He has badgered his father to let him join the Spanish army in the Naples campaign. His cousin Berwick is with him.'

'Berwick,' repeated Jenny slowly, remembering, and her eyes were bright with dawning excitement. The Duke of Berwick had fought beside his half-brother James in the French army – and Berwick's son was now fighting beside James's son Charles. It was an omen. The waiting had been long, too long, but Sir Ewen's words would be fulfilled. In spite of his reasoned pacifist arguments, Lochiel's news came as a breath of exhilarating outside air which nourished her patriotism, fed her starved spirit and filled the void which loneliness had made in her life. James's cause had been lost, she realized, in that winter of destitution in St Germain. But his son was a bright and certain hope. Already he was fighting in a war to win a crown – the crown of Naples for the Spanish king. What better apprenticeship for any prince?

And when he came, Lochiel would rise, in spite of all his arguments. He *must* – for when the *crosh-tarie* was carried through the Highlands, every chief must answer his King's call. She herself would answer for Glendessary, for Donald had that day brought her news of her brother Ewen's death in Leiden. Her brother John had died the previous year – now she felt the added responsibility which their going laid upon her. Her heart quickened with the old remembered fervour as she said quietly, 'Prince Charles will be the one.' She reached for her glass and raised it. 'Come, cousin. Let us drink to the King across the water – one day.'

When that day came eleven years later it was destined to split more lives than Jenny Cameron's asunder.

. .the Frigate stood in for the Coast of Lochaber and landed the Mock Prince and his Attendants on the Isle of Skye where he remained in private for some time, at the House of Mr McDonald of Kinloch Moidart; until he was joined by the Camerons, McDonalds, Stuarts and some other of the Clans in number about 150; then he set up his Standard on the 16th August and chose for his motto Tandem Triumphans i.e. At Length Triumphant.

Jenny was in her father's library when the news came, the room which Alan had monopolized and which Jenny now made her own. She worked at the desk under the window so that when she chose she could look out across the loch, or on the soft slopes of the hills which cupped the waters now in summer velvet. Once, she remembered, she could not have borne to spend an hour in a closed room when there was sunlight and space for the taking. Now she had responsibilities which she gladly bore – John, his tenants, his estate . . . For it was his, still, in name, and Jenny saw that her nephew was accorded proper deference. 'What shall I do, Aunt Jenny?' he would say, turning to her in helpless bafflement if a tenant asked for guidance, or a decision on a squabble with a neighbour. Jenny would tell him and, word for word, he would deliver his reply. It was a harmless charade, accepted without question by every Cameron in Glendessary. John Cameron was the mouthpiece, Miss Jenny the brains, and as long as Miss Jenny, straight-backed and striking with her dark green gown and scarlet petticoats, her clear eyes and jet-dark hair, was in charge at Glendessary, all was well.

If anyone remembered the untamed hoyden who had been packed off to Edinburgh so many years ago in disgrace, they did so with indulgence: 'She was aye a spirited lassie wi' a pair o' fine eyes.'

Those eyes were at the moment turned towards Achnacarry and they were very bright. Lochiel had sent her copies of various letters he had received, in secret, from the Continent, and one from his exiled father John, true chief of the Cameron Clan, whom she had last seen in the *auberge* in Sainte Marie de la Roche. He had been kind to her. He must be eighty years old now – as old as Uncle Ewen had been on that visit to

Glendessary when she and Hugh had ridden down from the hills to meet him. Uncle John wrote that Prince Charles was in Paris, in secret, preparing for invasion. That with England drawn into war again with France the time was ripe for an attempt, and that since the French defeat at Dettingen, King Louis XV was sympathetic. Things were falling into place. Donald was to hold the Cameron clan in readiness.

Her cousin had replied, warning of the dangers of a landing without foreign assistance. Nevertheless, he had pledged his support...

Donald, she knew, was unwilling, believing the attempt doomed as all the others had been, wanting merely to plant his trees in peace, she thought with a flash of rare contempt. But it was a flash soon doused: he meant no disloyalty. He wished only to guard his clan, to keep them safe from butchery and ruin. He cared deeply for peace, for civilized living and the welfare of his clansmen: yet surely when the call came, he must answer? With his own father, true chief of the Camerons, at Prince Charles' side, how could he do otherwise?

This time, thought Jenny fiercely, victory was certain. How could it be otherwise when so many had waited so long? When the cause was championed not by Old Mr Misfortune, as James was often known, but by young Prince Charles, as gallant, heart-stirring, and brave a champion as any cause could wish for? She thought with fleeting sadness of her nephew John, the same age as his Prince and yet how different. But John would support the Chevalier with as much fervour as his namesake Uncle who rode at the Prince's side – if Jenny told him to do so.

For weeks now, ever since that first letter from Uncle John, she had been making secret preparations, with Hugh's sons Ewen and Donald her eager accomplices. Hugh himself she had not involved, deeming, rightly, that with Lochiel's disinclination for any Rising without French support – and the uncertainty of such support being given – such orders from Miss Jenny would only lead to conflict.

She was glad that she had had the foresight to buy arms all those years ago and to hide them safely; glad that she had laid aside any money she could save from the estate. So while Ewen took out the weapons one by one from their concealment, greased and checked them, replaced them where they could be taken up at a moment's notice, and sharpened dirks and broadswords, Donald amassed stores of oatmeal, of powder and fuses, of *uisge beatha*, even bandages. Jenny, at her desk overlooking the loch, searched her memory for the long-buried detail of those campaigning days with Finn, made private notes, gave private orders and with gathering expectation made her own preparations ... A certain trunk was brought out from a closet, certain garments shaken out and checked for moth and mildew. The horses were given particular attention, their stores of fodder measured. And when Hugh was safely abed in the home farm, she took a key from its chain round her neck, unlocked the money chest and counted out the silver: so much to fee each man on the estate when he was called upon to leave his family and follow.

Not Johnny, of course. He must stay at home with Isobel or Jean. She would lead the men herself. If only she had Oberon ... But there was that bay gelding in the stable, the one she kept for Johnny though he was still nervous of its size and loath to ride it. And she knew what she would wear, checked and packed away again in camphor in Finn's campaign trunk, but ready to be snatched up and donned the instant word came ... everything that could be done had been done. All that remained was to wait.

She raised her eyes from the close-written page and gazed unseeing over the loch. All her life, she realized, had been a preparation for this – her childhood, her banishment to Edinburgh, even her first baby – for that had brought about her exile in France, led her to Finn and the Marlborough campaign. And then her years of waiting, here in Glendessary ... Now, at last, as Sir Ewen had foretold, she would ride in glory to her King. She remembered the firelight long ago when Finn and she had rested with the others after the day's march and he had talked of such a day. He, too, had known it would come. Dear Finn ... if only he were with her. She would have liked a man at her side.

The door opened at her back and without turning, she said with unguarded sadness, her thoughts still in the past, 'What is it?'

'The message has come.'

She whirled to see Hugh, grave-faced in the doorway, though there was an excitement about him which set her own heart pounding. 'What message, Hugh?'

'Prince Charles has landed in his kingdom. The clans are summoned to Glenfinnan for the raising of the Royal Standard.'

For a breathless moment Jenny stared at him in disbelief, then, with a cry of exultation, flung back her chair, ran to him and threw her arms around his neck in a transport of unthinking joy. Above her head, his eyes were as bright now as hers as he held her awkwardly for an unbelieving moment, then with a fierceness which half took her breath away.

'You should have done that years ago, Jenny.'

'I thought you did not want me.'

'*Not want you?*' At the groaning anguish in his voice she tipped her head back to look at him in dawning wonder. 'I have wanted nothing else . . .'

His face was alight now with a glory which had nothing to do with Prince Charles' landing and which burnt out the years of loneliness and sorrow as if they had never been, until she was looking into the same young eyes she had confronted on a hillside above Glendessary when they were both children – and, as she had done then, she drew his face to hers and kissed him, not clumsily now, but with a joyous giving, while he held her with the fierceness of one too long denied.

'It has been so long, Jenny . . . so many wasted years.'

'You always were a cautious lad, Hugh Cameron.'

'And you were the lass who never cried,' he murmured, kissing the tears from her brimming eyes.

But already she had broken away from him on a laugh of exultation. 'Why are you idle, haunchman? Have you forgotten our King has called us?'

'We must await the word from Lochiel. He is gone to Kinlochmoidart to urge caution. The Prince has landed with a mere seven men, Jenny. His supporting ship was attacked and forced to put back to Brest. He has no guaranteed support from France, or anywhere, and no army. In all honour, Lochiel must urge the Prince to wait . . .'

'He may urge him all he chooses,' retorted Jenny, 'but it will do no good. Prince Charles will finish what he has begun. He will not turn back. *I know*, as Uncle Ewen knew, so many years ago. Oh Hugh, how could I *not* know, when it is the moment I have waited for since I was a little child?'

'But if Lochiel should follow peace, and the path of caution . . . ' Hugh had learnt patience over the years.

'Lochiel will follow his Prince!' Jenny's voice allowed no contradiction, even from Hugh, so newly found. 'And so will we. Make haste and ring the bell to summon the household while I fetch the Laird to the great hall.'

John Cameron sat obediently in the Master's chair, his pale face nervous, his fingers plucking at the cloth of his coat, his bewildered eyes wandering from Aunt Jenny's exultant face on one side of him to Hugh Cameron's on the other. The room was full of people, all staring at him, but he did not know which way to look or what to say.

'What must I do, Aunt Jenny?' he whispered anxiously, his hand seeking hers under the great oak table. She took the tremulous fingers and held them firm in reassurance. 'I will tell them for you . . . .

'Prince Charles has landed!' Her ringing voice filled the hall. 'Charles, son of James, son of James, son of Charles, has landed in Kinlochmoidart to reclaim his kingdom. He came with but a handful of the chosen, knowing, and rightly, that his army awaits him here in his own land. If any doubt or hesitate, let him leave the hall, for he is unworthy of the name of Highlander. But I tell you all, as I will tell Prince Charles himself, that were there not a man in Glendessary who would draw his sword, I am ready to die for my King!'

'And I!' roared Hugh at Glendessary's side. 'And I!' 'And I!' His sons Ewen and Donald added their voices to those which gathered to a roar as more and more men crowded into the great hall till Jenny raised a hand for silence. Slowly she surveyed the gathering. Hugh, his sons, the estate workers, all the dear-loved faces of her childhood, and her nephew Johnny, waiting to be told what to do. Her face was radiant as, quietly, she spoke the dreamed-of words.

'Send out the *crosh-tarie*, Johnny, to summon the Cameron men.'

Then, forgetting protocol and all pretence, she rose to her feet and the whole hall with her while the rallying call of the Camerons shook the dust from the rafters and reverberated through the tranquil summer hills.

3

Lochiel sent an Order to Mr Cameron of Glendessary to raise his Men, and join the Family Standard. Mr Cameron, incapable of obeying such a Summons, his Place was supplied by his Aunt, Miss Jenny, who soon got together two hundred and fifty men and marched at the Head of Them to the Pretender's Camp.

Prince Charles Edward Stuart, son of James, stepped from the boat which had brought him the length of Loch Shiel to the appointed rendezvous, and looked on desolation. Glenfinnan was a natural mustering ground, a half-mile square of level land at the head of a loch flanked on all sides with mountains steep-cragged, rough-heathered, gaunt with pine and wheeling sea-birds; but on the summer-sweetened grass where the Highland army should have gathered were only a few thin cattle with their shepherds. To be sure, these latter wished the Prince God-speed, in unfamiliar Gaelic, but where were the clansmen who had pledged their support?

The Prince looked over the vast solitude of the mountains, the silence of his chosen, unpeopled arena, the shimmering emptiness of the loch, and retired to the seclusion of a nearby shieling where hope could revive and flourish, uncontradicted by the evidence of his eyes.

But it was afternoon before the mournful cry of the gulls was scattered by another distant sound which steadily strengthened to the unmistakable strains of the pipes. With a lifting of the heart, the young Prince hurried from the shieling to wait on the green-sward, his small band of attendants at his side, while the skirling music echoed from crag and gully in mounting splendour, the waters of Loch Shiel quivered in answering resonance, until, round the last curve of the masking hillside, came Lochiel at the head of the Cameron men, 700 of them marching three deep in two advancing columns, their kilts flashing scarlet and their claymores silver in the August sunlight, while the war-pibroch swelled to fill the valley with heroic challenge. Sandwiched between the two lines of Camerons, the first prisoners of the Rising stumbled, awestruck and afraid – soldiers captured by a contingent of Keppoch's men near Fort William.

Close on Cameron's heels came Keppoch himself with 300 Macdonalds from Glen Spean and Glen Roy – and a present of a captured horse for Prince Charles.

Now the clansmen spread in their ordered ranks from the water's edge to the hills, filling the vale with voices, with the strange cry of the pipes and the clash of metal on metal as weapons were assembled, stands of arms distributed to those who had none – for many had come unarmed – and horses tethered and tallies made. A thousand Highlanders had answered the call.

The young Prince stood on the raised ground outside his shieling-headquarters with the heathered crag at his back, the great loch of Shiel a deep and vibrant blue under the August sky; and where only that morning had been lush and empty grassland, a host of Highlandmen, plaid-bright, sun-browned, seethed with noise, activity and expectation. As he surveyed his gathering army, his own face glowed afresh with faith and happiness. Surely now it was time?

'Another half-hour,' said Atholl at his side. 'It is but early afternoon and there are more, yet, to come.'

McKinnon saw them first as a moving speck on the northern horizon. Then, as the column moved closer down the hillside from Sgurr Thuilm, the sound of pipes came clear across the distance, haunting, stirring the blood to dreams of glory, twisting the heart with longing. More patriots, he thought sadly, misguided as he was, marching to uncertain glory in a doomed cause.

He turned his back on them to return to the medical tent and his old friend Archibald Cameron. If it had not been for Archibald, McKinnon would not have come. A Prince, landing with only seven men on a remote Hebridean island and expecting to gather multitudes at every step: McKinnon could not credit his own gullibility. That he should allow himself to be persuaded to join such a harebrained enterprise!

But Charles had gathered men – not yet his multitudes, but men enough. And now here came more – 200 of them at least, moving with glory across the summer heather, sure-footed on the rocks and gullies of the hillside, with pennons streaming and pipes playing full and wild. There were horses in the forefront, then marching men, well ordered, in a winding column which flowed over the horizon and down towards the tranquil valley where the Prince's tents stood regal in the sunlight.

The near hills were sea-green velvet in the August sun, the waters of Loch Shiel a shimmering silver blue, and in the distance the purple haze of many mountains. The column which moved steadily across the lower slopes now to the meadow-land at the loch head was small as a trail of busy ants ... as small and as helpless. McKinnon, watching still in spite of his resolution, felt sudden anger at the futility of battle – and that there would be a battle he had no more doubt. Already Charles had gathered too many heroes about him, young men thirsty for glory, old men for the rights of kings. They, and hundreds with them, would fight and die while he and Archibald Cameron moved among the wounded, patching up their self-sought mutilation as best they could. It was a hopeless, agonizing business for which only his faith gave him strength.

He turned to look again at that approaching column before joining Archibald to make a tally of bandages and laudanum, and stopped, astounded, as by a thunderbolt from heaven. For riding at the head of the column on a high-stepping bay gelding, was a dark-haired woman in a sea-green riding habit with scarlet lapels, gold-trimmed, wearing a velvet cap with a scarlet feather, and a naked sword in her hand.

'Miss Jenny Cameron of Glendessary!' said someone, and sped to the royal hut to give the news.

Jenny sat her horse as in her dreams, riding in glory as Uncle Ewen had prophesied, to meet her King. Hugh rode at her side, her haunchman and her plighted love. When she looked at him, as she did often on that trek across the hills from Loch Arkaig into Glenfinnan, her heart sang with the joy of his company. For he had shed the carapace of sorrow which had isolated him too long from ordinary laughter; his face was young and eager as his grandson's, ten years old and left protesting at home.

But Hugh's son Ewen's eldest boy, named Hugh after his grandfather, had been entrusted with the care of the Laird of Glendessary in Miss Jenny's absence and had no choice. For the glen was emptied of all other men, except those too old or ill or young to fight. Only the women remained. 'I entrust those, too, to your care.' Knowing he would be loyal as his grandfather, Jenny left young Hughie with a light heart to ride out of her glen with his older namesake. In full Highland battledress, with claymore and targe, dirk and musket, Hugh was a warrior fit for the gods – and when he met her eyes as he invariably did, his own caressed her with a pride and tenderness she knew would never waver. He would fight their King's battle and come home again, to her. It was an unspoken, solemn bond between them.

On her bay gelding, in the riding habit Finn had dreamed of, with her man beside her, her columned clansmen following to the pipe-march of the Cameron's Gathering, Miss Jenny Cameron of Glendessary rode on to the royal meadow at Glenfinnan.

Jenny would have known her Prince in a crowd of twice the number, and though he was dressed simply as a private gentleman, in a plain dun-coloured coat with scarlet-laced waistcoat and knee-breeches, she rode up to him without hesitation and gave him a soldier-like salute.

'My nephew not being able to attend your Royal Highness,' she began in a voice which echoed the shining fervour of her eyes, 'I have raised his men in his stead and brought them to Your Highness. I believe every one of them as ready to hazard his life in your cause as I am myself, and though they are at present commanded by a woman, I hope there is nothing womanish about them. These men are yours. They bring you hearts as well as hands, and will serve you, to the death if need be, with both. Hugh! Order my men to pass in review before His Highness that he may judge for himself whether they are worthy to fight for Prince Charles and for Scotland!'

'If they be but half as worthy as their leader,' said her Prince gravely, 'I will be well pleased.'

Afterwards, when Hugh Cameron had led the Glendessary men in slow review before the Prince and he had pronounced them as well-drilled and well-accoutred as any in the field, he turned to her, bowed, and said, 'I will be honoured if you will dine at my table tonight, Colonel Jenny. You did well to make me wait, Atholl: but we need wait no longer. Let the ceremony proceed!'

To the end of her life, Jenny would remember that day. Her Prince had called her 'Colonel', had welcomed her among his trusted chiefs and, it seemed to her on that blazing afternoon, had waited only for her coming...

The Prince took up his position on the grass outside the shieling he had made his headquarters, those few who had accompanied him from France beside him, with her cousin Donald, Old Glenbucket, Keppoch and others of his escort. A hush fell over the valley as Duke William of Atholl took up the standard of King James and slowly, reverently, and with quivering hands raised it aloft. The afternoon breeze stirred the silken folds, spread them wider till the gold-tasselled banner of the Stuart Kings was clear for all the valley to see. Like the distant rumble of thunder, the roar gathered strength and

202

resounded echoing from crag to crag, 'Prince Charlie, King of the Gael!' – and, like a hiss of a thousand indrawn breaths, claymores flashed from their scabbards and stabbed the sunlight, bonnets flew jubilant aloft, and the pipers gathered breath to add the tribute of their skirling music to the general jubilation.

The Duke of Atholl read the King's Commission appointing his dearest son Charles sole regent in his Kingdom. The Prince himself addressed them in a short but eloquent speech, pledging his devotion to the welfare and happiness of his people and trusting in God's protection for a just and noble cause. Jenny found Hugh's hand and held it tight while her eyes brimmed with tears of joy as she drank in every word.

After the ceremony the Prince ordered brandy casks to be given to the men to drink the King's health, and the celebrations and singing lasted long after the sun had set. Jenny felt as light-hearted and as full of gaiety as if she had been a child again in her father's hall when Uncle Ewen visited them. But it was Scotland's own Prince Charles who was the guest of honour here and her heart could scarce contain her happiness. He called her Colonel Jenny before the entire company and when she caught Hugh's eyes, as she did often in the crowded tent, she knew he shared her pride – and her love.

'I am glad you found your man, Jenny,' said McKinnon from across the trestle table. 'May God go with you both.'

'And with you, Calum.'

They had been two days in Glenfinnan, two days of activity and confusion, every hour of which had been heaven to Colonel Jenny. There was ammunition to be unpacked and distributed – Lochiel's men, unlike Jenny's men, were woefully ill-armed – details of guards and watches to be settled, prisoners to be guarded; and as well as the newly-sworn soldiers, there were ladies, and gentlemen too, come merely for the spectacle, to add their voices and their silken colours to the general activity.

'It is like the old campaigning days, is it not?' laughed Jenny to McKinnon, forgetting the pain and sorrow, remembering only the excitement. 'How I wish I could stay with you all, ride with the column as I once did, and fight, in my woman's way, for my King.' Her eyes were young again and bright. 'I have Hugh beside me, as my Uncle prophesied – and my Prince. Why must I stay behind with the womenfolk, merely because I go in skirts?'

'There will be suffering,' reminded McKinnon quietly, 'as well as glory.'

'And you will alleviate it, Calum, as you always did.' Her face was sober, remembering Finn. Then with a laugh she raised her glass. 'But I drink to glory, not to suffering.' Her eyes sought those of the young Prince at the head of the table and she raised her glass. '*Au revoir*, Your Highness. God speed you all to victory!'

'Surely you do not desert us, Colonel Jenny?' called the Prince when the toast was drunk. 'You led your men to join my standard. I expect you to lead them on to victory.' He raised his own glass towards her. 'A welcome to the newest Colonel in my army!'

For a timeless moment Jenny hesitated, weighing on one side the immeasurable glory of leading the Cameron men, with Hugh beside her, in the King's cause, of riding as an equal in Prince Charles's army, of dining in the royal tent and sharing the royal Council; and on the other, poor, witless Johnny and a handful of women in an empty glen. There was a time when she would not have hesitated, but when at last she spoke it was without regret.

'You do me great honour, Your Highness, and I thank you for it. But my nephew has need of me and I leave my men in good hands.' Her eyes met Hugh's where he sat lower down the table. 'Hugh Cameron will lead them as well as any general in your army. I drink to your victory, Your Highness, and to our next meeting, in Edinburgh Castle.'

'Edinburgh Castle!' echoed the length of the table as glasses were raised and emptied, filled and raised again. But though he matched her toast, McKinnon could not match her optimism: he knew that this time when they parted, they would not meet again.

'I am glad you decided as you did, Jenny,' said Hugh that night as they stood quietly together at the lochside. Except for the sentries, the camp was asleep, the only sounds the occasional stirring of horses, a muffled cough, the distant bark of a deer or fox, the splash of a fish on the star-glittered surface of the water. Gently he kissed her ear. 'It was the right choice.'

'I know it . . . but I confess I was wickedly tempted!' Laughing, she raised her face to his. 'Take care, Hugh,' she whispered later, 'and come home to me, safe.'

Aftermath

The story of the '45 is too well-known to need retelling: the fervour and the loyalty, the mistakes, the waste, till the final butchery on Culloden Moor where a thousand clansmen died, Macdonald and Cameron, Stewart, Fraser and Gordon, Farquharson, Drummond, Clan Chattan ... and afterwards the hunting.

> The battle of Colloden, which put a final Period to the Rebellion, and all the Pretender's Hopes of sitting on the British Throne, was likewise fatal to vast Numbers of his Followers and Adherents, Multitudes of whose Carcases spread the bloody Field; and they that escaped were but reserved to suffer infinite Difficulties and Hazards. The Camerons behaved with their usual Bravery, and Lochiel their chief was sorely wounded in the Ankle. Being overpowered and obliged to retire before his Enemy, he was closely attended by his Brother the Doctor, who dressed and took all imaginable Care of his Wound, till it was healed. The next Day, Lochiel marched with his Clan to the Side of a Hill, where he drew them up, and ordered the Piper to play all the following Night, such Tunes as he knew would best divert and amuse them in their present melancholy Circumstances. The next Morning, finding there was no Likelihood of his being joined by any considerable Force, and that there was no Subsistence for his Troops, marched away for Lochaber ... and in two days came to Glengary where he found his unhappy Master.
>
> ... At length after much debate it was agreed that the Camerons should keep in a Body and march together to Achnacarry ... and the first thing they did on their Arrival there was to secure their best Effects in the Woods and subterraneous Caverns of which there were many in that Part of the Country; ... which being done and the Enemy approaching, the whole Company left the House, which was soon afterwards burnt down to the Ground.

Jenny saw the flames from the window and rushed to raise the

205

alarm. As the bell clanged its urgent summons over the waters of the loch, women came running with children, captured hens and hastily bundled possessions; old men stumbling to keep up with spryer daughters, old women with their men. Some had panniered horses, the basketwork creels creaking under the weight of babies or cooking pots, others bundles on their bent backs ... children, bare-legged, herded skinny cows in twos or threes; grandmothers helped with rowan switch or besom. There was snow, still, in the high hills, but there were soldiers in the valley.

In the yard at Glendessary Jenny Cameron waited, her face pale but calm, the Laird already safely mounted on his horse beside her, young Hughie standing guard over the bridle.

'What is it, Aunt?' asked John Cameron, bewildered. 'Where are we going?'

'To the high pastures, Johnny, to find clear air.'

But Jenny's eyes were on the skyline at the eastern end of Loch Arkaig, twelve miles away. How long would it take Cumberland's men to move twelve miles when fired with blood-lust for the fugitive Prince Charles? Why else would they burn Achnacarry? It was Lochiel's house, and Lochiel was known to be with the Prince. Where more natural then for the Prince to seek concealment than in Cameron country?

'Hurry!' urged Jenny, casting her eyes swiftly over the assembled flock, ticking off each new arrival against a mental list. The sky to the east was black now with billowing smoke, with, low at its centre, the leaping orange pyre of what had once been Achnacarry, house of her chief; first Uncle Ewen, who had torn out an English soldier's throat with his teeth, then Cousin Donald who had dreamed of an avenue of beech trees which would lend grace and natural beauty to the home of Lochiel for generations to come ... Lochiel was with Prince Charles, somewhere in the fastnesses of the Highlands where the English roads had not yet penetrated. He would be safe, but her heart wept for Achnacarry.

She looked at the grey keep of Glendessary at her back, home of her childhood, centre of her world ... then at the women, anxious, ragged, dogged women, their babies precious at their breasts, their children trusting, bare-legged, lithe, the boys straining higher to emulate their fathers who had gone to fight at Culloden field. How many of them had died?

The question which had haunted her dreams unceasingly since the news of Culloden had come flying like the plague to consume them, rose up in those leaping flames to fill her with dread. Was Hugh among the slain?

And she knew that Achnacarry was nothing to her, Glendessary a mere edifice of stones, their loss a trifle beside the loss of Hugh whom she had found again so short a time ago. Even her King was nothing to her beside Hugh Cameron, her haunchman and her pledged love. As she scanned the faces of those other waiting women, she felt unbearable compassion for all such widows and orphans, all such wandering, homeless bands who had lost home and hearth and husband, father, brother, son . . . in the cause of a single, would-be King.

'*Too many young men dead.*' Aunt Cameron's words came back to her with stabbing meaning. 'Please God,' she prayed, 'not here, not in Glendessary.'

'Is everyone assembled, Hughie?'

'Aye, Miss Jenny, as far as I can tell.'

'The cattle?'

'Ready.'

'The strong box?'

'Here.' The lad indicated a metal-bound casket strapped to Glendessary's saddle.

'You have meal and flour, dry tinder and the rest?' Her old campaigning days with Finn still served her well.

'Aye. And the Master's papers.'

'Then it is time.' She raised a hand in signal and the small procession moved away along the westward shore of Loch Arkaig towards the narrow valley of Glen Pean. Miss Jenny was in the lead, then John, Laird of Glendessary, whimpering quietly to himself at the unnatural haste, then, strung out in ragged, hurrying disorder, packhorse and cottar's wife, sharp-boned cattle, old-boned men, and the anxious, scurrying, silent children . . . she saw Ewen's wife and Donald's, with their children, Hugh's daughters Isobel and Jean, both decked with little ones, all following where she led, with faith and trust.

'Oh God,' she prayed in sudden knowledge of her burden, 'help me to lead them into safety.'

At the head of the glen, where the stream turned westward in a tumbling rise of white-foamed waters, she stopped, moved her horse a little up the hillside to wait, sentinel fashion, till the stragglers had safely passed. Then turned to look back and down, past the racing thread of white-frothed water which marked their climbing journey, past the greyed and green-mossed rocks, the bracken, brown from last year's autumn, its green unfurling tendrils hidden still, past the lichen-misted rowans at the foot where the flatlands of the loch-head opened in a spread of softer green, to the square tower of Glendessary, small now as an upended peat.

Wind funnelled down the gully at her back. Below her lay Loch Arkaig, its silver water untroubled, serene – but along the sand-thread of its shore moved the inexorable black-and-red-specked menace of Cumberland's men. She heard their voices, faint with distance, saw their smallness in the vast arena of the mountains as they drew closer ... closer ... until the heart of that little peat block glowed suddenly red, then leaping gold, and the first dark plume wound upwards to defile the sky.

Resolutely, Jenny turned her back to follow her band round the bluff, and onwards, west, into the high hills: Cameron country where no roads gave easy access, no stranger would betray them. It would be a long and bitter summer, but somehow they would survive, keeping a home and a welcome for those weary stragglers from Culloden, the lucky few ...

They came in ones and twos, Cameron men going wearily home to Fassefern or Dungallon, Loch Lochy or Lochiel. Some had news of relatives, all of slaughter and weeping. Oh God, oh God ... Young Ewen dead ... *Please God, not Ewen*..... Donald too .. and Isobel's husband ... Jean's left wounded, dying ... others young and old, mutilated, butchered, the scarce-dead bodies stripped and violated, the living beaten with musket butt to death ... The weeping spread, like the grey mare's tail when the first snows melted, to fill every vale with sorrow.

In the evening light the piper played his endless lament as each new traveller told his tale and moved on, leaving another heart drained of hope, another place empty ...

MacGillivray, chief of the Mackintosh clan had led the charge through cannon fire and grapeshot on to a sea of bayonets. Keppoch advanced alone to a hero's death and twenty of his followers fell in as many seconds after him. Seventeen Appin men fell round their banner till another ripped it from its staff and bore it to safety. The Cameron standard was saved in like manner, wrapped round the body of Lochiel's own standard-bearer. Lochiel himself, wounded in both legs, was carried from the field by his devoted followers, hidden safe. Young Fraser of Inverallochie lay where he fell, to be slaughtered in cold blood the following day. And a thousand clansmen fell ...

'But where is the glory?' Jenny asked over and over. 'Where is the justice? *Too many young men, dead* ...' Her aunt's words beat incessantly now inside her head, until she could not even remember the time when she had thought it glorious to fight and to die for a cause. Her cousin Donald had been right: life was too precious to be squandered for a dream. One should endeavour to preserve the peace of everyday existence, to care for the sick, to teach understanding and kindly tolerance. What did any king matter when a woman was widowed, a child un-fathered? Glendessary had lost too many men. Pray God she had not realized too late. Pray God . . . .

And still the fugitives came, with tales now of retribution and the endless hunting, though all agreed that the Prince was still free and Lochiel with him. Refreshed with sowans or broze and a draught of Miss Jenny's wine, they travelled on, leaving the little mountain community safe in its turf-roofed shieling, hidden away from prying Government eyes, wrapped in the silence of its grief.

Spring moved into summer, summer waned. Soon it would be time to move down again nearer the valley before the night frosts and the snows assailed them. Though in the daytime she maintained a strong and reassuring spirit for the Laird's benefit and for young Hughie's, Jenny's heart was cold now at night: too long had passed since Culloden field. Even Prince Charles had gone now, safe, from Borrodale to France.

So many she had known and loved were dead: her father, Uncle Ewen, Aunt Cameron, Calum McKinnon – killed, a fugitive told her, on Culloden field; so many others gone from her life for ever. Sister Cecilia. Andrew. Daniel and Colette. Finn's son had died – Finn too. Oh Finn, she thought with a rush of yearning, Finn . . .

She would bear no children now, whatever happened. It was too late. Too late for her King, for her children, for Hugh . . .

'What is it, Aunt Jenny?' asked a timid voice and a hand crept trustingly into hers. 'Why are you sad?'

She looked at the simple, guileless face of John Cameron, Laird of Glendessary, and knew she might not surrender to sorrow. When he said, as he always did, 'What must I do Aunt Jenny? Tell me and I will do it,' she saw her path clear and inescapable. Once, long ago, she had dreamed of being Laird in her brother's stead, had fought against the injustice which denied her all chance. Now she must *be* Laird, with all that that involved, and bear her private grief as a chieftain would do, in secret.

'You must go to bed now, Johnny,' she said gently. 'I will call Hughie to help you. Tomorrow we will decide what must be done, for soon we must go home.'

Home. If Hugh lived or if he died, she knew she must go on. Though she and the Laird himself were childless, her brothers dead, Hugh had left children and grandchildren, fit as their grandfather had been, and strong. There would be Camerons for generations yet in the glen of the Dessary, and one day a Cameron chief would rule them again from Achnacarry; Cameron children would range free and joyful as she and Hugh had ranged over the green, dear slopes which cradled Loch Arkaig...

' ... At length a small schooner of about eighteen or twenty tons arrived in the Harbour of Flota in the Isle of South Uist where the Chevalier, his Friend Lochiel and Dr Cameron happened to be. In the Vessel they joyfully embarked and the next morning which was September 17, they set Sail for Bologn, where, after a quick passage they safely arrived to the Surprise of their Friends and their own great Satisfaction. Lochiel had immediately a Regiment given him in the French Army and the Doctor was made Physician to the same...'

And those few who had accompanied the Prince in his passage through the Scottish hills turned weary steps, at last, for home.

He came out of the west on a September evening, the setting sun at his back, his silhouette haloed with burnished gold. She stood where she was, on a bluff above the camp, and watched him draw closer while her heart brimmed full with love and overflowing gratitude.

He had come back: his children would be her children, his grandchildren hers, and their children in turn ... there would be Camerons again in Glendessary and one day, peace.

'I promised to return to you,' he said as he gathered her quietly to him and held her close against his heart. 'A Cameron never breaks his word.'